4-01 *

mG

WITHDRAWN

Tenderness
and Fire

Also by Robert Funderburk
in Large Print:

The Fires of Autumn
All the Days Were Summer

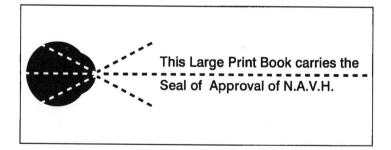

This Large Print Book carries the
Seal of Approval of N.A.V.H.

Tenderness and Fire

Robert Funderburk

Thorndike Press • Thorndike, Maine

Published in 1998 by arrangement with
Bethany House Publishers.

Thorndike Large Print ® Christian Fiction Series.

The tree indicium is a trademark of Thorndike Press.

The text of this Large Print edition is unabridged.
Other aspects of the book may vary from the original edition.

Set in 16 pt. Plantin by Juanita Macdonald.

Printed in the United States on permanent paper.

Library of Congress Cataloging in Publication Data

Funderburk, Robert, 1942–
    Tenderness and fire / Robert W. Funderburk.
        p.   cm.
    ISBN 0-7862-1299-3 (lg. print : hc : alk. paper)
    1. Large type books.   2. Football players — Fiction.
3. Louisiana — Fiction.   I. Title.
[PS3556.U59T43   1998]
813'.54—dc21   97-44891

To

Aaron McCarver

For giving me sound counsel
on the writing of this series
and
for being a steadfast friend.

Robert Funderburk is the author of the Dylan St. John Novels and The Innocent Years series with Bethany House Publishers. Much of the research for both series was gained through growing up in Baton Rouge and then working as a Louisana state probation and parole officer for twenty years. He and his wife have one daughter and live in Louisiana.

CONTENTS

Part One
Cherry

Part Two
Taylor

Part Three
Dalton

Part Four
Justine

PART ONE

★ ★ ★

CHERRY

ONE

The Wedding

★ ★ ★

"I'd *better* be sure, Mama!" Jessie Temple stood before the mirror of her dresser making last-minute adjustments to her bridal gown, a handmade artwork of taffeta, satin, lace, and pearls. "I'm getting married in two hours!"

Catherine's blue eyes held a private thought as she sat down next to the bed in a pink satin chair with a heart-shaped back. Her tan linen suit and silk blouse contoured her youthful figure, giving her an appearance of cool serenity that she felt not at all. "I know you are, sweetheart. I guess talking is just my way to keep my mind off the fact that my eldest daughter is actually leaving home for good."

"Mother, our house is just across town. Austin loves that old place so much, I'll never get him out of there."

The morning summer sunlight streaming in through the window splashed on Jessie's pale hair as she turned and plopped down on the side of the bed next to her mother.

"Careful! Don't wrinkle your dress!"

Ignoring her mother's warning, Jessie continued, as though trying to convince herself that agreeing to marry Austin had been the right decision. "Austin's always been your favorite. You know you've been wanting me to marry him for years!"

Catherine ran her hand idly over the chenille bedspread, smoothing a small wrinkle from years of habit. Then she stared into Jessie's warm brown eyes, a replica of her father's. "I surely have." For some reason, Catherine's thoughts suddenly turned to her own marriage and the silver wedding anniversary she and Lane had celebrated only a week before. Time seemed to have been thrown into another gear, the years racing by like the old "Burma Shaves" signs along a highway.

"Well, let's see your face brighten up a little, then."

"There were times," Catherine recalled, reaching over to pat Jessie on the hand, "when I thought you two weren't going to make it. Austin's been so patient with you, Jess. I'm glad you didn't lose him!"

"I always knew we'd manage to get through those rough days." Jessie gazed out the window at the cloudless sky. "Never a doubt in *my* mind."

"Hmm . . ." Catherine gave her daughter a skeptical look when she turned around.

"Well," Jessie confessed, "there might have been a time or two when I had just a *tiny* doubt." Before Catherine could agree with her, she jumped off the bed, grabbed a brush, and began putting the final touches on her hair.

Catherine found herself surveying the room. Memories seemed to inhabit every open space and every piece of furniture. "Guess I'll take these down after you've gone," Catherine said. She waved her hand at the color photographs of movie stars, cut from *Photoplay* magazine when Jessie's dreams of the Silver Screen were still untainted by the reality she had found once in Hollywood.

Jessie turned around, letting her eyes take in the yellowing remnants of her adolescent fantasies. Using her brush as a pointer, she flicked her wrist at the only eight-by-ten glossy on the wall. "I think I'll keep *this one*. Bob Hope's such a nice man! And he *did* write that sweet little note on it for me."

"You've certainly had an" — Catherine paused for a moment, staring at a mourning dove perched on a branch in the massive live oak outside the window — "*interesting* life for someone who's only twenty-four, Jess."

"I guess I have, at that."

Catherine's smooth brow furrowed briefly in thought. "I hope you don't expect marriage to give you the thrill-a-minute kind of life you've had since you got out of high school."

Jessie turned, the fingers of her left hand moving slowly over the silver-backed brush she still held in her right hand. "I haven't really done all *that* much." A reflective light filled her eyes. "Those few months out in California and over in Korea . . . then Memphis, and singing with Billy in all those churches . . ." Jessie let the words trail off, then smiled with her mouth, but her eyes still held the memory of that frantic, exciting, bittersweet season of her life.

"Jessie . . ." Catherine felt awkward asking, but somehow felt the question *needed* to be asked.

"Yes?"

"Did you love Billy?"

A smile tinged with sadness crossed Jessie's face. "I never could figure out how I really felt about him when we were on the road so much. We hardly had any time at all to ourselves."

"I shouldn't have asked," Catherine said,

her voice constricting in her throat. "This is a terrible time for me to bring up the subject of another man."

"No . . . no, it's not. I've thought a lot about Billy in these past few months." Jessie took a deep breath, letting it out slowly. "I think Billy knew he didn't have much time to do the work he was called to do — especially there at the last. He put his whole heart, his whole life, into preaching. There wasn't much of Billy left over for me — or any other woman, for that matter."

"You still didn't answer my question."

Jessie's eyes now joined in with the smile her mouth had started. "Mama, I love Austin, and I want to spend the rest of my life being a good wife for him. He's the only man in my life from now on. Does that answer your question?"

"I guess it'll have to, won't it?"

"Good." Jessie stood up straight in front of her dresser. "Mirror, mirror, on the wall, who's the fairest bride of all?" she asked, playfully winking in the mirror at her mother.

Catherine smiled at her daughter's antics.

"Well, you're supposed to play the part of the *mirror*, Mother dear."

"Why, *you are*, Miss Temple, soon to become Mrs. Youngblood!" Catherine answered, joining in the game.

"That's more like it!"

"Jess, you've been away from home so much these last few years. . . ."

"And?"

"Well, I was just wondering . . ."

Jessie finished applying deep-pink lipstick, grabbed a tissue from a box on the dresser, and blotted her lips. Then she turned to face Catherine, batting her eyes in wide-eyed innocence. "Yes, Mother. I'm *still* a good girl!"

"You sure you want to go through with the ol' 'ball-and-chain' routine, Austin?" Cassidy Temple, a tomcat grin on his lean face, eyes like polished pieces of sky, sat in a folding chair in the room where he, his brother, and sisters had all attended Sunday school at one time or another over the years.

Dalton punched his little brother good-naturedly on the shoulder. At six-one and a shade under two hundred pounds of muscle and sinew wrapped around an iron determination, Dalton looked every inch the college halfback that he was. "Bad time for jokes like that, Cass," he muttered in disapproval.

"Not if I can make him change his mind," Cassidy quipped, brushing his sun-bleached hair from his forehead. "I thought this boy had good sense till I found out he was marrying *our* goofy sister."

Austin, laughing at Cassidy in spite of his nervousness, turned away from the window he had been using as a looking glass to adjust his black bow tie. His black hair looked like the negative image of Cassidy's, his gray eyes light and clear. "I have to admit, I had some doubts about one thing."

"See, Dalton?" Cassidy said, nodding toward Austin. "Maybe there's still some hope for his sanity if he's talking like this about Jessie. She'll be flitting around so much, he'll think he's married to a *rumor* of a wife."

"I don't worry about Jess," Austin said, glancing at Dalton.

"What are you talking about, then?"

"You."

"You lost me, Harvard-boy."

"Well, since I'm going to be in the family" — Austin brushed a piece of lint from his lapel — "they'll expect me to keep you out of Angola Prison, and I don't think I'm that good a lawyer."

"That's about as funny as a crutch," Cassidy commented. He leaped from his chair and faked a punch at Austin's midsection.

Austin blocked the punch and stopped his own right cross two inches from Cassidy's chin. "You better pick another way to come at me, little boy."

Sparks flashed in Cassidy's eyes, then vanished above his grin. "You might have been state champion in the ring, Harvard-boy, but you'd never take me in a *real* fight!"

Austin returned the grin and stepped closer. At six feet even, he was two inches taller and fifteen pounds heavier than Cassidy. "You're a fifteen-year-old, hundred-and-fifty-pound baby."

"You'd never take me."

"Why's that?"

" 'Cause *you* follow the rules."

Dalton saw the cold light that began to fill Cassidy's eyes and knew it was time to step in and put an end to the joking. "That's enough, Cass."

Cassidy spun around to face his big brother, then his face relaxed. "I have to give him credit for one thing, though. He talked his mama out of having the reception down at the Heidelberg. I can't stand that hotsy-totsy place."

"Ain't that the truth!" Austin, never failing to see the humor in the pretenses of his upper-crust family, joined in with Cassidy. "And she'd already put a deposit down on the 'I'm-So-Much-Richer-Than-You-Are Room'!"

"See there, Dalton," Cassidy beamed. "Austin *can* take a joke. If I can't kid around with my brother-in-law, then who can? He'd better get used to my warped sense of humor if he's gonna be a part of *this* family."

"Why don't we let him get used to his new role a little at a time, Cass?" Dalton had been concerned about his little brother as far back as he could remember. Even as a child, Cassidy had shown an unhealthy interest in pushing things to the point of danger. It had fallen to Dalton to get him down from tall trees, keep him out of street fights, rescue him from deep water, and generally act as his shepherd and overseer. In this, his third year as a teenager, he continued to show an ardent and growing affection for danger and breaking the rules.

"It's all right, Dalton." Austin patted Cassidy on the head as if he were an errant toddler. "Besides" — he threw Dalton a knowing glance — "the runt here just *might* be making a valid point about Jessie."

Dalton looked as though someone had just told him the muddy Mississippi had started flowing back upstream toward Minnesota. "You mean you *don't* want to marry her?"

"No — no," Austin quickly assured him, "nothing like that." He sat down on one of the tiny wooden chairs used by the Sunday school children, his legs splayed out in front, elbows resting on a low table stacked with

Bible-story coloring books and an assortment of crayons. "I just mean that everybody facing a decision that will affect them for the rest of their lives needs to take a final, long look at what they're about to do. That's all."

"Well" — Dalton crossed his muscular arms across his chest — "what did you see in this long look?"

Austin grinned at Cassidy, then turned to Dalton. "The same thing I've seen since that day I first met your big sister. It's just me and her from now on."

Merely nodding, Dalton stepped over and extended his hand. "Well, let me be the first to welcome you to our family while you're still a carefree bachelor." Although he had never told him so, Dalton felt a sense of relief that Jessie was marrying Austin Youngblood — someone who had loved her for years, who would take care of her, someone she could depend on when times were rough.

Dalton remembered the early, wild days of their relationship when Austin had courted danger and Jessie as if he couldn't decide between them. But that had all slowly changed after one ordinary evening when he had had an extraordinary encounter with an elderly couple on the lakeshore across from his home. Austin had told him of this chance meeting, and it had explained for Dalton the new course Austin's life had taken since asking Jesus into his heart. He had graduated from Harvard law school and embarked on a career as an attorney. You couldn't get much more stable than that. Dalton could hardly believe this was the same Austin Youngblood who liked fast cars and taking chances.

"I think it's time we got this show on the road, boys," Cassidy volunteered, glancing at his watch.

Austin stood up. He rotated his shoulders, let his arms hang at his sides, hands swinging back and forth as if to shake off his nervousness, or as if he were trying to stay loose between rounds the way he had done so many times during his high-school boxing days.

"You look like you're about to step out into the ring, Austin," Dalton observed.

"He is." Cassidy's eyes crinkled in a half-smile. "And my money's on Jessie for a KO in the first round."

Freshly cut flowers brightened the heavy crystal vases resting on linen-covered tables in the shade of a live oak. In the center of the brick patio, a fountain made tinkling music as it flowed from one level to the next, sparkling in shafts of sunlight that filtered down through the canopy of leaves.

Huge bowls of boiled shrimp chilling on ice were flanked by others holding mounds of salad. Cakes, pecan- and sweet-potato pies, and long, flat pans of warm bread pudding rested on the service tables near the back gallery. The rich aroma of crawfish etouffee and seafood gumbo simmering in deep pots on the stove wafted out through the open screen door that led into the kitchen.

In the back corner of the yard, next to an ivy-covered wall, Jessie and Austin Youngblood stood together beneath a bower cascading with purple wisteria. The photographer, his hands like pale birds in flight, directed the couple into their proper poses.

"Isn't she just the most beautiful bride you ever saw?" Cherry Lovell asked Dalton in an excited whisper. She had worn her honey-blond hair in a bouffant twist since her high-school days in the tiny North Louisiana town of Dry Prong when the drama teacher had told her it gave her "a charming air of sophistication." She also wore an almost perpetual expression of delight, as though invisible friends were whispering marvelous secrets in her ear all during her waking hours. Brushing a wisp of hair away from her forehead, she slipped her arm inside Dalton's, reaching down to squeeze his hand.

Feeling the warm pressure of Cherry's hand on his, Dalton glanced down at her upturned face. "Not any prettier than *you* are," he whispered. He tried to act casual, but Cherry's touch always stirred him in a way that he often found himself fighting. With her air of defenseless innocence, she also made him feel as though she had reserved him a place at the round table along with Arthur's other knights.

"You're sweet," Cherry cooed, patting his arm. At five feet two, she barely reached his shoulder, even in heels. Tall men had always given her a feeling of security, ever since that day as an eight-year-old she had watched her short, plump, and abusive father storm out the front door, never to return.

"He *is* sweet, isn't he?" Cassidy, overhearing her remark, reached over and pinched Dalton on the cheek. "I'm always telling people what a really *sweet* big brother I have! Just stick a football helmet on a stalk of sugarcane — that's ol' Dalton."

Dalton, scowling at Cassidy, felt his face glow with embarrassment. He sometimes wished he could be as nonchalant and unperturbed as his younger brother always seemed to be. "Cool" was the accepted word for it. Social situations proved to be awkward for Dalton. He much preferred the bone-jarring tackles and muscle aches of the football practice field over the feel of starched shirts and the discomfort of having to make polite conversation.

"You're awful, Cassidy Temple!" Cherry rushed to Dalton's defense. "You ought to try being a little more mannerly yourself, like your brother."

"Maybe you could teach me," Cassidy suggested and winked. "I'm not doing a thing after the reception!"

Now it was Cherry's turn to blush.

"Hey, Uncle Coley," Dalton said, changing the subject. He waved at the blade-slim, dark-haired man gliding down the walk toward them in his wheelchair. Dalton felt relieved that his father's best friend and law partner had arrived to interrupt what was proving to be a tense moment. "Where's Maria?"

Coley Thibodeaux wheeled up next to them, locking the brake on his chair. "She's inside, helping your mother with the food." Having lost the use of his legs to Japanese shrapnel in a bloody island invasion during World War II, and completing the marine rehabilitation program, he had then gone to law school. Dalton was proud to know a hero like his uncle Coley.

Coley's cool gray eyes settled on the couple getting their picture taken. "Little Jessie," he said, resting his elbows on the arms of his chair, "finally getting married. Seems like yesterday she was wobbling around in her first pair of high-heels."

"You and Maria have been married almost a year now, haven't you, Uncle Coley?" Cassidy asked.

"A year last month."

"So many girls and so little time," Cassidy remarked smoothly. "I don't know if I'll *ever* commit to marriage."

"I'm sure that bit of information would put some mother's heart at ease," Coley drawled, giving Cassidy an oblique glance. Although no blood kin to the Temples, Coley had long been considered as a member of the family. As a four-year-old, Cassidy had shown a remarkable fondness for him and began calling him "Uncle," with the other three children following suit. Cassidy had remained Coley's favorite since those first days.

"Oh, yeah," Cassidy shot back. "Well, I heard Maria's daddy took to wearing a black armband since the day he found out y'all were getting married."

"Don't believe everything you hear, squirt." Coley grimaced slightly, rubbing his thighs with both hands to stimulate the blood circulation. "He only wore it for *six months.*"

"When we going fishin'?" Cassidy always seemed to speak whatever popped into his mind, bouncing conversations around like tennis balls. He stepped over closer to Coley's chair. "Well, what do you say?"

"About what?" Coley watched the photographer pose Sharon, Jessie's younger sister and maid of honor, with the bride beneath the bower.

"*Fishin'!* When we goin'?"

Coley glanced up. "Soon as you recover, I expect."

"Recover?" Cassidy looked at Dalton, then at Cherry, as though asking if they could see anything wrong with him. "Recover from *what?*"

"Why, from your period of *grieving* over your big sister leaving home," Coley said with mock gravity. "Oh, you put up a good front, but I can tell you're crying inside."

"Yeah, I'm crying, all right," Cassidy replied and snorted. "Only thing that bothers me is Austin might get fed up with her triflin' ways and send her home before the week's out."

Dalton gazed over at Austin, standing a few feet away from Jessie and Sharon. The expression on his face resembled that of a little boy at the bottom of the stairs on Christmas morning. "No danger of that, little brother."

Jessie's histrionics as she had flounced and buffeted and cried her way through her teens had always fascinated Dalton. From behind the upstairs bannister, he had watched her discard boyfriends like used tissues, ending each relationship with late-night, living-room performances that rivaled Vivian Leigh's portrayal of Scarlett O'Hara in *Gone with the Wind*. The next day she would be clinging to the arm of a new beau, who'd gaze at her all wide-eyed and unsuspecting, actually believing that Jessie Temple adored *him* above all others. Three weeks was the record, as far as Dalton could remember. That was before she met Austin Youngblood.

Jessie had found her match in the unpredictable and sometimes violent banker's son from south Baton Rouge, who preferred the wrong side of the tracks to the elegance and moneyed ease that was his birthright. He had touched something in Jessie that had drawn her inexorably over the years toward this inevitable meeting at the altar.

Unlike Cassidy, Dalton Temple knew that Jessie was gone for good. Also, unlike his younger brother, Dalton knew he would miss the living, breathing theater that was Jessie Temple Youngblood.

"How's next week suit you for a fishing trip?"

"Great!"

"That okay with you, Dalton?"

"Huh?" Dalton turned his thoughts away from his older sister. "Oh, yeah. That'd be just fine."

"Good. We'll catch enough fish to feed us all for a month." Coley took a deep breath, smelling the gardenias that filled the corner of the backyard with their sweet, heady aroma. "Gardenias always remind me of my mama. . . ."

Lane Temple, his brown eyes showing the fatigue of the long day, untied his shoes, slipped them off, and propped his feet on a plant stand next to the porch swing that hung from the high ceiling of the back gallery. Undoing his bow tie, he rested his arm on the back of the swing, allowing Catherine to lean back into the hollow of his shoulder. "Well, that's *one down* and three to go!"

"You make it sound like some kind of contest," Catherine remarked as she sat up and gazed at him. "Like the first quarter of a football game, with three more to go."

"Raising children *is* like that, in a way, I guess," Lane admitted and yawned. "You have to give it your best shot while they're with you, 'cause it's the only chance you've got."

Catherine pulled her knees up, placed her stockinged feet on the slats of the swing, and leaned back against Lane. "Well, I think we've done a pretty good job so far."

"Hmm . . ."

"What's *that* supposed to mean?"

Lane shrugged. "Just hmm . . . that's all."

"You mean 'hmm,' as in Cassidy, hmm, Temple?"

Lane, staring at the aftermath of the reception in their backyard, remained noncommittal.

Catherine sat up again in the swing, crossing her legs in front of her, Indian fashion, and smoothed her skirt over her knees. "A lot of boys get in fights at school, Lane."

"With their P. E. teacher?"

"Well, they suspended him for a whole week." Catherine found herself coming to the defense of her youngest and most exasperating child, just as it had seemed she had done all his life. "Wasn't that enough punishment?"

Lane shook his head slowly back and forth. The night wind rippled through the white folds of linen cloths hanging down from the sides of the tables still out in the yard, giving them the appearance of great birds spreading their wings to lift off into the night. "Cath, the only reason they didn't expel him for the remainder of the year is that the track coach begged the principal to let him run in the state finals."

"And he did a fine job, too, didn't he?" Catherine knew she had Lane on her side now.

"Well, let's see: he won the hundred, came in second in the two-twenty, and anchored two relay teams," Lane admitted, trying not to sound too proud of his often-wayward son. "I'd say that's a pretty good day's work."

"He runs like a deer. I've never seen anybody make running look so pretty." Catherine stared at the lighted window just beyond Lane's head. "It's almost like . . . ballet."

"He's got that God-given speed, all right. No doubt about it." Lane glanced at Catherine and chuckled. "I wouldn't talk about that ballet stuff in front of him, though."

"No, I guess I'd better not," Catherine agreed. "Somehow I think Cass wouldn't see the beauty of it."

Lane's thoughts returned to the prospective marriages of his remaining children. "Maybe Dalton and Cherry will be next,"

Lane suggested out of the blue. "What do you think?"

"Goodness!" Catherine said. "Let's not hurry them into anything! We just got this one over with."

"What's the matter?" Lane wondered what had prompted Catherine's guarded reaction. "Don't you approve of her?"

Catherine thought of how Cherry always gushed when she was around Dalton. It had been her experience that young women who fawned over their men, as Cherry did, were just as quick to latch on to someone else when the relationship hit some rough spots. "It's not that," Catherine replied, her eyes following the erratic flight of a moth as it thumped the windowpane, seeking the light inside the kitchen. "I don't really know her well enough yet to have an opinion."

Lane closed his eyes, speaking slowly. "*Dalton* sure seems to approve of her."

Catherine remembered how Cherry's dress clung to the generous proportions of her figure and commented, "I'm not sure that he's thinking too clearly at this point."

"Well, she's certainly friendly enough."

"Maybe *too* friendly." Catherine regretted the words as soon as they were spoken.

Lane opened his eyes and fastened them on Catherine's, a slight frown on his face.

"What's *that* supposed to mean?"

"Oh, I don't know . . . nothing, really." Catherine couldn't truly understand why she had said what she did. "It's just that girls who grow up without a daddy sometimes —" She paused, then added, "Dalton said they never knew where their next meal was coming from."

"Sounds like she'll fit right in with this family, then," Lane offered.

"Why's that?"

"Mississippi's full of little towns like Sweetwater, where one or two families have all the money," Lane continued. "Since neither of ours had any, she's probably just the North Louisiana version of the Temples and the Taylors."

"Maybe you're right," Catherine admitted. She tried to push aside her doubts and inner reservations about Dalton's girlfriend. "I guess all mothers think that no girl's good enough for their sons."

A smile crossed Lane's face. "Well, I know for a fact that no *boy's* good enough for Sharon."

As always, the mention of Sharon made Catherine think immediately of her daughter's health. She felt a gratitude beyond expression that it had been good the past year. "She looked so pretty today, didn't she? The perfect maid of honor for her sister."

Lane knew the question didn't require an answer. "Leukemia's still in remission." His voice carried a tone of thanksgiving. "I think she looks better now than she has in years. Her color is so good, and she's even put on a little weight."

"You know what's amazing about this whole thing?" Catherine's tone echoed her husband's.

"Yep," Lane replied, his face holding a deadpan expression. "We both managed to stay out of the insane asylum."

A trace of a smile lit Catherine's blue eyes. "That, too, but I was thinking more of Sharon's grades. She stayed on the honor roll, in spite of everything she's been through."

"She'll be a writer, for sure." Lane nodded thoughtfully. "Maybe even win the Pulitzer or the Nobel someday, like Faulkner did. Who knows?"

"Writing's where her heart is," Catherine agreed. "There's no mistaking that. Although I think her writing's more like Eudora Welty's than William Faulkner's."

"Well, enough about the children," Lane said suddenly. He placed his feet on the floor and began pushing the swing gently back and forth.

"What do you want to talk about, then?" Catherine asked, surprised that he would leave his favorite subject.

"Grandchildren!"

TWO

Sound and Fury

★ ★ ★

Its ironlike talons grasping a limb in the crown of a towering cypress, the vulture gazed southward toward the Gulf. From his vantage point, he could see the dark purple-gray wall building rising steadily from the rim of the earth. Above, a few puffy clouds floated like pieces of torn cotton in a soft blue sky. The day was warm and dry and almost perfectly still. Even so, the giant carrion bird shifted restlessly on his perch high above the lake.

Shaped like a rough oval a hundred yards wide, the lake beneath the huge black bird ran south for a quarter of a mile in the trackless network of bayous and bays and islands that formed the Atchafalaya Basin. A ragged company of cypress knees stood in the shallows; low-limbed willows crowded the shoreline. On the high ground of the basin, giant oaks, sycamores, and tupelos formed a canopy above the twilight region of the forest floor where palmetto grew in stiff, fanlike profusion.

The vulture fanned its great wings, restless, agitated, its relentless stare fixed southward. Suddenly it soared outward, in dark silhouette against the sky, and banked into a long, sweeping turn and headed toward the north.

Far below on the dark, mirrored surface of the lake, a white-haired boy in cut-off blue jeans fished with a cane pole. He sat crosslegged in the bottom of a pirogue, his eyes fastened on a cork floating on the water's surface. An invisible finger tapped the cork once, then three more times in rapid succession, pushing it just under the water. Suddenly the cork vanished.

Cassidy jerked upward on the pole, setting the hook hard. "I got you this time! That's the last shiner you'll steal off my hook, you big rascal!"

"What's all the noise about?" Dalton, his hard, tanned frame clad only in a red bathing suit, woke up from his nap in the bottom of the fragile little craft, both legs dangling over opposite sides of the low gunwales.

The pirogue wobbled dangerously, rocking back and forth. Water shipped over one side.

"Don't turn us over, you big dummy!"

36

Cassidy held the pole with both hands, arms outstretched above his head as he fought to keep the fish away from the thick tangle of a partially submerged treetop. The line jerked back and forth, cutting the water like a thin blade as the fish battled to free itself.

Smiling at his little brother's hysterics, Dalton calmly reached out with one hand and took hold of a limb reaching up through the water from the fallen tree. The little craft immediately stopped its rocking.

"Whatcha got there, Cass?" Dalton added with a grin. "I bet it's another choupique."

"Uh-uh." Cassidy was on his knees now, fighting the fish in earnest. "Bass . . . a *big* one!"

Dalton turned the limb loose. The pirogue suddenly wobbled back and forth beneath Cassidy's twisting and turning as he strained against the erratic pulls of the fish.

"You stupid . . . !"

But Dalton had already taken hold of the limb again.

Finally the fish broke water, creating a green-and-white fountain that sparkled in the morning sunshine.

Cassidy's face grew slack with disappointment. "Another choupique."

Tiring now, the fish let himself be drawn toward the boat. With anger sparking in his

37

eyes, Cassidy grabbed the short-handled paddle at his feet. He stared at the mottled-green, prehistoric-looking fish at the end of his line. Holding the pole with his left hand, he brought the paddle crashing down on the fish's head, crushing it.

"A little rough on that poor thing, weren't you, Cass?" Dalton asked, resting his elbows on the gunwales. "*He* couldn't help it if he wasn't born a bass."

"He won't be stealing any more shiners from me," Cassidy stated, slipping the heavy K-bar knife from his belt. Every time he grasped its ribbed handle, he wondered if his father had used it to kill Japanese soldiers in the South Pacific. Even as a child his blood had raced at the thought of taking his father's K-bar knife into battle someday. Unwilling to touch the choupique, he cut the string and watched it turn over slowly and slide downward, its white belly fading gradually out of sight into the depths of the lake.

"You have any luck while I was asleep?" Dalton lay back, resting his head on a boat cushion jammed between the gunwales where they came together to form the sharp prow. In the warm June shade, his skin glistened with a thin sheen of perspiration.

With a smug expression, Cassidy lifted the fish stringer hanging over the side of the pirogue and dangling down into the cool water. Fashioned from a slender willow branch, it held five shining, flapping sac-a-lait strung through their gills.

"Not bad. Pound, maybe a pound and a half each." Dalton appraised his little brother's afternoon catch. "Coley can fix us a good supper with that many."

"Whadda you mean, 'us'?" Cassidy untied the cotton bowline from a willow branch next to his hip. "All *you* did was lie around like a big bear all afternoon."

A sudden memory, sharp and clear as a well-focused photograph, flashed at the back of Dalton's mind. *The black bear charged straight at him. He could see its long white canines and the fiery little eyes across the few feet of air that separated them. The shotgun roared its own lethal anger, fire and smoke bursting from the barrel, its butt thumping heavily against his shoulder. He watched a red blossom spring to life on the bear's chest. It tumbled head over heels, then rose on its hind legs, stalking doggedly toward him.*

Dalton saw himself break the barrel open, eject the spent shell, dig frantically in his pocket for a fresh one — but there wasn't enough time. Then Cassidy appeared directly behind the bear, the heavy K-bar gripped tightly in both hands. He quickly raised the knife above his head, plunging it down into the bear's back at the base of its neck. . . .

"Careful how you talk to me, little brother. Bears can be pretty dangerous." Dalton saw by the glint of recognition that Cassidy had been remembering too.

"Tell you what," Cassidy offered. "I caught 'em. Coley's gonna cook 'em. . . ."

Dalton could tell what was coming, so he finished the sentence for him. "All right, all right. I'll clean 'em, then."

Cassidy grabbed the short paddle at his feet and dipped it into the dark water, sending a slight swirling on the surface as the pirogue slid away from the shade into the late June sunlight winking on the surface. The leaves on the cypress far above caught the light in a bright green shining. The air was heavy with moisture, perfectly still, and carried a slight smell like singed copper.

"Think Coley's up from his nap yet?" Dalton shielded his eyes with the flat of his hand, squinting at the tiny cabin ahead of him. Built of rough-cut logs, it rested on pilings seven feet above the shallows and forty feet out from the shoreline. A set of steps ran down the five-foot drop from the front gallery to a small pier. Tied to one of the supporting posts, an aluminum bateau with a ten-horsepower Evinrude clamped to its stern floated at the end of its rope tether.

As though in answer to Dalton's question, the front screen door pushed open slowly. Coley rolled through in his chair, let the door gently close, and rolled over to the head of the steps. He stretched, yawned, and brushed his dark hair, still tousled from sleep, back from his face.

"Whadda you think about this, Uncle Coley?" Cassidy rested the paddle across the gunwales and lifted the dripping string of sac-a-lait from the water.

"I think they're gonna taste mighty good tonight with some hush puppies and French fries."

Cassidy grinned as though he could already taste the white flaky fish that almost melted in the mouth after Coley had battered and fried them. "Dalton has *graciously*" — Cassidy made an open-handed sweeping motion as if to introduce an honored guest — "agreed to handle the cleaning duties for us. Isn't that right, big brother?"

"*Somebody's* got to handle the dirty work." Dalton placed one hand on a piling, the other on the weathered decking, and stepped carefully out of the little pirogue. "I notice that you always manage to keep *your* hands clean."

Tapping the side of his head with a forefinger, Cassidy winked at Coley. "Well *some-body's* got to do the thinking." Then he tied off the bowline, lifted the string of sac-a-lait onto the pier, and stepped out.

Dalton picked up the string of sac-a-lait and walked to the end of the pier. "I saw your report card this year, Cass. As a *thinker,* you're about two notches below Daffy Duck."

Cassidy opened his mouth for a quick retort, but there was no refuting such an obvious truth. Instead, he hurled a verbal javelin, seeking a chink in his brother's armor. "Oh, yeah! Well, I think Cherry might just go out with me, if I asked her."

"Ask away," Dalton replied, supremely confident in his girlfriend's fidelity.

"If you weren't *Mr. Football* in this football-crazy town, that girl wouldn't look at you twice," Cassidy pressed as he walked the length of the pier and sat down next to the workbench. Leaning back on a piling, he let his bare feet dangle down into the water. "Yes, sir," he continued smugly. "Miss Cherry Lovell and me would be a hot item if good looks and charm meant anything to her."

"You're probably right." Dalton obviously felt he had won this battle with his little brother. Grabbing the butt of the willow stringer, he slipped the first fish off the end and placed it on the makeshift table built from a two-by-twelve nailed across the tops of two pilings.

Cassidy's acceptance of defeat came in the form of a quick change of subject. "Hey, Uncle Coley!" he called over his shoulder. "We got any Cokes left?"

"One apiece. I'd save mine for supper, if I were you, though." Since he had come to know the Temple family, Coley had enjoyed bringing Dalton and Cassidy on these fishing trips with him. Over the years, he had come to think of them as his own nephews and had enjoyed watching them go about the business of growing up. That had given him as much pleasure as savoring the beauty of the basin itself.

"Yeah, I will." Cassidy nodded toward Dalton. "We may not *have* any supper if Slowpoke here doesn't speed up his fish-cleaning a little."

Dalton ignored the remark. Using a slim-bladed knife left on the table, he scaled the fish on both sides, carved a quick crescent to get rid of the head, and slit the belly open.

Cassidy lay back on the weathered cypress decking, hands clasped behind his head, feet moving lazily back and forth in the cool water below.

Dalton, a quick smile crossing his tanned

face, glanced at Coley. Raking the fish remains off into the water, he watched several small turtles rise slowly into sight from beneath a cypress log. Their mouths working with uncharacteristic speed, they began feasting on their free supper.

"Owww!" Cassidy jerked his legs from the water, holding one foot in both hands as he skidded backward away from the edge of the pier.

Dalton kept at his work, trying to suppress the laughter welling up inside. After two or three seconds, he gave up, sat down on the decking, and let it roll out of him.

"That's not funny!" Cassidy scowled at Dalton, then at his foot, as though disappointed that only a tiny red spot marked it instead of a generous flow of blood.

Dalton's laughter spoke for him.

"You think it's funny?"

Dalton rubbed his face with both hands and took a deep breath before replying. "I think it's the funniest thing I've seen since that goat butted you in the Christmas play!"

Cassidy glanced up at Coley, his eyes still lighted with the afterglow of laughter. A grin spread across Cassidy's face. "Maybe you're right. You know, it was my idea to glue cotton balls on that goat to make it look like a lamb, too."

"A goat in sheep's clothing is still a goat, Cass." Coley glanced toward the southern sky, a slight frown crossing his slim face. "Why don't you come on up here and get the Coleman stove fired up? Dalton's gonna have those sac-a-lait cleaned and gutted before you know it."

"Your cookin' just gets better and better, Uncle Coley," Dalton praised. He leaned his ladder-backed chair against the wall of the cabin and placed both hands over his stomach. "That's the best fried fish in Louisiana."

"You say that every time, Dalton." Cassidy sat on the edge of the gallery, his legs hanging seven feet above the water.

"Well, it is."

Coley gazed at the late western sky, the sun now a red smudge behind the treeline. Both lake and swamp seemed suffused with firelight, the sky washed with lavender. Then Coley turned his gaze toward the south, a shadow crossing his face.

"Wow! Look at *that!*" Cassidy pointed toward the sky at the southern end of the lake.

The first of the vultures cleared the treeline, wings pumping slowly in flight, then the birds held rigidly outward, catching air currents as they cleared the treeline and sailed out over the lake. Behind the leaders, others came on in endless dark waves, shadowing the sky with their numbers.

"Man!" Dalton, a metal cup of steaming black coffee in one hand and a half-eaten devil's food snack cake in the other, stared up into the darkened sky. "I didn't know there were that many buzzards in the whole world."

"What's happening here?" Cassidy stood abruptly, glancing at Coley before looking back toward the south.

Trailing the vultures at lower altitudes, snowy egrets, blue herons, crows, and a few hawks flew north in close rank and file across the open space of lavender sky. Mixed in with and trailing behind, smaller blue jays, mockingbirds, sparrows, and scores of other species brought up the rear guard.

Dalton stood up and walked over to stand next to his brother. "Looks like Noah opened up the ark, don't it? I wonder what'll be heading this way next?"

As though in answer to Dalton's question, four armadillos scampered out of the underbrush on the far shoreline, entered the water, and began paddling frantically toward the north shore of the lake, their barely discernable V-trails fanning out behind them.

Coley took his eyes from the hundreds of birds flying overhead. He shook his head slowly back and forth. "I should have paid more attention hours ago."

"What are you talking about, Uncle Coley?" Dalton, his face cloudy with concern, turned around and took two steps toward him. "Paid more attention to *what?*"

"That yellowish color the sky was taking on down toward the south."

Cassidy joined in, walking over and plopping down in the chair Dalton had just vacated. "What's a yellow sky got to do with anything?"

"It *can* be a sign of a hurricane brewing out in the Gulf." Coley rolled his chair over to the south end of the gallery. "In fact, I think that's *exactly* what it is."

"You mean all those buzzards and —" Dalton studied the bird-filled sky.

"Storm's driving them north."

Cassidy was on his feet again. "Well, what're we sitting around *here* for? Let's get things together and get on home." He started gathering up rods, reels, cane poles, and other fishing tackle hanging on the walls and stacked on the floor of the gallery.

"Too late for that," Coley stated flatly. "Sorry. It's my fault. I should have gotten us on the move earlier, while we still had time." He gazed longingly across the lake at the small channel, the only way out of the swamp and toward home.

"We got time. Let's just hurry." Cassidy reached for another rod hanging across two nails driven into the cypress wall of the gallery.

On the horizon's rim, the tops of clouds — dark purple and green — pushed upward, roiling and rising and climbing to the north. Coley pointed at the ominous bank of clouds.

Cassidy turned around, gazing wide-eyed at the billowing outriders of the coming storm. "What do we do now?"

Dalton bounded down the steps and began untying the bateau, pulling it along the length and around the end of the dock to the north side of the cabin.

"Help your brother get the bateau and the pirogue around on that side, away from the wind, and tie them between the trees as good as you can." Coley spun his chair around, opening the screen door of the cabin. "I'll see what I can do inside to make things a little more secure."

Cassidy grasped the bowline of the pirogue, then stared down at the side of the pier. "Hey! It looks like the water's come up six inches on this piling!"

"That hurricane's been pushing toward landfall for a while now. Water's backing up all the way from the Gulf." Coley's explanation grew more faint as he wheeled his chair inside the cabin and disappeared.

Dalton pulled the bateau between two thick cypress trunks and began tying it off. A sudden wind from the southwest swept across the surface of the lake, sighing high in the trees above him and ruffling the smoothness out of the water. A scattering of leaves and small branches tumbled and drifted and swooped downward onto the lake and the dock and clattered onto the tin roof of the small cabin.

By the time he had finished securing the bateau and had moved to help Cassidy with the pirogue, a trackless shadow had marched across the lake beneath the tumbling clouds. In a matter of minutes, a sundown darkness dropped around them and the temperature dipped fifteen degrees.

The screen door bolted open, and Coley rolled out onto the gallery. He called out to the boys, "If you're finished with the boats, pick up everything that's not nailed down and bring it into the cabin." With a worried glance at the sullen sky, he wheeled back inside.

Dalton pushed the mattress aside and gazed out the window. A stillness had settled over the lake and the swamp. The air had grown breathless, so close and heavy and wet that he felt almost as though he took a warm liquid down into his lungs with each breath. In the thin, pewter-colored light filtering through the clouds, everything appeared still and waiting. Even the long silvery tendrils of Spanish moss hung perfectly motionless from the trees.

Then the world outside the little cabin changed. The first heavy drops began to fall, dimpling the water's surface. Abruptly, the rain swept down in torrents, hissing loudly on the lake and clattering across the tin roof like gravel. The wind rose in gusts, flinging the downpour horizontally against the windowpanes, moaning around the eaves of the cabin and wailing high in the tops of the trees.

As the last of the light faded away, Dalton stepped back from the window and grabbed the mattress to push it back into position as a protective covering of the windowpanes.

"Wait! I wanna take a look!"

Dalton turned and gazed at Cassidy, who was getting up from his seated position on the metal springs of one of the iron single beds that had lost its mattress. In the flickering yellow light from a coal oil lamp standing on a shelf, his brother's face had taken on an expression he had never seen before — excitement mingled with a strange and, or so it appeared to him, *unnatural* pleasure.

"Let me see!" Cassidy stepped over to the low window, knelt down, and pushed the mattress aside.

Dalton listened to the wind, increasing in intensity as it began to howl across the flat stretch of water that separated them from the forest. "There's nothing to see. It's black out there."

"I can see a little bit with this." Cassidy's voice had taken on a hushed tone, as though he were whispering secrets in church. He pulled a green marine-issue flashlight from the back pocket of his jeans, slipped the switch on, and shined its beam of light through the rain-splashed windowpane. "Boy! What a show!"

Dalton glanced over at Coley, sitting in his chair next to the closed and barred door. The pale light shadowed the lean planes of his face. Coley merely shrugged at Cassidy's unusual interest in the storm. Dalton thought Cassidy's behavior must at least seem mildly amusing to Coley, considering the things he had seen during his combat experience in the South Pacific.

"Look at those waves! They're coming all the way up to the porch now!" Cassidy, his eyes sparking in the lamplight, turned toward Dalton. "You gotta *see* this! It looks like the whole *world's* gonna blow away!"

A shrieking of tearing metal and a slamming against the cabin wall pierced the storm's fury. Next, they heard a bumping along the floor of the gallery and a crashing sound.

Dalton jerked around, staring at Coley.

"There goes the screen door," Coley said a little too casually, in answer to Dalton's unasked question.

"Can I go out on the porch, Uncle Coley?" Cassidy turned his head from the window, his eyes bright with a private affection for the power raging outside in the darkness.

Coley gave Cassidy a level stare. "Don't even *think* about it, young man. That wind would blow you all the way over to the Mississippi River."

"Aw! C'mon. Let me take a peek."

Coley dismissed Cassidy's second request with a wave of his hand.

Above the shrieking of the wind and the slapping of the waves against the pilings and floor of the cabin, Dalton heard a tiny scratching. Listening closer, he found that it appeared to be coming from the bottom of the door that let out onto the gallery. "What's that noise?"

Coley glanced behind him. "Don't know for sure, but I've got a pretty good idea."

"Maybe we ought to take a look." Dalton walked over to the door and knelt on the floor.

"All right," Coley agreed, "but be careful not to let the wind get ahold of that door." Lifting the age-darkened two-by-four that barred the door, Dalton eased the door inward just six inches. A half-grown rabbit, soaked and shivering, scurried inside, bumping up against Dalton's tennis shoes. "Look at this pitiful little thing, would you?" He eased the door to and picked up the half-drowned rabbit, cradling it in his arms. Then he walked over to the corner behind him and sat down on a battered footlocker. "This poor thing is nearly scared to death."

Cassidy tore his eyes away from the window, giving the shivering rabbit a skeptical gaze. "Maybe you better not get too attached to little 'Thumper' there, Dalton."

"Why not?" Dalton picked up a soiled towel from the floor next to the footlocker and began rubbing the rabbit's wet fur. It struggled briefly, then seemed to relax.

" 'Cause we just might have to eat him if this storm leaves us stranded back here."

Dalton turned the rabbit over on its back, rubbing the soft white fur of its underside with the towel. "Nah. This storm won't last much longer. Sounds like it's dying down some already."

A sudden rush of wind howled above all the other storm noises, followed by the crash of shattering glass. Dalton turned just in time to see a wall of water cascading in through the broken window. With a sickening thud, a piece of driftwood as big as his leg rammed against Cassidy's skull. The door made a loud banging noise against the inside cabin wall as the wind slammed it open.

"Cass!" Dalton leaped toward his brother, now scraping along the floor beneath the surging water. Struggling in water up to his knees, Dalton grabbed Cassidy under his armpits, lifted him up, and pushed him onto the top bunk still standing firmly against the wall. "Cass! Are you all right?"

Cassidy moaned softly, turned his head to one side, and lay still on the damp army blanket.

The wall of water, pushed forward by the surging wind, suddenly collapsed. Dalton wrestled the mattress back in front of the gaping window, blocking it in place with the heavy bunk bed. Then he turned to see the last of the water slosh past Coley's empty wheelchair, folded half inward, caught against the doorjamb.

"Uncle Coley!" Dalton rushed over to the door and stared desperately out into the howling madness of the storm.

"Uncle Coley! Where are you?"

THREE

The Wind-Torn Darkness

★ ★ ★

Catherine walked softly along the upstairs hallway, faintly aware of the muted conversation drifting up the stairwell from the kitchen. A dim shaft of light fell through Sharon's partially opened door, forming a pale yellow trapezoid on the hardwood floor. Reaching the door, Catherine placed her hand on the jamb and peeked in.

Sharon knelt beside the chair at her writing desk, lamplight gleaming on her soft brown hair. Her head was bowed, hands clasped around the Bible that she pressed against her breast. A faint smile crossed Catherine's face as she took the scene in: *The Ponder Heart* by Eudora Welty lay on the desk in a pool of lamplight next to a legal pad and two yellow pencils; the bookshelf Lane had built for her when she was eight years old, crowded with volumes by America's best writers, stood against the wall; through the partially opened Venetian blinds, tree limbs swayed and danced outside in the gusts of wind spawned by the storm.

Catherine's mind turned to a scripture that had been a mainstay for years: "The effectual fervent prayer of a righteous man availeth much." What then of a righteous seventeen-year-old girl who had come to know Jesus as a child? A sense of peace filled Catherine's heart as she thought of Sharon's prayers, rising like incense toward the portals of heaven.

"The boys will be all right, Cath." Lane, the strained expression on his face belying the confidence of his words, stared at his wife over his coffee cup. His time-worn marine undershirt and threadbare khakis had seen him through other troubles over the years, and tonight he took comfort in the feel of the clothes, remembering. "Coley will take good care of them."

Catherine brought to mind the scene she had just witnessed upstairs — Sharon praying for the safety of her brothers and Coley. Standing at the sink, she picked at a thread on the sleeve of her cotton dress, cornflower blue and matching the color of her eyes almost perfectly. It had always been one of her favorite colors. "I know he will." She lifted several dinner plates from the drain and walked over to the cabinet to put them away. "I just wish they could have gotten out of there. This hurricane came up so suddenly."

The sound of high-heels clicking on the hardwood floors in the hall drifted into the kitchen. "Well, the telephone's still dead." Maria, her large brown eyes shadowed with concern, walked into the kitchen and joined the others. She wore a gray skirt and a silk blouse the color of summer plums. "Even if they made it out of the basin, they wouldn't be able to let us know," she said, trying to think up any good excuse for not hearing from Coley and the boys.

Lane picked up his cup and walked over to the stove. "Look, Coley grew up in those swamps," Lane reminded them as he poured steaming coffee from the white enameled pot into his cup, "and this isn't the first hurricane he's been through."

"I know," Maria said softly, pushing her long dark hair back from her face with the fingers of her left hand. "It's just . . . just that he always thinks he can do more than he's really able to do."

"I think you're right about that," Lane agreed, taking his place at the table across from Maria. "That's probably how he managed to survive Tarawa."

Catherine picked the teakettle up from the

stove and walked over to the sink. "Lane's right, Maria." She turned the water on and let it run into the kettle. "Coley always seems to get the job done regardless of his limitations and no matter how bad things look."

Outside, the wind groaned around the eaves of the house. A lid from a garbage can clattered along the driveway, banging into the garage door.

Maria flinched at the sound, then sat up straight in her chair and lifted her chin slightly. "Like proving that Lane was innocent of those trumped-up charges that Andre Catelon . . . arranged against him."

"Coley had a lot of help from you, Maria," Lane reminded her, his eyes taking on a remote gaze.

Standing at the stove, Catherine turned the knob for the burner, its blue flames making a soft popping noise as they circled the bottom of the kettle. She gazed at her husband, knowing that his mind had leaped northward into the Tunica hills, bringing back those agonizing weeks he had spent in Angola State Prison, accused of a crime he didn't commit. "We'll always be grateful to you and Coley, Maria," Catherine said softly.

Maria smiled at Catherine, sitting down beside her. "Coley did all the work," she admitted. "I just happened to be in the right place at the right time to give him some information."

Catherine reached over and placed her hand on top of Lane's, giving it a gentle pressure. She watched the darkness fade from his eyes as he came back to the present.

"Catelon had everything going his way," Maria continued. "I thought there was no way we were going to be able to prove that Lane was innocent."

"Well, however bad it was back then, it brought you into our lives, Maria." Catherine gazed at her, thinking that she truly did, as Coley had once described her, bear a strong resemblance to a Titian madonna.

A loud cracking sound, followed almost immediately by a heavy thud, pierced the night beyond the bank of windows that looked out onto the backyard.

Catherine and Maria flinched, jerking their heads toward the stormy darkness outside the brightly lit kitchen.

Lane sat relaxed in his chair, slouched down, hands clasped in his lap. "There goes another limb." He sat up, resting his elbows on the table. "There's going to be *some* kind of mess to clean up out there in the morning."

"Well, you've got two strong boys to help

you." Catherine somehow took comfort in the sound of her own words, as though merely speaking of her sons would bring them safely home to their usual family routine.

"Yep." Lane sipped his coffee, both hands folded around his cup. "Dalton will be the first one out there." He smiled at the sound of his son's name. "He'll have half the yard finished before Cass finishes rubbing the sleep out of his eyes."

The teakettle's whistle shrieked. Catherine got up, took it off the burner, and turned the fire out. "Sometimes I think Cass never really wakes up until after noon." Taking two cups down from the cabinet, she dropped tea bags into them, added water from the kettle, and brought them over to the table. She seldom bothered with saucers when serving family or close friends in her kitchen. She put one of the cups in front of Maria.

"I've been fond of these cups since the first time we had tea together, Catherine." Maria traced the delicate grapevine pattern circling the outside rim of her cup with the nail of her forefinger. "It's a shame you can't replace them, especially since they were given to you as a wedding present."

"Three," Catherine said with a sigh.

"That's all I've got left." A soft light filled her eyes as she glanced at Lane, then down at her cup. "But it doesn't bother me like it used to."

Maria squeezed out her tea bag against a spoon and added sugar and cream. "Really? I'd think the older they got, the more valuable these cups would be to you."

"I don't really know how to explain it," Catherine admitted. "Maybe it's just that I'm getting older. Things that were so important to me at twenty-five or thirty don't seem to mean as much now that I'm forty-two."

Maria turned toward Lane as though searching for an explanation of his wife's statement.

Lane shrugged and nodded toward Catherine.

"I guess 'things' is the word that really explains it all." Catherine gazed thoughtfully at her husband. "Eventually, we're going to lose all the *things* we've accumulated, so why place so much value on them?"

"That sounds pretty logical to me," Maria agreed.

Catherine took the tea bag out of her cup, adding sugar and lemon. "Oh, I don't mean it's wrong to have nice things. I enjoy them as much as anyone." She took a sip of tea and lifted the delicate china, admiring the way the light gleamed off its surface. "Like having tea out of my favorite cup."

Out in the wind-torn darkness, another heavy limb came crashing down into the backyard.

Lane stared at the windows, his face shadowed with his own private thoughts. "I hope Coley gets those boys back here in time to help."

"I'm sure he will," Catherine assured him.

Lane turned toward his wife. "Maybe you ought to finish your little philosophical discussion for Maria." The corners of his mouth formed a half-smile. "I'd kind of like to see where it's leading, myself."

"I don't think it's philosophical at all," Catherine defended. She lifted her cup in both hands, changed her mind, and set it back on the table. "It's simply common sense."

"Elucidate, my dear." Lane grinned.

"Our families," Catherine began and turned toward Maria, "and our friends are the only truly eternal things we have. So why make a fuss over anything else we happen to lose?" Thinking of her sons riding out the hurricane deep in the Atchafalaya Basin, she felt the reality of her own words sink deep into her heart, as though such thoughts had never occurred to her before this raging night.

"I'd say that's pretty deep stuff for a little backwoods Mississippi girl," Lane commented, with a wink in Maria's direction.

"Maybe it's this hurricane." Catherine took a swallow of tea, savoring its rich taste and the sense of comfort tea always seemed to bring her. "Or maybe I'm beginning to understand for the first time what the apostle Paul meant when he said that the things we can see are temporal, while the things we can't see are eternal." She laughed softly as though to herself. "Or, maybe as I said before, it's just that I'm getting older."

The kitchen lights flickered, dimmed to a soft glow, and then came back to full brightness.

"You might be a little older," Lane added, "but you still look like that same seventeen-year-old girl I married — except you're a lot prettier now."

"Now you can see firsthand, Maria." Catherine opened her hand palm upward toward Lane.

"See what?"

"The secret to a happy marriage."

Maria gave Catherine a puzzled frown. "I must be missing something here."

"It's simple," Catherine explained, gazing

directly into Maria's eyes. "The secret to a happy marriage is to simply stay married until your husband gets a little senile." She nodded at Lane. "They say the nicest things at that stage of life. It also helps if their eyesight is failing."

Dalton's hands felt frozen to the doorjamb as he stared into the darkness. "Uncle Coleeey!" The wind roared like a mad beast, whipping up the water, shrieking in the tops of the trees, ripping limbs off and hurling them out into the wet darkness. Waves broke onto the gallery, flooding it with rushing water. In the dim flicker of the coal-oil lantern, the storm appeared to Dalton as if it would tear the very world off its course. He stood in the doorway, in the iron grip of fear and uncertainty, his mind unable to come to terms with the churning fury that confronted him.

Realizing he had very little time, Dalton shook off his fear as he would a hard tackle. He spun around and grabbed the flashlight still clutched in Cassidy's hand, wondering how he had managed to hang on to it. He leaned over his brother for a moment to check his breathing. It appeared normal, and his eyelids fluttered slightly. Then he snatched a length of hemp rope from a nail on the wall, secured one end to the rail of the iron bunk bed, and tied the other around his waist.

Dalton flicked the flashlight on, forced all thoughts about the possible consequences of what lay ahead of him from his mind, and stepped out onto the gallery. Instantly, the wind blew him heavily against one of the posts supporting the roof. Pain flamed inside his left shoulder. Clinging to the post, he called out, "Uncle Coley! Can you hear me?"

The storm answered with sudden breaking waves that thrust him toward the end of the gallery. Shuddering slightly, he glanced behind him at the dark, swirling lake that had almost engulfed him.

Although it had been only a matter of seconds since the wall of water had crashed through the cabin, it seemed like hours ago to Dalton. His heart sank within him as unbidden fears forced their way into his mind. *Uncle Coley must be on the bottom of the lake by now!*

Reaching just above his head, Dalton jammed the flashlight between the ceiling joist and the bottom plank of the cabin's roof, pointing the narrow shaft of light out and downward to illuminate as much of the area before him as possible. The beam revealed the storm's fury so clearly that he almost wished he hadn't brought the flashlight along.

Bracing himself against the heavy surge of windblown water across the gallery, Dalton took two steps and latched on to the handrail that led down the steps to the pier. He had no clear course of action in mind, but the overwhelming urgency to do something — anything — to find Coley forced him forward. Reaching tentatively downward with his foot, he placed it on the first step. Then, still holding on tightly to the post at his side, he slid his hand downward along the rail.

"Uhhh . . ." Beyond his control, the sound leaped from Dalton's throat. His hand had touched something firm and cold and fleshy, straining against the rail.

Turning loose of the post, Dalton slipped and felt himself being washed away until he grasped the rail with his free hand, using all his strength to hang on. Water slapped against his face, burning in his throat as it forced its way down into his lungs.

He braced against the waves with his legs spread and slipped his hand farther along the rail. Grasping the wrist with a grip made powerful from years of lifting weights, Dalton felt Coley's slim fingers wrap around his own wrist, exerting a pressure that sent pain up his forearm. *He's alive!*

Joy, like the sun blazing through dark clouds, rose up in Dalton's heart as he realized that he was part of a miracle. Nothing less could explain what was happening. *Uncle Coley's alive!*

Dalton leaned backward, straining with his legs and using his left arm for leverage. Coley's head broke through the surface of the lake, his mouth open wide as he took a great, gasping gulp of air down into his lungs. With a final effort of his right arm, Dalton pulled Coley against his own body, guided the deathlike cold arms around his neck, and turned back toward the cabin.

Feeling Coley's arms securely around his neck, Dalton grabbed the rope with both hands and began the slow, deliberate pull across the gallery to the cabin. He skidded along the floor, feeling the muscles of his biceps and upper back burning with the effort.

The storm shrieked on, voicing its displeasure at losing a victim. The rain stung Dalton's face and arms with a cold spray, but he stayed with his hand-over-hand work to pull the two of them toward safety. The twenty feet angling across the gallery to the cabin seemed more like the mile-wide span of the Mississippi River in Dalton's pain-numbed mind. He felt himself in a dreamlike state when he finally reached the door and carried Coley inside, out of the driving rain and howling wind.

"What's going on?" Cassidy, rubbing the back of his head, sat up unsteadily on the bunk.

Dalton carried Coley over to another bunk and sat him down, kneeling next to him. "How do you feel, Uncle Coley?"

Coley raised one hand to his head, pushed the sopping dark hair back from his face, and took a deep breath. "Kind of like Lazarus did when he walked out of that tomb, I imagine."

"What happened?" Cassidy shook his head, turned his slightly out-of-focus blue eyes toward Coley and Dalton, and asked, "Did I miss something?"

Dalton glanced toward the back of the cabin. The rabbit huddled in a corner, shivering from fright and cold, its eyes glowing in the flickering light of the lantern that still burned bright on its high shelf. "Not much," Dalton answered, grabbing a clean towel off a shelf and rubbing it briskly over his head and shoulders. He felt a sense of peace and safety, knowing that the worst was past. Already, he could hear a difference in the sound of the wind, its high-pitched screaming tuning down to a slightly lower key. "Uncle Coley went for a swim, and the rabbit decided to stay with us a while."

Cassidy rubbed his head again, then jerked around toward Dalton. "A swim!" He then turned his gaze on Coley, soaked through and through.

Dalton walked over to the corner, picked the rabbit up, and wrapped the towel around him. "Yeah. We'll tell you all about it as soon as we get some dry clothes on."

"Daddy, would you pass the eggs, please?" Dalton wore a white LSU football jersey with gold lettering. His brown hair was towel-dried, straight from the shower, and had not encountered a comb's teeth on the way to the kitchen table.

Lane handed his son the large platter of scrambled eggs and watched him rake a huge portion onto his plate, next to a stack of bacon and four homemade biscuits dripping with butter. "Don't be shy now, son." He glanced around the table at Catherine, Sharon, Maria, and Coley who were happily eating, sipping coffee, and sharing in the homecoming celebration of the three hurricane survivors. "You go ahead and eat all you want."

Dalton smiled around a mouthful of eggs and bacon. Washing everything down with a big swallow of milk, he grinned. "Food never tastes as good as it does after I've eaten Coley's cooking for a few days."

Coley, wearing a soft, faded-blue cotton shirt Lane had let him borrow, his body canted slightly to the left in the damaged wheelchair, sipped his coffee and turned his gray eyes on Dalton. "Next time, I'll let Cassidy do the cooking. You might appreciate me more after that."

"Never mind." Dalton took another long swallow of frothy-cold milk from a tall glass. "I appreciate you already, just thinking about having to eat *anything* Cassidy cooks."

"Somebody in here taking my name in vain?" Cassidy, barefoot and wearing only faded Levi's and a black T-shirt, his white-blond hair slicked down on his head, walked across the black-and-white tiled floor and sat down at the table next to his mother.

Catherine kissed her son on the cheek, smiling at the funny face he made in Coley's direction. She gently rubbed the lump on the back of her son's head. "You sure that doesn't bother you, Cass?"

"Not a bit." Cassidy served himself from the heaping dishes passed to him, then spooned sugar into a cup of steaming black coffee. "I'd have given Dalton's right arm for a cup of this Community coffee last night." He stirred the sugar in and took a sip, closing his eyes as he swallowed. "Hmm . . . that's worth waiting for."

Sharon wore a maroon jersey, legacy of Dalton's Istrouma High days, and a pair of white shorts. "Tell us again how you managed to keep from drowning in that terrible storm, Uncle Coley. I missed that part when I went to answer the phone."

Coley eased his hand over and clasped Maria's. She gave it a gentle squeeze. "Well, to tell you the truth, I thought my days on this terrestrial ball were finished," he began, smiling at his wife, who sat next to him. "They would have been, too," he nodded toward Dalton, "except for the nation's number one halfback and lifeguard over there."

"My brother, the hero," Cassidy mumbled toward his plate as he shoved a forkful of hot, buttered grits into his mouth.

Glancing at Cassidy, Coley spoke in a more somber tone. "Don't forget, Cass," he reminded, "I saw you flopping across that floor like a rag doll when that wall of water hit the cabin. If Dalton hadn't grabbed you and put you up on a bunk, you'd have been right out there in that storm with me."

Cassidy stared at Dalton, a sly glint in his blue eyes. "I'll remember him in my will."

Dalton didn't look up from his eating. "What are you gonna leave me — an autographed copy of your rap sheet?"

"That's enough, boys." Lane didn't raise his voice, but it still held that unmistakable ring of authority.

"Come on, Uncle Coley," Sharon pleaded. "I want to hear the rest of your story."

"Not much to tell, really. That big wave the storm kicked up came right through the window, knocked me backward out of my chair, and washed me out the door."

Maria, her eyes glazing with sudden emotion, leaned over and kissed Coley on the cheek. "You don't have to talk about it if you'd rather not, sweetheart."

"Doesn't bother me a bit," Coley replied. "Anyhow, Sharon — who just has to know — I slid right on across the gallery and banged into the railing that runs along the steps. You know, the one you like to slide down when your mother's not watching."

Sharon glanced at Catherine, a slight flush coming to her cheeks. "Yes, sir, I know."

"Well, I just grabbed at thin air a time or two and finally latched on to that railing with both hands." Coley wrapped his hands around an imaginary rail in the air in front of him. "But the wind was pushing the water up in big waves and they kept breaking over my head."

Cassidy leaned over and gazed down the length of the table at Dalton. "I'm glad you grabbed *me* in time, big brother. If I'd got washed out that door with Coley . . . one of us wouldn't be sitting here right now."

"That's for sure," Coley agreed quickly. "Anyway, I managed to lift my head up for a breath of air two or three times before my strength gave out. Then my arms started to lose feeling, and just when I thought I was finished . . ." He alternately rubbed both forearms and continued, "I felt Dalton's big hands wrap around me and pull me up out of that cold . . . darkness." His eyes grew dark with the memory of his brief glimpse of death.

Silence settled on the storm survivors and their families. Coley's words had brought home to each of them how very fragile and fleeting life was and, as after every near-tragedy, how much they depended on one another.

Beyond the bank of kitchen windows, the early sun cast long shadows across the storm-littered yard. From the limb of a live oak, a thrush sang in celebration of the new morning. Gusts of wind from the tail-end of the hurricane whined around the house like the last dying gasps of some great beast.

Sharon's soft voice finally broke the extended silence around the table. "What happened next?"

"The rabbit made it through all right."

"What rabbit?"

Coley told them the part of the story that he had left out. "Yep. He stayed with us the rest of the night, just like he was part of the family. Then in the morning, we let him go."

Sharon's brown eyes lighted with renewed interest as this part of the story unfolded. "I bet he was cute!"

"Looked like a drowned rat," Cassidy muttered, finishing his last bite of grits.

"And . . ." Coley let the word trail off, adding more suspense to his story, "your little brother over there killed a snake."

"You did?" Sharon gazed at Cassidy, who quickly feigned disinterest in something as common as snake-killing.

"Yep."

"How?"

"Just whacked his head off with Daddy's ol' K-bar. Nothing to it."

Dalton shook his head slowly, a rumor of a smile on his face. "Wasn't much left to whack at."

"Why? Wasn't he a big one?" With a writer's appreciation of a story, Sharon seemed disappointed that some of the danger had been taken out.

"Oh, he was big, all right," Dalton continued, scraping his chair back from the table. "That hurricane had already done a pretty good job on him, though. Wasn't much fight left in him."

Cassidy took offense at his brother's demeaning his part in the hurricane heroics. "There was enough left to make you holler like a stuck pig when you saw it . . . hero."

"He just startled me." Dalton refused to admit to something as pedestrian as fear. "That's all."

Gazing around the table at her friends and family, Catherine felt a warmth spreading inside her breast. Her sons had proven themselves able to stand up under adversity, just as their father had done in two wars and other troubles that would have easily defeated someone of lesser courage and character. She listened to the conversation and took pleasure in the smiles and laughter, even in the long-running rivalry between Dalton and Cassidy. Her sons were safe, Sharon seemed to be as healthy as ever, and the storm had passed them by.

FOUR

A Pile of Old Bones

★ ★ ★

"I just love all this excitement!" Catherine gazed at the LSU players clad in gold-and-white uniforms with purple trim as they broke from the huddle, spreading out in their precise offensive formation. The brilliance of the arc lights towering above the stadium gave the field an appearance of midday in summer. "I was so disappointed LSU lost last week." She gave a quick look around the half-empty stadium. "Apparently there were a lot of other disappointed fans."

"Don't worry about it. If half the team hadn't been sick, we could have held on to that 14–0 lead Taylor gave us in the second quarter. This week's going to be different, though," Lane assured his wife, admiring the soft curves of her purple sweater. After twenty-five years of marriage, her youthful beauty could still be a distraction for him, even in the midst of a football game at Tiger Stadium. "Maybe part of the problem was first-game jitters, but that's all behind us now."

Down on the field, Win Turner crouched over the center, glanced to his left and then his right, barking out the signals. Taking the snap, he whirled around and slapped the ball into Cannon's midsection.

Catherine was instantly on her feet, shouting, "Run, Billy! Run!"

Standing now, Lane smiled at his wife's enthusiasm, then turned his eyes back to the playing field.

Cannon was carrying out Catherine's instructions as though he had heard them. Turning the end, he simply outran all his pursuers and galloped fifty-three yards into the end zone.

"Way to go, Billy!" Catherine's hands were clasped at her breast as she jumped up and down, her face glowing with excitement.

The stadium roared with the cheers of LSU fans. When the noise had subsided, Lane leaned over toward Catherine. "Did you watch Dalton on that play?"

"Why . . . no." Catherine's face held a perplexed expression. "Billy had the ball."

"Well, he wouldn't have scored if Dalton hadn't thrown that block on the cornerback," Lane explained. "He had a dead bead on Billy, until Dalton cut his feet out from under him."

"Why don't you tell me these things while I still have time to see them for myself?"

Lane was about to tell Catherine how to watch the plays unfolding when her attention wandered.

"Look at Cherry doing cartwheels with the other cheerleaders! She's so pretty!" Catherine reached over and took Lane's hand. "We've got so much to be thankful for with our children . . . our family, Lane."

Trying to bridge the gap in Catherine's thought processes between cartwheels and thanksgiving, Lane simply agreed with her. He had ceased long ago spending undue time trying to decipher the unique and mysterious workings of his wife's mind. "Yes, we do."

Catherine, watching the teams line up for the extra point, took her seat. "I wish Sharon would have come with us."

"Since Jessie got pregnant, Sharon's been like an old mother hen with her." Lane sat down next to his wife.

"Isn't that the truth?" Catherine clapped her hands as the kick cleared the goalposts for the extra point. "I've told her that a little morning sickness is normal, and that Jessie's going to feel a little run-down for a while, but that it's just temporary." She kept her eyes fastened on Dalton as he walked back to the Tiger bench. "You know what she told me?"

Lane shrugged.

"She said Jessie doesn't have enough sense to take care of herself, much less a baby."

"That sounds just like Sharon," Lane laughed.

"So I expect every time Austin goes out of town on business, she'll be insisting on staying with Jessie."

"By the way . . ." Lane paused to watch the kickoff. At the other end of the field, the Alabama receiver took the ball, sprinted ten yards, then disappeared beneath a mound of white-and-gold jerseys. "Way to stick 'em, Tigers!"

Two minutes later, after being held to an eight-yard gain in three tries by the Tiger defense, Alabama lined up in punt formation. Sailing off the foot of the red-shirted punter, the ball spiraled high in the dazzle of the arc lights.

"I hope Dalton gets a chance to run this one back." Lane leaned forward toward the field, intent on the game.

Cannon reached up for the ball, juggled it for a long second before gaining control, and exploded toward the far goal line. Slicing in from across the field, Dalton threw a bone-jarring block to cut down the first defender, a stocky linebacker who had his sights fixed on the ball carrier.

Lane leaped to his feet. "Way to go, son!" Then with Catherine cheering next to him, he watched Cannon like a thoroughbred among mules simply outrace the Alabama team for a seventy-three-yard touchdown.

"This is so much fun!" Catherine squeezed Lane's hand, then sat back down. "I have to be honest with you, darling. I'm enjoying this more than I did when you played up at Ole Miss."

Joining her, Lane remembered out loud. "Well, you were either pregnant or trying to take care of a baby. Either one doesn't leave much time for enjoying football."

"That's true. It's been so long, I'd almost forgotten babies are a full-time job."

As the teams left the field for halftime, Lane stood up and stretched, then looked down at Catherine. "How about a hot dog and a Coke?"

"I'd love one . . . both."

"Back in a minute." Lane walked down the steep concrete steps of the stadium, turned into one of the exits, and shouldered his way through the crowded landings and ramps leading from one level to another. Fall fashions were on display, even though the mild September weather testified against them. Men perspired freely, and the women used their football programs as fans.

Shoved from behind by a surge in the crowd, Lane jostled a young woman standing in front of him in the long line that eventually reached the concession stand. "Excuse me."

The woman turned around, her face lifted upward. "That's all right. This crowd is —"

Lane gazed down into the oval-shaped face framed by a familiar mass of dark, shoulder-length hair. He remembered it from years ago, a time that had almost cost him his marriage. His face felt warm with shame as he spoke to her. "Hello, Bonnie. It's been a long time." *Of all people in this town to bump into.*

Bonnie Catelon's eyes took on a remote light. "Hello, Lane. I see your son's become quite the football star."

"Not yet, but it looks like he might be on his way." Lane felt awkward, wishing for a graceful way out of the situation he now found himself in.

Bonnie stared at something in the air to the right of Lane's face. "Jessie married that Youngblood boy, didn't she?"

Lane nodded, glancing anxiously around

Bonnie at the concession stand they were inching toward.

"I thought I saw it in the newspaper."

"He's a fine boy."

"How's your little girl?"

"Sharon?"

"Yes. She's such a smart little thing."

Lane wondered how Bonnie could have known anything about his youngest daughter. "Thank you. She's had a few stories published in national magazines." Unwanted memories of his brief affair with Bonnie crowded back into his mind. He fought against them. An aching like that of an old war wound began inside his chest.

"She's doing well, then."

Lane suddenly saw Sharon's face the night he and Catherine had told her about her illness. Guilt stabbed at him like a cold knife blade. "She's had some health problems, but she's been doing much better this past year. How have you been?"

"The same." The delicate skin beneath Bonnie's eyes looked bruised. "I still live in Daddy's apartment in the Pentagon most of the time. . . ."

Lane fought against the scenes that were forcing themselves to the front of his mind, then flashing on its viewing screen.

". . . use the little place in the French

Quarter when I'm visiting down there."

"I'm so sorry, Bonnie." Lane heard the words spilling out before he could stop them. "I was —"

"Lane!" Bonnie closed her eyes, the long lashes dark against her pale skin. She opened them and placed her hand gently along the side of his arm. "It's all right. I don't blame you anymore for what happened."

Lane stepped up to the counter, ordered two Cokes and two hot dogs, and paid for them. His hands full, he turned and said, "I hope you find what you're looking for, Bonnie." Lane felt weak and useless and undeserving of all the blessings he had received. "I have to go now."

Bonnie, a single tear tracing a shining path down her cheek, watched him hurry away and disappear into the crowd.

"What'll it be, miss?"

Startled, she turned to the man behind the concession stand. He wore a toothy smile and a white paper hat with Coca-Cola printed in bold red letters on its side. "Nothing . . . thank you."

The man watched her turn, swept away by the river of people flowing along the landing that followed the curve of the stadium.

"Here you are, sweetheart." Lane handed

Catherine her Coke in its red-and-white cup and the hot dog wrapped in wax paper. "Sorry it took so long."

"I was starting to get worried." Catherine took a swallow of her drink, then gazed at Lane. "You've got the strangest look on your face. Is something wrong?"

Lane sat down beside his wife, trying to hide from her questioning eyes by taking a big bite of his hot dog. "Nothing's wrong," he mumbled through the bread and meat, then lifted his cup and drank deeply from it.

Catherine looked away at the Tiger Marching Band down on the field. The drum major strutted out front as the musicians moved with the precision born of long hours spent on the practice field. John Phillip Sousa would have approved of their performance.

Lane felt an urgent need now to confess. "I saw Bonnie Catelon."

Taking a sip of her Coke, Catherine continued to stare down at the band, prancing with the speeded-up tempo.

The words poured out of Lane now, seemingly of their own volition. "I couldn't help it, Cath. I just bumped into her and said a few words." He stared at Catherine's profile, lips slightly compressed, and added, "And I got out of there in a hurry."

Catherine seemed to find the band fascinating.

"C'mon, Cath." Lane leaned forward, elbows on his knees, trying to capture her full attention. "I didn't even have a real conversation with her."

"Do I look worried?" Catherine turned her face toward him, a bright smile fixed on it that didn't quite hide the shadow of concern in her cornflower blue eyes. "Now, quit digging around in that pile of old bones and eat your hot dog."

Jerry Lee Lewis's high-voltage voice blasted from the loudspeakers with his driving, piano-pounding version of "Whole Lot of Shakin' Goin' On." Purple and gold crepe paper and balloons of the same colors decorated the walls and ceilings. The Sigma Chi house vibrated with the sounds of music, laughter, conversations at a scream pitch, and dozens of sock- and stocking-clad feet pounding on the hardwood floor.

The college men wore a hodgepodge of styles: suits and ties, chinos, jeans and T-shirts, even bermuda shorts in a variety of bright plaids. Their girlfriends' apparel was just as varied, ranging from elegant party dresses and high-heels to pedal pushers and shorts worn with sweater and brown penny loafers or flats.

A makeshift bar, well-stocked with bottles of liquor and wine, had been set up in the corner. A galvanized tub full of beer, swimming inside a larger one of crushed ice, rested on the floor. Several rows of paper cups were stacked next to it, and the beer rocked with miniature waves from the constant dipping of the revelers into its foamy surface.

"Have a beer!" One the Sigma Chi pledges, eyes shining with alcohol, filled a cup with the foamy brew and stretched his arm in Dalton's general direction.

Dalton frowned slightly at the alcohol-charged breath that hit him across the four feet of smoke-filled air separating him from the Sigma Chi pledge. "No thanks. I don't drink."

The boy's mouth gaped open in surprise that bordered on shock. "You don't drink?"

"That's right." Dalton smiled down at Cherry standing next to him.

Persisting, the pledge acted as though he received a commission from every drink he gave away. "Aw, c'mon. You deserve it, after the way you played tonight. Nobody thought we could beat Alabama."

"Taylor made all three touchdowns. He didn't need my help to do that." Dalton glanced around the bedlam of the huge room, wondering why he continued to come to these fraternity parties after every game.

"I just love these parties, don't you?" Cherry cooed at his shoulder. "They're so much fun!"

Now I remember. Dalton put his arm around Cherry's waist, escorting her across the room to a table covered with a white linen cloth and set with a punch bowl and cut-glass cups. He noticed several of the other players and fraternity members eying Cherry's black party dress with its almost nonexistent straps. It retained a certain amount of modesty, but not enough to keep Dalton from feeling discomfort in her company.

Jerry Lee Lewis had apparently shaken enough, and was replaced by the smooth baritone crooning of Pat Boone, singing "Love Letters in the Sand."

"Can we dance, sugar?" Cherry held her arms toward Dalton, her long lashes drooping slightly over her pale blue eyes, giving them a sleepy look. "It's such a pretty song."

Dalton stopped the ladle in midair, set it back in the bowl, and led Cherry out onto the crowded floor. As she pressed into his arms, her fragrance drifted around him like spring flowers, and the rounded softness of her body seemed to melt into his own. He let his body move in time with the music almost of its own accord as thoughts blew through his mind like a gentle wind. *What could be better than this? I'm playing football, and that I love to do more than anything in the world — and LSU is giving me a free education to do it. I've got a beautiful girl who's crazy about me, a family that I wouldn't trade for anything. . . . Well, maybe I'd let Cass go if someone made me a pretty good offer. Who could have a better life?*

When the song had ended, Dalton took Cherry by the hand and led her back to the punch bowl. He filled two cups and handed her one just as someone put "Blueberry Hill" on the record player. The unmistakable voice of Fats Domino, accompanied by his own chubby fingers on the ivory keys, now blared from the speakers.

"Wanna cut a rug, babe?"

Dalton glanced at the tall, gangly young man wearing a Harris tweed jacket on his sparse frame and a leer on his long face. He stood opposite Cherry, gazing down at her with plain-spoken eyes.

"No thanks." Cherry's soft voice carried a slight edge.

"Aw, c'mon, sweetpea! Don't be a square," the thin young man insisted. "You don't know what living is till you've had a turn with me out on the dance floor."

Cherry took a half-step, turned her body slightly, and slipped her arm around Dalton's waist. "No, really. I'm perfectly content right where I am."

"So you are . . . so you are." Spotting a brunette in pink shorts across the dance floor next to the bar, he made a fake bow and edged away. "Maybe sometime when your bodyguard has the night off." He turned and began shoving his way toward the brunette, whose face was out of sight now behind an upturned cup of beer.

"There's something about that guy that I don't like," Dalton said through clenched teeth.

"I don't even know him," Cherry admitted, with a glance at the man's back. "Who is he, anyway?"

"I don't know him either. I think his last name's Amara, or something like that." Dalton's eyes narrowed, then relaxed as the first sparks of anger were quenched by Cherry's spontaneous show of affection for him in front of the stranger. "Somebody told me he moved here from New York at the first of the semester. They said he's supposed to be getting a graduate degree in business . . . lots of money in the family."

Cherry shivered as if she were suddenly

chilled, then said, "Let's not talk about him anymore." She went up on tiptoe and kissed Dalton on the cheek. "We certainly aren't going to let some rude Yankee spoil our fun."

Dalton looked down into her eyes, a deep blue color in the dimly lighted room. "You're right. Nothing's ever going to spoil our fun," he agreed, thinking that life was just too good to be true.

Built by a pioneer settler in the 1840s, Rowan Oak is situated deep in a grove of oak and cedar trees south of the Lafayette County Courthouse in the center of Oxford, Mississippi. Made famous in the novels of William Faulkner, the courthouse was burned, along with the rest of the town, by Federal troops in August of 1864, then re-built in 1873.

Faulkner bought Rowan Oak in 1930 and named it for the legend of the Rowan tree recorded in Sir James Frazier's *The Golden Bough*. According to the legend, Scottish peasants placed a cross of Rowan wood over their thresholds to ward off evil and give the occupants a place of refuge, privacy, and peace. Faulkner was known to have sought these qualities most of his life and most especially after the fame that winning the 1949

Nobel Prize for Literature brought him.

On a sunny afternoon in the autumn of 1957, with the smell of woodsmoke drifting on the brisk air, Lane and Catherine Temple strolled along Old Taylor Road on their way back to their hotel located near the square.

Lane wore a gray tweed jacket with a tie that matched the deep red color of the sweetgum leaves on the trees growing along the side of the road. "That isn't who I think it is, is it?"

"Who else would be coming from Rowan Oak?" Catherine, sporting a purple-and-gold scarf with her gray wool suit, gazed at the slight man as he walked down the steps of Rowan Oak and out into the sun-dappled lane. The lofty, white-columned house was one of Oxford's architectural treasures. Rowan Oak's treasure was the one who inhabited it. He wore a houndstooth topcoat over his suit and carried an unlit pipe in his right hand. His gait and bearing were unmistakably those of a gentleman-farmer from the Deep South.

"Well, young lady," the man greeted Catherine, "there's no doubt who you'll be cheering for in today's football game." The dark brows were finely drawn above his even darker eyes that had spotted the school colors of her scarf.

"My son plays for LSU."

"Does he, now? And what's his name?"

"Temple," Catherine responded, certain now of who she was talking with, and slightly uneasy because of it. "Dalton Temple. He plays — "

"Halfback," the novelist interrupted with a smile.

"You've heard of him?"

Faulkner smoothed his neat mustache with the back of a forefinger. "We have access to an occasional newspaper . . . even up here in the sticks."

"Oh, I didn't mean —"

"I know you didn't," Faulkner smiled, "and I don't follow football closely enough to know what kind of player your son is, but I recognized the name. Why, I think I even recognize this fellow standing next to you" — he turned toward Lane — "that is, if you have the same last name as the boy's."

"Yes, sir."

"Quarterback . . . am I right?"

Lane nodded, a little awed that he would be recognized by arguably the greatest living writer in the country. "I'm surprised you remember. That was a long time ago."

"Early thirties, but then, how could I forget?" The gold autumn light glinted on Faulkner's silver-gray hair. "Ole Miss

93

doesn't make it to the Orange Bowl or that other one — can't remember the name — out in California very often."

"It's called the Rose Bowl. The only other bowl game in the country when I was playing ball was the Sugar Bowl, down in New Orleans. The first one was held the year before I graduated." Lane decided to cut his brief epistle on football short. "I try not to think about that Orange Bowl much. We lost."

"Twenty-to-nineteen, as I recall, but I still admire your accomplishment, just leading your team to a bowl game. That's why I remember it, I expect. We didn't play in another bowl for seventeen years."

"I appreciate the compliment," Lane replied.

Faulkner turned toward Catherine, his eyes crinkling into a smile. "I also admire your choice of wives. I hope you don't mind my saying that you look perfectly lovely today, Mrs. Temple."

Catherine flushed slightly. "No, I don't mind at all."

"Well, what does the Ole Miss quarterback think of LSU's chances against his old alma mater?"

"I don't really know. We got off to a pretty bad start this year. Half the team came down with the flu, and Rice beat us twenty-to-fourteen. Since then, we've won four and lost two. I guess it could go either way."

"With running backs like Jimmy Taylor, Billy Cannon, and of course, Dalton Temple" — Faulkner glanced at Catherine — "I'd say you've got a pretty good chance."

It suddenly occurred to Catherine that she and Lane were probably boring this great man of letters. "We're all just so proud of you, Mr. Faulkner."

"Well, thank you," he grinned. "Just anyone my age couldn't take a walk all by himself."

"Oh, you just hush now!" Catherine found herself lapsing into the friendly, drawling dialect of her Southern childhood. "Everybody from Mississippi who can write his own name knows about the Nobel Prize you won in forty-nine."

"Hmm." Faulkner pursed his lips in obvious thought. "That must be at least forty or fifty people." Then he abruptly turned around and began to walk away. "I've got to get my walk in now. Company's coming in a while. But I'd be glad to have you join me."

Lane took Catherine by the arm and caught up with him.

A little breathless from the quickened pace, Catherine asked, "I know you must have answered this a hundred times, Mr. Faulkner, but I'd like to know — "

"Which of my books do I like best," Faulkner finished the question for her. "I've naturally given this a lot of thought . . . and I always come up with the same answer — *The Sound and the Fury.*" Tiny clouds of dust, pale brown and fine as face powder, puffed out from his shoes as he walked. "I truly believe if it had been given a better reception by the public, I might never have written another word."

"*Absalom, Absalom!* was always my personal favorite," Lane offered.

Faulkner gave him an oblique glance, then nodded his head. "I think we may be kindred literary spirits, young man. That's my second favorite. It may have come out number one, but the pain and grief that *The Sound and the Fury* caused me to get it delivered puts it always in first place."

Intrigued by the legend as much as the man himself, Catherine joined in the abbreviated literary seminar. "Do you enjoy writing — I mean the actual physical part of sitting down at your desk and turning it out?"

"At first, I did. Now I hate it so much, I hardly even write letters."

"I'm afraid we're making nuisances of ourselves, Mr. Faulkner," Catherine said politely. She could hardly wait to get home and tell Sharon about meeting one of her favorite writers. Sharon had always wanted to meet him. She had heard how reclusive Faulkner was and decided not to come with her parents to the game, as she felt there was little chance of seeing the great writer — much less of actually getting to take a walk with him.

"Nonsense! I asked you along, didn't I? Besides, it's not like you were journalists. You're not likely to misquote me . . . not in print, anyway. Are you?"

"I heard this rumor" — Lane winked at Catherine as he spoke — "about how you wrote one of your short stories. I think it was 'Red Leaves.' "

Faulkner smiled at the memory. "It just may be the truth. I never wrote that much at one sitting, before or since."

"How long did it take you?" Catherine asked.

"Don't recall for sure. I just took pencils and paper, crawled up into my hayloft, and didn't come down till I finished. The story is about five thousand words long."

"That's not exactly how I heard it," Lane said.

"Oh, did I forget to say that I also brought along a good-sized jug of corn whiskey?"

Catherine discovered that she had already come to think of William Faulkner in much the same way as she would her own grandfather or one of her uncles, in spite of his literary acclaim. "Mr. Faulkner, my youngest daughter, Sharon — she's seventeen now — absolutely loves the written word. Do you have any advice to give her about becoming a writer?"

"Does she have any talent for it?"

"She's had articles published in the *Saturday Evening Post* and some other magazines, and she wrote a weekly column for the local newspaper during the summer."

"She probably has enough talent then." Faulkner stopped, gazing briefly at the western horizon. "Tell her to treat it as I still do . . . as a hobby."

"A hobby?"

"Yes, ma'am. Writing is my true passion, but my job is farming."

Catherine thought he was joking with her at first, but his serious expression told her differently.

"She needs to get a real job," Faulkner continued, verbalizing his short course for aspiring writers, "and write in her spare time — *but* she's got to *keep* writing, no matter what."

"I'll certainly tell her that." Catherine

thought it was odd advice considering that it came from one of the most widely known writers in the world.

"Well, it's been nice visiting with you folks, but I've got to get on home now. Company's coming." With a quick nod of his head, Faulkner ended his walk with Lane and Catherine as abruptly as he had begun it. Then he stopped in his tracks and turned back toward the couple he had just met. He said, looking straight at Catherine, "Do you have a scrap of paper — just anything at all to write on?"

Catherine rummaged around in her black patent leather bag and found a scrap of paper — an old electric bill — and a fountain pen. She handed them to Faulkner, who used Lane's back as an even surface to write:

To Sharon — Keep writing, no matter what.
W. Faulkner

He handed the note to Catherine and without another word turned and continued his walk.

Catherine watched him walking briskly back down the road. "What a charming man! Sharon will be thrilled. But I wish she could have been here to meet him."

PART TWO

★ ★ ★

Taylor

FIVE

The Miracle

★ ★ ★

The tires of the black 1939 Ford coupe hissed along on wet pavement in front of the old State Capitol, which stood majestically on a bluff overlooking the Mississippi River. The neo-Gothic castle, completed in 1849, was gutted by a fire started by Union troops in 1862 and rebuilt in 1882. Glistening with winter rain in the glow of the streetlamps, it brooded over the city, archaic and alone behind its heavy piked-iron fence, appearing out of place and uncomfortable with the twentieth century.

"You done your Christmas shopping yet?" Dalton, both hands on the steering wheel, glanced to his left at the long line of Ionic columns forming the facade of the Yazoo and Mississippi Valley Railroad passenger station. He thought the train station looked more like a flattened and elongated Antebellum mansion than a commercial building.

Cassidy, brooding in his black leather

jacket, slouched in his seat, a matchstick dangling from the corner of his mouth. "Nah. Hadn't thought much about it."

"You wanna go with me tomorrow?"

"Yeah," Cassidy replied, sitting up suddenly in his seat. He rolled down the window six inches and flipped the matchstick out onto the wet street, its slick surface winking with the reflection of headlights. "I'm not buying much this year."

"What's the big news?" Dalton grinned at his brother. "You never buy much."

Cassidy kept a deadpan expression on his face. "It's the thought that counts."

Turning right on North Boulevard, Dalton drove up the bluff that the city was situated on, past the hundred-foot-tall Lafayette Street Standpipe, still in service after more than half a century, and the Confederate statue at the head of Third Street. He made a left turn onto Fourth Street and drove to the second block, parking in front of the massive Gothic Revival church constructed before the turn of the century. Mrs. Zachary Taylor, wife of the general, had been one of its founders.

Dalton shoved the gearshift up into reverse, turned the ignition off, and pulled out the key. He gave his brother a level stare. "Cassidy, have you been drinking again?"

"You must be losing your mind!" Cassidy immediately jumped on the offensive, a habit that seemed almost congenital with him. "You think I'd drive Daddy's car all the way out to the campus to pick you up if I'd been drinking?"

"Yep."

Cassidy, apparently expecting a detailed diatribe from his older brother, hadn't marshaled his thoughts quickly enough for a counterattack. "You must be crazy!"

"You already said that."

Cassidy opened the door abruptly and stepped out of the car. Raindrops danced with light as they fell into shallow puddles on the sidewalk.

Dalton walked around from the driver's side. Glancing upward, he saw that the belltower and the cross on its peak were lost in the misty night. He then followed Cassidy beneath the arched entrance and on into the foyer of the church.

Sitting down against the opposite wall on a pew made from heart pine, Cassidy stared across at the door he had just entered, his white-blond hair giving off light in the gloom. Through the closed door leading into the sanctuary drifted the faint sounds of children's voices lifted in song.

"You gotta get ahold of yourself, Cass,"

Dalton wisely advised as he sat down next to him. "If Daddy found out about this, you wouldn't be able to sit down for a month."

Cassidy took out a pack of LifeSaver wintergreen mints, peeled one off the roll, and popped it into his mouth.

Oh, little town of Bethlehem . . .

"You've been lucky so far," Dalton continued, staring at his brother's profile. Having lost his summer tan, the pale, smooth lines of his face gave it a childlike quality. "But I can tell you this, breath mints won't cover up alcohol, and not standing too close to people when you've been drinking won't work forever."

"A drink or two never hurt anybody."

Dalton watched the expression on his sixteen-year-old brother's face grow sullen, his eyes taking on a remote, distant stare. "I think your drinking's gone past one or two, Cass."

"How about that Russian Sputnik, huh?" He crunched the mint in his mouth and swallowed it. "You think the good ol' U.S. of A. will be able to catch up with them Russians in the space race?"

"I'll tell you what I think," Dalton said flatly, his eyes level on Cassidy's face. "I think Sputnik doesn't have a thing in the world to do with your drinking."

Cassidy suddenly sat up straight, turning toward Dalton with a half-smile still forming on his face. His voice had lost its sharp edge, taking on a lighter quality. "Hey, big brother" — he glanced around the foyer — "you don't have to preach me a sermon just because we're sitting here in church."

Over the years, Dalton had grown immune to Cassidy's charms. "This is serious, Cass." Knowing his brother's high tolerance for pain, Dalton decided to threaten his freedom. "I'm not kidding you, if Daddy finds out, you'll be lucky if you see daylight by the time you're twenty-one. . . ." He paused, listening to the high, pure sounds of the children's voices, then used his biggest gun. "And you know yourself, it would just break Mama's heart."

"Awright, awright," Cass muttered, "you don't have to pile the guilt on with a shovel. I'll knock it off."

"Good," Dalton said, expelling his breath with the word as though some great burden had been hoisted from his shoulders. "Now, let's go inside and listen to the choir."

They eased the door open, walked softly into the sanctuary, and took seats in the third-to-last row. Jessie, wearing a red plaid jumper made of wool, sat at the piano, playing the accompaniment. Occasionally she would lift one hand from the keys to direct the children as their timing began to slip away from the music.

Dalton relaxed in the pew. Enjoying once again the story of the Christ Child told in song, he let his eyes wander up to the three Tiffany stained-glass windows spilling out colored light above the altar. He loved this time of year, with the sharp bite of the cold fronts moving down from Canada. Even the winter rains that preceded them gave him pleasure, as they were soon replaced by dry air and the bright blue-and-gold days with temperatures that warmed quickly into the sixties and seventies.

The city celebrated the season with lights: along the lampposts and store fronts of the downtown streets, strung high on the towering facade of the State Capitol, on trees and shrubs in front yards, and along the windows and doors and rooflines of houses all over town, from clapboard shacks to lakefront mansions. Most of all, Dalton loved the colorful bubbling lights that had decorated the tree in his own living room for as long as he could remember.

. . . *abide with us, our Lord Emmanuel.*

Jessie stood up from the piano. "That was very good, children. You all have voices like little angels." The five- and six-year-old girls giggled shyly, and the boys made faces and shuffled their feet as she ushered them around to the side of the podium.

Through the opened door leading into an anteroom, Dalton watched the waiting mothers and fathers bundling the children into their coats and opening umbrellas against the weather before they stepped out into the dark.

"That sure was pretty, sis." Cassidy stood up first to greet Jessie as she walked down the aisle.

"Oh, I bet you say that to all the choir directors!" She gave him a quick hug.

Dalton stepped over and kissed her on the cheek. "I sure enjoyed it, Jess. Made me feel like I was back in the fourth grade at good ol' Istrouma Elementary."

"I'm glad you did, Dalton. And I sure appreciate your offering to give me a ride home. Austin had no idea that trial down in New Orleans would last this long."

"Anytime," Dalton shrugged. "Cass had to come out this way to pick me up anyway."

Jessie sat down and patted the pew next to her. "And I'm especially glad I finally got the two of you together."

Dalton sat down. "What do you mean?"

Jessie glanced up at her younger brother. "Cass, you want to sit down too?"

"Nah." Cassidy folded his arms across his chest. "Whatever it is, I can handle it standing up. I don't even need a blindfold."

"I'm not going to shoot you, Cass!"

"There's worse things than getting shot."

Jessie shook her head slowly back and forth. "Do you always have to expect the worst, Cass?"

Still seated, Dalton grabbed his brother around his slender waist and lifted him bodily off his feet, setting him down on the pew between himself and Jessie. "Just sit still and listen to your sister, you little twerp!"

Cassidy's face flushed with anger as his right hand balled instinctively into a fist.

Jessie lay her hand on Cassidy's flexing arm, holding it back. "Now, that's enough, boys! Y'all just sit still and listen to me, or I'm going to tell Daddy on both of you." She waved her hand, palm upward, in an abbreviated arc in front of her. "You might show a little respect for your surroundings too."

"Sorry, sis." Cassidy scowled at Dalton. "I just never like being . . . handled."

Dalton had noticed the black anger blaze instantly in the depths of his brother's blue eyes. He had been aware of Cassidy's reputation as a street-fighter for several years. Even as a sophomore, few of the rough-and-tumble North Baton Rouge brawlers were willing to take Cassidy Temple on. It seemed strange, though, that he had never seen that icy stare of Cassidy's until tonight, and it bothered him in a way he didn't want to think about. But then, Dalton reasoned, maybe he was making more of it than he should.

"Well, now that both my brothers are acting like such gentlemen, I have some news for you." Jessie smiled at each of them in turn. "You're going to be uncles."

After sitting a stunned second or two, his mouth an open reflection of Dalton's, Cassidy reacted first, sitting forward, hands resting on the edge of the pew. "Pregnant already!"

Dalton closed his mouth, staring behind Cassidy at Jessie. "But how — ?"

"How?" Cassidy cut him off. "You're nineteen, and you're still asking how?"

Pushing Cassidy back against the pew, Dalton ignored him and spoke again to Jessie. "When's it due?"

"*When*'s the right word, big brother," Cassidy jumped in. "Grown people ask when, not *how*."

Jessie shook her head at Cassidy in mild disapproval, even while the corners of her mouth reached for a smile. "It's due in April. I'm already four and a half months along. I'm surprised neither of you could tell."

"I thought you were just turning into a fat old married lady," Cassidy answered for both of them.

"Can you knock it off for a second, Cass?" Dalton defended his sister. "And you don't look fat either, Jess."

"At least I've got one brother who's civil," Jessie teased, pinching Cassidy's ear.

"Let's see . . ." Cassidy held his chin between thumb and forefinger. "The baby's due in April . . . you got married in June. That means . . ." He paused in mid-sentence, then shrugged. "Well, you had ol' Austin chasing all over the country after you for so long, I guess he had to make up for lost time."

"You're terrible, Cassidy Temple!"

"Don't blame me," Cassidy protested, raising his right palm outward toward Jessie. "You married him." His brow furrowed slightly.

"What about Mama and Daddy and Sharon . . . and everyone else?" Dalton asked.

"Well, I told Mama and Daddy first . . . then Sharon a little later the same day."

"Why'd you wait so long to tell us, then?" Dalton's face slackened, the excitement draining away. "Didn't you think we wanted to know too?"

"Of course, silly." Jessie reached across Cassidy and patted Dalton on the hand. "It's just that I wanted to tell the two of you at the same time, but privately, and this is the first chance I've had to do it. Remember, you were out of town on that hunting trip at Thanksgiving, Dalton."

Dalton nodded his head slowly. "Yeah." He stood up. "This calls for some kind of celebration. What can we do?"

"Let's go home, and I'll fix us some hot chocolate," Jessie offered, standing up, waiting for her brothers to do the same. "I've got some good homemade cookies to go with it too."

"Sounds good to me." Dalton popped out of the pew and stepped into the aisle.

Cassidy remained seated, his head tilted up toward his sister. "I don't know, Jess," he groaned. "Hot chocolate and cookies! That's more Dalton's speed."

As they walked up the aisle toward the church foyer, Jessie placed her arms around her brothers' shoulders. "I'm so glad I've got such handsome and strong brothers! And you're both so thoughtful too."

A look of mild shock on his face, Cassidy turned his head toward Jessie. Then abruptly, he slid her arm from around his shoulder. "Oh no!" he said, hurrying ahead of them toward the empty foyer. "I'm not babysitting for your little crumbsnatcher! You can just forget about buttering me up for that!"

". . . time!" Austin rolled over sleepily, forcing one eye open to gaze up at Jessie. She sat up next to him in bed, a slight grimace on her face, both hands on her mound of a stomach. The amber light from the lamp on the nightstand gleamed through her pale hair, tumbling down past her face. "Time for what?" Austin asked sleepily.

Jessie gave him an incredulous look. "It's one o'clock in the morning, Austin! Why do you think I woke you up?"

Realization surfaced from the depths of Austin's gray eyes, and for just a second he felt like a diver rising slowly to the water's surface to ward off the bends. Then the knowledge hit him as quickly as a bursting bubble. "Oh, Lord!" He threw back the quilt and sheet. Rolling over quickly he banged his toe on the bedpost. "Owww!"

"Be careful, sweetheart." Jessie eased over the side of the bed and slid her feet into her slippers.

"Where's the suitcase?" Austin, wearing only white boxer shorts, hopped around on one foot, holding his damaged toe in both hands. "We've got to get your things ready!"

"The bag's already packed and waiting by the front door, Austin. Don't you remember?"

"Oh, yeah. What can I do to help you?"

Jessie suppressed a smile and walked deliberately over to her closet. "Nothing. Just get yourself ready."

"All right," Austin muttered, sitting down on the side of the bed, still holding his foot with one hand and rubbing his throbbing toe with the other.

Jessie quickly slipped into a navy maternity dress with a lace-trimmed bodice, then put on her shoes and added a tan topcoat. "Hurry now, darling."

"Sure." Wincing with pain, Austin hobbled over to his dresser and opened the second drawer. After fumbling through it for a few seconds, he called over his shoulder, "Hey, Jess! Where's that white polo shirt of mine? You know, the one you bought me down in Florida."

"It's in the wash," Jessie replied from the bathroom. "Just find something else."

Austin returned to his search, tossing shirts of all colors and styles from one side of the drawer to the other and back again. "*Everything* must be in the wash."

Jessie stood in front of the bathroom mirror, stabs of pain shooting through her as she brushed her hair. "Hurry now, darling."

Austin slammed the drawer and rushed over to his closet. Racking hangers back and forth, he jerked a pale blue oxford button-down off its hanger and threw it on. Then he grabbed a pair of well-worn khakis, his Bass loafers and white socks, and carried them to the bed.

Jessie stepped out of the bathroom, dressed, hair brushed, and wearing fresh lipstick. "Honey, I'm ready to go."

Pulling his trousers on, Austin sat back down and stuck his foot into a sock, wincing again at a fresh bolt of pain as he pulled it against his injured toe. "Be right with you."

Two minutes later, Austin rushed into the living room, looking frantically around for the suitcase. "I guess she didn't have it packed after all," he said to the open door. "Jess, where are you?"

A faint voice carried through the screen. "I'm in the car, waiting for you."

"On my way." Austin stepped onto the porch, locked the door, and ran across the grass, wet with dew that sparkled in the glow of the streetlamp. He hopped behind the wheel of the white '55 Thunderbird and revved the engine to life. "Well, we're on our way."

"Not yet."

"What?"

Jessie gazed down at his feet.

Austin followed her eyes down to his sock-clad feet, soaked through from the hasty trek across the wet grass. "I thought something felt funny. Hang on — I'll be right back."

As he opened the door and stepped out, Jessie stopped him. "Austin —"

"What did I do now?"

"It's what you didn't do." She glanced at his thick, dark hair, still tousled from its battle with the pillow and quilt. "At least run a comb through your hair."

"Oh . . . okay."

"And you might want to get a light jacket."

Austin glanced around as though the early April chill was creeping up on him from behind, and shivered in agreement with his wife's suggestion as he ran for the house.

Both hands on her stomach, Jessie watched her husband clear the front steps, leaping all the way onto the porch. As he hit the slick surface in wet socks, his feet shot out in front of his hips. A split second after his feet lifted into the air, his behind bounced off the pine flooring.

The pain Jessie felt now was from holding

back her laughter in front of Austin's somber, clumsy attempts to rush her to the hospital. When he disappeared inside the house, she let it spill out, shaking with glee even as another contraction hit her.

Catherine glanced at the big schoolhouse clock on the wall for the fifth time in the past ten minutes. *Why do babies have to take their own sweet time getting into this world?* she wondered as she cast a thoughtful glance at the hallway that would bring the doctor to them with his good news. *Maybe they just want a few final hours of peace before facing their new lives.*

Sighing with pleasure as well as weariness, Catherine let her eyes wander around the hospital waiting room. Her family, in various degrees of hurried dress except for Sharon sitting next to her in neatly ironed jeans and her boyfriend's Istrouma letter jacket, sat on couches and chairs, along with Austin's parents.

Lane, his World War II marine field jacket still fitting him perfectly, and Marvin Youngblood, a slight man with neatly combed brown hair wearing his banker's starched white shirt, sat side by side in leather and chrome chairs, talking in hushed tones.

Connie Youngblood — tall, angular, with

jet-black hair and high cheekbones that spoke of her Houmas Indian heritage — sat quietly next to her husband. Her ermine-edged wrap lay on the chair next to her. A cigarette dangled from her fingers, their nails long and gleaming with carmine-red polish, as she thumbed through a tattered copy of *Better Homes and Gardens.*

Catherine smiled at Cassidy, who was fast asleep on a couch across from her, then glanced at Austin and Dalton standing next to the plate-glass window that looked out onto the parking lot and the lake beyond. Its dark surface mirrored the lighted limestone tower of the State Capitol, and Catherine could see the twin sets of light winking back through the colorless glass.

"Mama, how much longer do you think it's going to be?" Sharon's blue eyes held an intense light as she looked at her mother from behind her gold-rimmed glasses.

Patting her daughter's hand, Catherine glanced once more at the clock on the far wall. "Whenever the little thing decides he's ready to take a look at us, I guess, sweetheart. Even after four children, birth is still a mystery to me." She smiled away Sharon's nervousness. "Oh, the doctors can give you all the medical reasons, but I think it's still up to the baby to decide when he's ready to trade his safe, warm home for a new one. Maybe that's kind of silly, but it makes as much sense to me as anything else."

"I just wish he'd hurry."

"You know something, sweetheart?" Using the backs of her fingers, Catherine gently brushed the soft tendrils of brown hair along Sharon's temple.

"What, Mama?"

Catherine leaned over and whispered, "I think this pregnancy has been harder on you than on Jessie!"

Sharon gave her a puzzled frown, then laughed softly. "You may be right! I don't think I've ever been so concerned with anything in my life."

Not even your own sickness. Catherine felt love for her daughter welling up deep within her. *I hope God blesses you with many children, my most sensitive and caring child. You so richly deserve it.* "Well, it'll be a big help to you later on."

"How?"

"Having your own child ought to be easy, after what you've been through with this one."

Placing her hand on her mother's wrist, Sharon laughed again. "Oh, Mama, it hasn't been that bad."

Catherine stood up, walking across toward

120

the big plate-glass window. She glanced down at Cassidy as she passed him on the couch. He was snoring lightly and totally oblivious to the mixture of anxiety and expectation that filled the room. *Cass, Cass, what a handful you are! Sometimes I wish I could just keep you like this. You're such a little angel when you're asleep.*

"How's the new father getting along?" Catherine asked brightly, stepping between Austin and Dalton and placing her hands on both their shoulders.

"Hey, Mom." Austin's dark hair bore only a trace of neatness left by his raking a comb hurriedly through it on the way back to the car. "Still waiting to *be* a father. I think this baby is going to be as slow about everything as his mama."

Across the room, Connie Youngblood flinched slightly and dropped her magazine just below eye-level at the sound of her son calling another woman *mom*.

Catherine patted Austin on the back. "Don't worry, it'll all be over before you know it." She stared out at the lighted reflection of the capitol in the lake. "And the new little Youngblood will be more than worth all the turmoil and anxiety."

As though to confirm Catherine's confidence in the outcome of this ordinary and miraculous event, at that precise moment the doctor walked down the hall and into the waiting area, his step sluggish and his eyes reddened with fatigue and lack of sleep, but smiling. He wore a green surgical gown and bore a remarkable resemblance to Henry Fonda. In seconds, he was surrounded.

Austin stood directly in front of the doctor, his face open, eyes glazed with the strain of waiting.

"Congratulations, Mr. Youngblood. It's a boy." The doctor shook Austin's hand, gave everyone a positive report about the mother and child, then disappeared back down the hall.

More congratulations, handshakes, and overlapping conversations ran through the well-wishers.

Dalton glanced over at Cassidy, lying placid and undisturbed on his couch bed. "Somebody better call the doctor back. Cass's going to have a stroke with all this excitement."

After the clamor among the waiting-room crowd had subsided to a mild drone, Catherine walked back to the window by herself. The first rose-colored streaks of dawn were beginning to tint the eastern sky. Stars still crowded the heavens as though they could last all day. She closed her eyes and let joy flood through her like a gentle river. *Thank You, Lord, for little Taylor Youngblood, another miracle in our lives. May we never take Your blessings for granted!*

SIX

A Lone Defender

★ ★ ★

"My history professor told us that mound-builders lived here about the time of Julius Caesar," Cherry commented as she walked beside Dalton up one of the Indian mounds across from the LSU Field House. It was a crisp fall evening, and the weather complimented the success of the evening and the new football season. Behind the couple, the dazzling lights of Tiger Stadium drove the stars out of the sky.

Dalton, his arm draped casually around Cherry's shoulders, stopped at the top of the mound that had overlooked the floodplain of the Mississippi River at the time of its builders. It now overlooked the stragglers, in cars and on foot, leaving the stadium after LSU's 32–7 victory over Kentucky. "It seems funny to be standing on something built that long ago. It kind of makes Valley Forge and Gettysburg seem like current events."

Cherry stepped in front of Dalton, facing him, her arms encircling his waist. "I'm so proud of you, Dalton!" Her eyes took on that drowsy quality. "I yelled so much I thought I'd lose my voice when you ran for that touchdown."

"I had some good blocking," was all Dalton could think of to say as he lost himself in the depths of Cherry's deep-blue eyes. It seemed as though his thought processes slowed down dramatically, or that they simply went on vacation every time he got this close to her. He found himself growing fond of the sensation.

Suddenly Cherry slipped her arms away and sat down on the damp, cool grass. Shivering slightly in the cool October night, she opened her purse and dug into its tangle of contents. "It's in here somewhere. I was looking at it right before we went out onto the field."

With the image of Cherry and the other cheerleaders running ahead of the team underneath the goalposts and out into the electric glare of the playing field, Dalton sat down next to her. Taking his letter jacket off, he placed it over her shoulders. "What's so important all of a sudden that you have to find it right now?"

"Oh good, here it is!" She unfolded a sheet

of pink stationery, holding it close so it would pick up the glow of the streetlight. "The national rankings."

Dalton leaned on his elbow, staring at the short column of dates and numbers she had scribbled on the sheet of pink paper. "You've been keeping up with this for all the games we've played this year?"

"Certainly." Cherry sat cross-legged, adjusting Dalton's jacket around her shoulders. "Look." She placed the perfectly manicured nail of her left forefinger next to the first row of figures. "At the beginning of the season, we were ranked thirty-five."

"Yeah. I remember that one, for sure," Dalton said, staring not at the scores but at the delicate curve of Cherry's small hand. "Coach Dietzel said that suited him just fine. It meant that nobody would be taking us very seriously — at least, for the first game or two."

"And then you beat Rice sixteen-to-six and jumped up to sixteen in the rankings." Cherry seemed more excited than Dalton at the progress of the team. "Next was Alabama thirteen-to-three, and we went up to number thirteen."

"I remember what Coach Bear Bryant said about our new formation," Dalton added and smiled.

Cherry kept her place with her fingernail-pointer, brushed her soft honey-blond hair back along her neck, and looked at Dalton with sleepy eyes. "What did he say?"

"Somebody asked him if he thought the wing-T helped LSU. He said, 'I think LSU helps the wing-T.' "

"Wing-T?"

"It's just the way we line up on offense, honey," Dalton explained.

"Oh." She returned to her list. "Next we beat Hardin-Simmons and went to number eleven. Then —"

"Do you keep up with all the statistics, Cherry?" Dalton interrupted her.

"Oh no. Just the national rankings." She lowered her eyelids until they were almost closed. "I *have* been keeping a scrapbook on you, though . . . ever since you were a freshman."

Dalton felt a sudden sense of pride, blended with a liberal portion of confusion, that Cherry would show such an interest in him even before they met — but also wondered why she would do this for someone she may, in fact, have never met. "Three years you've been keeping a book on me?"

A touch of color rose in her cheeks. "Yes. I just knew you wouldn't have anything to do with me because I was such a little nobody and you were this big football star."

Dalton just looked at her, a puzzled smile on his face.

"And then I made the varsity cheerleaders last year and — well, you know what happened after that."

Nodding in agreement, Dalton glanced back at the pink paper trembling slightly in her hand. "We might as well finish up the rankings," he suggested.

Cherry's face brightened as she returned to her work. Running her fingernail down the list, she continued. "We beat Miami forty-one to nothing." She glanced at Dalton. "Boy, was that a fun game! I could hardly keep my mind on the cheers because I was trying to watch all the touchdowns y'all were making. They put us at number nine in the nation after that one."

"We'll go up a few more notches after tonight too," Dalton predicted. "I heard somebody say we might even make it as high as the number three or four slot."

"Wouldn't that be wonderful?"

"I guess," Dalton said and shrugged. "I don't usually think much about rankings and things like that."

"Why not?"

"I don't know. It just never seemed that important to me." Then he added quickly, thinking that his words made him sound almost ungrateful, "I do *love* the game, though."

"Oh, me too." Cherry folded her Fighting Tigers progress report and placed it back in her junkyard of a purse. "You know that I still have no idea how y'all got the names for the three teams that Coach Dietzel uses. I never can remember to ask anybody."

Dalton turned on his back, lying on the damp grass, staring up at a canopy of stars. Down the slope of the Indian mound, cars hummed by on the pavement. The drone of conversations mixed with laughter and a few victory shouts drifted on the cool October air. He rose up on one elbow to face Cherry as he prepared to talk more football. "Pretty simple. The first unit always works out in white jerseys, so we're the White Team. The team coach decided to make our offensive specialists work out in gold jerseys."

"But they're not called the Gold Team," Cherry protested, "they're called the *Go* Team."

"Some sportswriter misunderstood and used the term 'Go' instead of 'Gold,' and it just stuck."

"Then why don't y'all call the defensive team the 'Red Team'? I've seen them coming in from practice, and they always have red jerseys on."

Dalton crossed his arms over his chest against the chill of the night air. "Well, I admit that one is different."

"See, it's not so simple after all!"

"You're right," Dalton agreed and smiled at Cherry's little-girlish, told-you-so response. "Coach was trying to come up with something to brighten up the practice sessions for our defense." He turned his eyes upward toward Cherry. "Defensive teams usually just get a lot of hard work and not much glory. He read a line in the comic strip 'Terry and the Pirates' about Chinese bandits being the most vicious people in the world." He stood up, took Cherry's hand, and helped her to her feet. "And that's how they got their name."

"Well, at least I know now, in case somebody asks me." Cherry brushed a few stray pieces of dry grass from her skirt. "A cheerleader ought to know these things." She took a step forward, standing with her feet together inside Dalton's stance, and placed her head against his chest. Holding both his hands tightly, she murmured, "I'm so glad we met, Dalton."

"Me too." Dalton breathed in her fragrance, calling back the summers he spent as a boy on his grandfather's farm in Mississippi and the honeysuckle vines that grew along the fence rows. He placed his lips against the silky texture of her hair.

Cherry let her arms slide around his waist, pressing closer to him as she tilted her chin upward, opening her mouth slightly and closing her eyes.

Dalton touched her cheek with the fingertips of his left hand and leaned down, placing his lips on Cherry's, feeling their moist warmth pressing against his, savoring the taste and fragrance and softness of her.

Pushing slowly away from him, Cherry gasped, "Goodness! I don't think that's ever happened to me before."

"What?" Dalton placed his hands on her shoulders. "Is something wrong?"

Cherry smiled up at him. "Oh no," she said softly. "Something's very right! It's just that I actually felt as if I was going to faint for a second."

"Oh."

Taking Dalton's hand, Cherry squeezed it tightly. "I think we'd better be going."

"Sure thing."

As they walked down the side of the grassy mound, Dalton gazed at the few remaining cars moving slowly up North Stadium and along Fieldhouse Drive, as though the drivers were reluctant to leave the rush of excitement they had found at the football game and return to their homes. "Looks like everybody's finally clearing out of the parking lots," Dalton noted, trying to get his bearing after Cherry's last remark. As he gazed toward the western sky, the huge arc lights began shutting down, one by one, in Tiger Stadium. The gathering darkness reminded him that tonight's victory was already a thing of the past.

"We'll find out what they're made of tonight!" Lane, wearing his tan topcoat against the November chill, sat next to Catherine in the near frenzy of the Tiger fans that had packed the stadium to overflowing.

Catherine took her calfskin gloves from the pocket of her navy jacket and slipped them on. "I thought they'd been doing that all season long."

"They have," Lane agreed quickly, "but when it comes to this game, you can throw away the record book. There's no telling what's going to happen tonight."

Glancing at the scoreboard, Catherine rubbed her gloved hands nervously together. "I just wish we could score at least once in the first half."

After three straight losses to Florida under

Coach Paul Dietzel, LSU had pulled off a 10–7 win over the University of Florida Alligators the previous week, sweeping them past Army and Ohio State all the way to the number one spot on the AP poll. On this November night, they faced their arch rival, Ole Miss. Johnny Vaught's Ole Miss Rebels, unbeaten in six games, held the number six spot. The stage was set for the first sell-out crowd in the history of the 67,500-seat Tiger Stadium. People began lining up outside the ticket office shortly after midnight. One fan offered eight hundred dollars for eight good sideline seats.

The first quarter ended with neither team scoring. At the beginning of the second quarter, Ole Miss drove the ball to the two-yard-line and a first down. With four tries to score a touchdown, not one person in the stadium believed that the Rebels, behind their huge line, could be stopped. Eleven men out on the field had a different view of things.

"Oh, they'll never be able to hold them now!" Catherine shifted uneasily from one foot to the other, holding on to Lane's arm for comfort.

Lane shook his head slowly back and forth. "It's going to be tough, all right." His expression grew intense as he gave the formation a close inspection. "That Ole Miss line

133

looks heavier than their listed weights."

Catherine opened her program, scanning the list of LSU squad members to see how the players weighed in. "I just noticed this. On the White Team, our line is about the same size as our backfield. That's not normal, is it?"

"No, it's not. They all run right around two hundred pounds — some a little more, some a little less."

Catherine seemed appalled at the knowledge that had escaped her all year. "That's not big enough!"

"It's big enough to get us to the number one spot in the nation," Lane answered, laughing. "We just have to make up for it with speed and deception . . . and heart."

Down on the field, Dalton stood behind his defensive tackle, his body pumping adrenaline. The quarterback crouched behind the center, took the snap, and lunged forward. Dalton slashed across the line at the ball carrier. With grunts and groans and leather popping loudly, the Tigers stopped the Rebel quarterback on the one-foot-line. Now Ole Miss had three plays left to move the ball a scant twelve inches.

On second down, the halfback, Lovelace, charged up the middle where he was greeted by a stone wall. The big fullback hit the line on third down, but barely made it to the line of scrimmage.

Pacing behind his linemen, Dalton stared at the Ole Miss huddle. *This is it! Last chance. We've got to stop them this time!*

Ole Miss broke their huddle, digging in at the line of scrimmage for their final all-out effort. The center snapped the ball. With the quarterback whirling for the hand-off, Dalton read the play, shot forward, and slammed into Lovelace, stopping him in his tracks for a two-yard loss.

As pandemonium broke loose in the stands, it seemed that the fighting spirit of the Rebel team had broken as well. Late in the second quarter, after recovering an Ole Miss fumble on the twenty-one-yard-line, the Tigers scored, leading 7–0 at the end of the first half.

Minutes later in the locker room, deep in the bowels of the massive concrete-and-steel arena, Dalton sat on a bench, listening to Dietzel give one of his famous halftime pep talks. The words finally became little more than a drone in his ears as his body and mind sought rest, gathering strength for the second half.

"Goooooo . . . Tigerrrrrs! Goooooo . . . Tigerrrrrs!" The LSU cheerleaders stood single file along the sidelines, clenched fists pointing toward the goal line, cheering their team to victory. All around the blazing-bright stadium, Tiger fans stood to their feet, waving pennants and flags, chanting in unison with the cheering squad.

Dalton stood downfield, watching the Rebel formation, waiting to receive the punt. He let his hands hang loosely at his sides, shaking them to throw off tension. Glancing to his left he saw Cannon, hands on hips, eyes trained on the Ole Miss punter. Letting his eyes wander beyond the big halfback, he caught a glimpse of Cherry in the line of cheerleaders. Then, as the Ole Miss line hit their three-point positions, he cleared his mind of everything but the job he had to do.

The ball lofted high into the air, making a perfect spiraling arc in the dazzling glare of the lights. Dalton focused on it completely, arms extended, hands spread wide for the catch. A blur in his left peripheral vision told him Cannon was moving into position to run interference for him.

Dalton, already on the move as soon as the ball smacked into his arms, instinctively scanned the spread of Ole Miss defenders rushing downfield toward him. Looking to pick up blockers, he sprinted directly up the middle of the field. A fleet-footed back, eager for a big play, charged full-speed at Dalton. Cannon cut him down like a sharp scythe through ripe wheat.

Faking to his left, then cutting right, Dalton avoided a burly linebacker. Picking up another block, he sprinted for the sidelines. Two red-and-blue-clad defenders barred his way. Lowering his head, Dalton rammed his helmet into the solar plexus of the first, then broke the tackle of the second. Slowed down by the second defender, he saw three more charging in from his left side. With a burst of speed, he outran two of them, but the third, in a desperate dive, grabbed his ankle, almost making the tackle.

Fighting for balance now, Dalton saw the goal line ten yards ahead of him. He did not see the lone Rebel back who had now closed the gap between them. Dalton took three more strides, picking up speed, confident now of the touchdown. The final Rebel defender charged at full speed from Dalton's blind side, lowered his shoulder, and slammed it into the outside of Dalton's leg.

Pain exploded in Dalton's knee as it crumpled inward. He heard a dull popping sound, then felt something rip and tear loose deep inside his leg. He thudded to the ground. Grasping the ball tightly, he saw the blurry end zone marker, wavering five feet away.

With all his strength, he fought against the nausea and pain-filled darkness that seemed to blanket the whole world.

"It surely was a happier occasion that brought us to this hospital last time," Catherine noted sadly as she walked over to a chrome-and-leather chair in the emergency waiting room. As she sat down, she felt an unwarranted sense of comfort that the chair was exactly like the one she had used in the maternity waiting room at the birth of Jessie's baby. *It's silly to think the chair has anything to do with it, but maybe we'll get good news anyway.* "How long do you think the doctor will take with Dalton?"

Lane's mind still carried the picture of his son crumpling beneath the bone-jarring tackle of the Ole Miss defender. His face winced as though the pain were his own as he saw again Dalton's leg cave in. During his playing years as the Ole Miss quarterback he had seen many injuries, but only a few as severe as Dalton's. "Can't say for sure. I don't think he'll take too long, though. The doctor's just going to examine him."

"And if he needs surgery?"

Trying to push that possibility aside, although the picture that kept flashing in his mind told him differently, Lane strained to keep his voice level and confident. "He'll just schedule it at a later date. I'm sure he sees injuries like this one all the time."

"I expect so."

Lane determined that he would do his best to keep Catherine's mind off their son's injury. "That was some football game out there tonight, wasn't it?"

"Yes, it was," Catherine agreed absently, her eyes staring at the schoolhouse clock on the wall. "Dalton could have . . . I wonder how it turned out?"

"I don't know." Lane glanced at the swinging double doors the doctor would come through once his examination of Dalton was completed. "I don't think there's much doubt who won, though."

"LSU?"

"Certainly." Lane remembered the encouraging remarks and handshakes of Dalton's teammates as he was carried from the sidelines on a stretcher. "Those boys said they'd win it for Dalton, no matter what — and they meant it!"

"Why don't you come sit down, sweetheart?" Catherine patted the chair beside her.

Pacing back and forth in the restricted space of the waiting area, Lane cupped his hands together, rubbing them back and forth in the same way he had done just before going into combat. "I think I'd rather stand up. Sitting makes me feel . . . helpless." He smiled weakly at his wife. "That's kind of stupid, I guess. What difference does it make whether I walk or sit?"

"Men pace." Catherine gazed at the sturdy middle-aged nurse in the glassed-in reception area, poring over a stack of forms. "Women sit."

Catherine jerked involuntarily at the sound of the phone ringing across the room.

"Phone call for a Mr. or Mrs. Temple." The nurse held the phone like an auctioneer waiting for a final bid. *Going once, going twice, going . . .*

"I'm Lane Temple."

The nurse-auctioneer went back to her forms, thumbing through the tall stack left-handed, with the telephone held aloft in her right.

"Thank you." Lane placed the receiver to his ear. "Hello . . . Sure, everything's fine here. . . . Can't say for sure, but we'll let you know as soon as we hear something. . . . Okay, I'll give her a call, and then we'll come right on home."

Lane returned the telephone to its keeper, then walked over and sat down next to Catherine.

"Sharon?"

Lane nodded. "She still wants to come down here, but I told her we should be home pretty soon." Lane blinked his vacant stare away as another thought formed in his mind. "Remind me to call Jess."

This time Catherine nodded, reached over, and slipped her hand inside his. In another half hour that seemed more like days, the orthopedist pushed through the swinging doors, glanced about, and stepped briskly over to where Lane and Catherine were sitting. They rose to hear the news.

Having never met the doctor, Lane glanced at the name tag on his white lab coat — Palermo, J., M.D. About thirty-five years old with the build of a sprinter, Dr. Palermo wore horn-rimmed glasses and a crew-cut.

Dr. Palermo motioned for them to sit and squatted down on one knee next to their chairs. "I wish I had better news for you folks."

"He's going to be able to walk, isn't he, Doctor?" Catherine asked, then stared at him, her blue eyes intense and unblinking.

Attempting a smile that didn't quite come off, Palermo patted Catherine gently on the back of her hand. "I'm sorry. It must have sounded awful the way I said it." He took his glasses off and pinched the bridge of his nose between thumb and forefinger. "If he wasn't an athlete it wouldn't be all that bad."

Lane's face appeared etched in rock but for a small ridge of muscle working under the skin of his jaw. "Give it to us straight, Doctor."

Palermo took a deep breath. "Dalton sustained an injury in three major areas of the knee. He has a tear in the anterior cruciate. . . ." Noticing the creased brows of his listeners, Palermo explained, "That's a primary ligament." Seeing nods of approval he continued, "There's also a tear in the medial meniscus" — he demonstrated with his hands — "that's a crescent-shaped cartilage in the knee joint."

Catherine's face held an expression of pain. "This doesn't sound good at all, Doctor."

Nodding quickly in agreement, Palermo continued his medical treatise. "Finally, there's also a tear in the medial collateral ligament."

"Will he be able to play ball again?" Lane sounded hoarse, as if he had to force the question out.

Palermo shrugged, using the time-worn phrase that asked more questions than it answered, "Only time will tell."

Catherine reached for Lane's hand, holding it tightly. "What do we do next?"

"The only option is surgery. I'll schedule it as soon as you give me the word."

Lane and Catherine exchanged glances, with Lane asking, "Can you tell us what's involved?"

"Sure." Again, Palermo drew pictures for them in the air with his hands. "First, we remove the meniscus."

"That's the cartilage, right?" Lane asked.

Palermo nodded. "Then we debris the ligament stubs."

Again, the twin puzzled frowns.

"Clean them out."

Waiting for more, Lane finally asked, "That's it?"

"That's it." Palermo stood up, rubbing the back of his neck with his left hand. "For the surgery, that is. After that, he'll be in a cast for about four weeks."

The answers she was getting had made Catherine wary of asking more questions. "And after that?"

"Twelve weeks or so of physical therapy to restore motion and strengthen the injured area." Palermo rushed ahead as though eager to finish. "This kind of trauma usually results in an extremely unstable knee."

"But the physical therapy should help, shouldn't it?" Lane asked, grasping for encouragement.

"It should, but this can be a career-ending injury for a football player." Palermo folded his arms across his chest as if protecting himself against reprisal for the bad news he had just delivered. "One final thing — degenerative arthritis may develop in the joint as he grows older."

"You haven't painted a pretty picture." Lane felt the news press down on him like an unspeakable burden.

"No, I haven't."

Catherine joined Lane as he got up from his chair and asked, "May we see him now, Doctor?"

"Certainly." Palermo motioned for them to follow him. "He's going to be a little groggy from the shot we gave him."

Lane pushed the swinging door open, holding it for Catherine and Palermo as they entered the emergency room, sectioned off by curtains hanging from grooved tracks in the ceiling. A low, moaning sound came from behind one cubicle they walked past. Bloodstained jeans and a green plaid shirt lay on a white metal table standing next to it. "He can come with us now, can't he?"

"I guess it would be all right," Palermo answered, with some reluctance, "but you must be very careful with that leg. I'll make arrangements to have him admitted tomorrow night for surgery on Monday. We should be able to get a wheelchair from the hospital for you to use until then."

"Thank you."

"Sure." Palermo stopped and pointed to the hospital bed behind a partially closed curtain. "There's your boy. I'll come by tomorrow night and check on him." He shook hands with Lane and Catherine before hurrying off.

Against the fresh white pillowcase, Dalton's face looked pale and drawn. His brown hair, sweat-soaked as he had been carried off the field, had dried in the disheveled style left by his helmet. A cleat had left an abrasion, caked now with blood, across the top of his left hand.

Catherine, brushing at the corners of her eyes with the fingertips of her left hand, slowly approached the bed. She placed her hand softly on Dalton's, feeling the crusted blood scrape against her palm.

Opening his eyes slowly, Dalton managed a weak smile. "Hey, Mama."

"How do you feel, baby?" Catherine didn't see her son as a one-hundred-and-ninety-pound college halfback. In her mind, he was eight and coming through the back door into her kitchen with another skinned knee.

Dalton's reply was as weak as his smile.

"Pretty good." He tried to laugh but gave up on it. "Have the police put out an arrest warrant on that Ole Miss back, will you?"

"We'll let you take care of him when you get that knee back in shape, son." Lane glanced at the oblong mound made by Dalton's left leg beneath the sheet.

Dalton, a flicker of pain tracing across his brow, closed his eyes and nodded.

"You ready to go home now?" Lane asked.

Nodding, Dalton kept his eyes closed.

Catherine ran her fingers through his matted hair, brushing it back from his face. "We're waiting for them to bring us a wheelchair. Then we'll take you home for a nice rest."

"Sounds good," Dalton said weakly through taut lips that barely moved.

Catherine's hand gently stroked the side of his face. "We'll be coming back tomorrow night, and the doctor's going to operate Monday morning."

"Gonna fix you up good as new," Lane said with a note of optimism in his voice that almost rang true. "That Heisman Trophy's still gonna be there next year."

Dalton slid his hand over against the side of his leg. "That guy gave me a pretty good pop tonight. What did the doctor say about it?"

Lane cleared his throat. "After the surgery, you'll be in a cast for four weeks, then you'll go to physical therapy for a while to get the strength back."

"Did he say I'd be able to play again?"

"He didn't say — not for sure." Lane looked down at the floor before continuing, "But you know how doctors are; they never tell you *anything* for sure."

"Yeah." It was the last word Dalton spoke until Lane rolled him through the back door into their kitchen where Sharon, Cassidy, Coley, and Maria waited to greet him.

SEVEN

Pulling the Cork

★ ★ ★

Cassidy, his black leather jacket worn over a heavy, red flannel shirt, hurried out of the December wind into the steamy weight room. He rubbed his hands together and blew out his breath. "I think North Stadium is the coldest place on earth. Some people say the north wind's permanent home is right around here somewhere."

Dalton feverishly pumped iron. He wore white tennis shoes, gold sweat pants that were cut off above the knee, and a white T-shirt, soaked through and through. Perspiration poured off his face, arms, and shoulders as he sat on a bench, heaving a weighted lever up and down with his left leg.

"You gonna wear that leg out if you don't let up a little. C'mon, Dalton, it's the Christmas holidays." Cassidy stared at his brother, teeth clenched, eyes narrowed and intense, dedicating himself completely to restoring his damaged knee. "I don't want to spend 'em hanging around in some smelly weight room." Making a face, he glanced around at the bare walls and concrete floor littered with barbells, dumbbells, weight racks, and benches.

Dalton kept his eyes focused on his knee, forcing the iron bar in its quarter-circle, up-and-down motion.

"Besides," Cassidy added, "I don't think you're supposed to be working out so hard now." He walked over to the bench and stood directly in front of Dalton. "Dalton, the campus is deserted. People are home, going out on dates, buying Christmas presents, drinking egg nog. There's an actual *world* outside this room, with a lot of fun things to do!"

Dalton let the bar down one final time, lifted his leg free, and collapsed on the bench, his arms dangling over the sides, his breath coming in hard, fast gasps.

Looking around, Cassidy saw a smaller bench, dragged it over next to Dalton, and sat down. He noticed that the bar Dalton had been using held only one twenty-pound-plate on each end. His brother's left leg, bent at the side of the bench, twitched with muscle spasms. The knee itself, scored with angry red scars, looked fragile and atrophied, as if it belonged to an accountant rather than a college halfback. "You 'bout ready to get out of this dungeon?"

"Let me catch my breath first."

Cassidy snapped his fingers. "I've got an idea —"

"No," Dalton interrupted him, "I'm not going to stop by the liquor store and buy you a bottle."

"What an ingrate you are!" Cassidy feigned a hurt tone. "I'd never ask you to compromise your sterling character."

Dalton grunted in response. "Sure."

"Now, if you'll allow me to continue," Cassidy said, twirling the ends of an invisible mustache. "What I have in mind has to do with the fairer sex." He stared at Dalton, eyes closed, resting limply on the bench. Getting no response, he went on, "You get ahold of Cherry, and I'll pick somebody at random from my little black book, and we'll double-date. You like the sound of that? *Double-date,* just like the teenagers do."

"You *are* a teenager," Dalton muttered. "Last time I checked, sixteen qualifies you as one."

Ignoring the rebuke, Cassidy asked, "Well, what do you think? Sounds like fun, huh?"

"Cherry went home for the holidays."

"Why would she do a thing like that?" Cassidy asked incredulously. "Christmas in

Dry Prong. Even Dickens couldn't make *that* interesting."

Dalton sat up, grabbed a towel lying on the floor next to the bench, and mopped his face. Then swiping at his shoulders and the back of his neck, he draped his elbows across his thighs and turned to Cassidy, a look of despair crawling across his face. "I don't think I'm going to make it, Cass."

"Are you nuts?" Cassidy grew immediately incensed at his brother's defeatist remark. "Whadda you mean, you're not gonna make it? You just got the cast off two weeks ago! Now, you're already saying you ain't gonna make it! What kind of sissy —"

"All right! All right!" Dalton stopped his brother's tirade. "You've made your point."

"Man, I thought you had more guts than this!" Cassidy stood up abruptly, stuck both hands into the back pockets of his jeans, and began pacing back and forth.

"How long have you known me, Cass?"

Cassidy stopped, stared at his brother, and asked, "What's this, some kind of trick question?"

"No, I just wanted to get your attention." Dalton gave him an oblique glance, then twisted the towel in both hands as he spoke. "Have you ever known me to give up on anything before?"

"Well," Cassidy admitted reluctantly, "no." Then he took his hands out of his pockets, crossing his arms over his chest. "I hate to admit this, but I think you've got more guts than anybody I've ever known — except maybe for Daddy."

Dalton stared at the towel and said nothing.

"That's the reason I got so mad when you said you didn't think you were gonna make it."

"Watch this." Dalton stood up and walked slowly across the room.

Cassidy kept his eyes on his brother's left leg. It wobbled slightly from the knee outward, with the calf and thigh forming a small but very significant angle. "So what?"

Dalton returned to the bench, favoring the injured leg. He sat down and gazed up at his brother. "So, this knee feels like there's nothing there to work on — nothing left inside it to work any strength back into." He grabbed the towel and wiped his arms. "That's *so what*, Cass. That's precisely *so what*."

"Yeah, well . . ." Amazingly, Cassidy seemed at a loss for words. Even more amazingly, he walked over and placed his hand on Dalton's shoulder in a reassuring gesture. "Well, it's still the holidays, and we never did get to go shopping together last year."

Dalton smiled weakly and stood up. "You got any money with you?"

"I thought I'd mooch off you," Cassidy grinned. "Why change things this late in life?"

"Downtown or Delmont Village?"

"Let's hit 'em both. We'll make the stores on Third Street on the way home, and Delmont's right by the house, anyway." Cassidy made a face at his brother as he pulled the sweat-damp T-shirt over his head. "You *are* going to take a shower, I hope."

"Nah," Dalton grinned. "I think it'll be real easy getting through those Christmas crowds if I don't."

The December wind blew from the north across the open field, made a lonesome sighing sound high in the tops of the pines swaying slowly back and forth along North Stadium Road, and lowered its pitch to a moan as it struck the massive concrete facade of the stadium. A sky sealed with clouds stretched over the city like the underside of an iron gray circus tent.

Dalton, his hair wet and combed from the shower, walked with Cassidy toward Lane's black Ford coupe parked on the side of the road. He had changed into brown penny loafers, Levi's, and his LSU letter jacket. "I think you're right about this wind. This has gotta be the coldest place in town."

"You're telling *me*," Cassidy muttered as he slid in behind the steering wheel. "This place would give an *Eskimo* pneumonia!"

As he stepped into the car, Dalton's foot clunked into a hard object that had slipped partly out from under the seat. Picking it up, he gazed at a half-full bottle of Jack Daniels sour mash whiskey. "You buying the good stuff now?"

"Christmas present," Cassidy answered tersely.

"Somehow I find that hard to believe." Dalton slipped the bottle back under the seat.

Cassidy stuck the key into the ignition, started to turn it, then leaned back and held his hand out toward Dalton. "Whadda you say we have a shot of Mr. Daniels? He's just the thing to knock the chill out of our bones."

"You're driving, Cass."

"One drink, Dalton." Cassidy rolled his eyes toward the car's low ceiling. "Who am I sitting here with — the new president of the Ladies' Temperance League?"

Dalton reluctantly reached for the bottle and handed it to his brother. "Just one drink."

154

"Scouts' honor." Cassidy smacked his lips, popped the cork out of the bottle, and turned it up to his lips. After three swallows, he pulled it away from his mouth and grimaced, shuddered involuntarily, and blew his breath out.

"You said one drink, Cass."

"You know they kicked me out of the Boy Scouts, Dalton." Cassidy grinned, corked the bottle, and handed it back to Dalton. "Why don't you have one?"

Dalton shook his head.

"Aw, come on. It'll do you good, help you, too, besides the benefit you get out of it —"

"That didn't make a lick of sense, Cass." Dalton glanced at the bottle gleaming in the weak, tin-colored light seeping through the windshield. "One swallow of this stuff, and you already sound like somebody needs to measure you for a straight jacket."

Cassidy turned the ignition key, firing the engine to life. He pressed the accelerator, revving it just enough to warm it in the cold weather. "One swallow might just take the edge off the pain in that knee. Whadda you got to lose?"

Dalton stared at the bottle, pulled the cork, and sloshed it around a little before holding it beneath his nose. "Whewww! This stuff smells like rubbing alcohol!"

"That's the good stuff." Cassidy's eyes registered a sudden thought. "You're twenty years old, boy! You never had a drink of whiskey?"

Staring at a sparrow huddled on the hard ground near the gnarled root of an oak, its feathers ruffling in the wind, Dalton mumbled, "Well, there was that time we found Papaw's jug of corn liquor in the hayloft."

"That was almost ten years ago!" Cassidy spoke as though Dalton, by abstaining from drink, had betrayed the sacred trust of all the young men who had grown up in the South. "You mean, that's all the liquor you ever had?"

"Yep."

"What kind of example is that to set for your little brother? It just makes me so mad I could —" Cassidy jerked the gearshift down into first, glanced to the left, and shot out into the road with a shrieking of tires that left twin black trails of rubber behind on the pavement.

"Are you crazy?" Dalton gaped at his brother, teeth clenched, frenzied eyes staring dead ahead.

Cutting his eyes at Dalton, Cassidy immediately eased his foot down on the brake. "Just foolin' around," he said, breaking into laughter. "Had you goin' for a second there, didn't I?"

Dalton leaned back on the seat, blowing his breath out slowly. "I think I will have that drink, after all." He raised the bottle toward his mouth, then stopped. "By the way, could you make one stop for me?"

"Sure. Where to?"

"The coroner's office. I'd like to have him examine you." Dalton sat the bottle on the seat between his legs. "I think you're *way* overdue."

Cassidy made a U-turn, drove past the cage located across the road from the stadium where LSU's mascot, Mike the Tiger, made his home, and turned right on Nicholson, heading downtown. "You gonna have that drink or not?"

Dalton shrugged. "Might as well. Like you said, what have I got to lose?" He put the bottle to his lips, turned it up, and took a long swallow, feeling the whiskey slide like liquid fire down his throat and hit his stomach. He struggled not to gag in front of Cassidy.

"Well, how was it?"

"Not bad," Dalton rasped.

"Don't worry," Cassidy encouraged him, "it'll get a *whole* lot better."

"I hope so." A soothing warmth began to form in the pit of Dalton's stomach, radiating outward and upward like small, benign tendrils of comfort, tiny invisible friends sent to bring him good cheer as they traveled inexorably toward his brain. He took another drink and corked the bottle. "Hey, why don't we take a ride out by the lakes? I bet they're real pretty now."

Cassidy glanced up at the heavy clouds hanging low over the city. "You think so?"

"Sure."

"Whatever you say, big brother." Cassidy shrugged, making a quick U-turn.

Dalton relaxed, letting his worries slide away like the road beneath the humming tires. Glancing out the window minutes later as they passed Allen Hall, he thought that facing another semester of English in one of its dreary classrooms wouldn't be so bad after all. *It seems funny how I dreaded it so much. What could be so bad about Victorian poetry anyway?*

"Well, what do you think?" Cassidy sped past the Indian mounds on his left.

Suddenly, the dark clouds that had settled on Dalton's future without football vanished like vapors. The knife-blade uncertainties that had haunted him now seemed blunted and dull, no longer able to inflict their insidious pain. "You know something? This stuff ain't half bad."

Cassidy negotiated the curve that led into Dalrymple Drive, then grabbed the bottle, pulled the cork with his teeth, and took another long swallow. He nodded to his left at the Greek Theatre, its rows of concrete benches curving down the slope toward a stage set back in a stand of pines. "Remember that night Jess won the talent contest here, singing 'September Song'? Who'd have thought our big sister would ever go on tour with Bob Hope?"

"I think Jessie's whole life was kind of like one long tour after the other till Austin finally settled her down."

"Yeah, that girl's had her head full of stars and bright lights ever since I can remember," Cassidy said, adding the role of maturity and vast experience to that of tutoring his brother in the fine art of moral decline. Handing the bottle back to Dalton, he glanced downward. "How's the knee feel?"

Dalton realized that his knee still throbbed with a dull ache, still felt numbed and useless, but that somehow it didn't seem to matter any longer. "What knee?"

"I hate to say I told you so, big brother," Cassidy laughed, "but I did. All you have to do is follow Dr. Cass's prescription, and you'll find out this is really a fun world."

Dalton laughed for no particular reason he could think of, but that it seemed like the thing to do.

"I bet it wasn't much fun sitting on the sidelines, watching those last three games, was it?"

Remembering how badly he had wanted to grab a helmet and run out onto the field during those games, Dalton now wondered why he had let being benched bother him so much. "Nah. It wasn't so bad. Besides, we ended up the number one team in the country, and I'm still a part of it. What's so bad about that?"

"Now, *that's* the way to look at things, boy," Cassidy encouraged, his eyes shining with alcohol. "You get that leg back in shape for next year, and you'll make all those pro scouts sit up and take notice. And . . . in the meantime, you still got the prettiest girl on campus to make things sweet while you're waiting. Yes, sir, you got it made."

"Yeah." Dalton grinned, wondering why he had let his football injury bother him so much. "I guess I do, don't I?"

"When's Cherry coming back?"

Dalton's face brightened even more at the mention of her name. "After Christmas."

"She going down to the Sugar Bowl with you?"

"You think that Cherry would miss a chance to be on national television?"

"No, not Miss Dry Prong of 1956."

Dalton ignored his brother's remark. He pictured Cherry as he had last seen her — at the bus station, leaving for the holidays, her honey-colored hair tumbling past her face as she leaned over from the bus doorway to kiss him good-bye. Her eyes, soft and blue and smiling, closed as she pressed her mouth against his. *Man! I gotta quit thinking about her so much! Gotta concentrate on getting back in shape.*

Stopping at the traffic light on Highland Road, Cassidy gazed out at the parade ground, its flat, grassy expanse stretching between the Memorial Tower on the western side to the massive, stone-columned Law Center on the east. "I wonder what kind of scheme I can come up with to finagle my way out of R.O.T.C. Somehow, putting on an army costume and playing soldier two days a week doesn't sound like a whole lot of fun to me."

"It's not all that bad." Dalton took another swallow of whiskey. "Some of it's kinda fun."

"You mean, like all the freshmen getting their heads shaved?" Cassidy gunned the engine, darting across Highland and on past the blocks of fraternity houses on their left. "They better not try that with me."

"Everybody does it, Cass."

"*Almost* everybody." Cassidy's eyes narrowed, the hard glint in them matching the flinty edge to his voice as he glanced back at Dalton. "I ain't."

From years of experience, Dalton knew there was no use explaining to his brother that he couldn't take on the power of the university bureaucracy as well as the Army Cadet Corps. "Maybe you'll be the first one, Cass."

"Count on it." Cassidy pushed the rising anger out of his voice as he drove past the Sigma Chi house and on between the University Lakes. "Well, there they are." He gestured toward the shining lakes with his hand. "Hope you enjoy them."

Dalton had forgotten that he had asked his brother to drive by the lakes on the way to town. "Enjoy what?"

"The lakes, dummy!"

"I've seen 'em a thousand times. Why would I want to look at them on a dreary day like this?"

Cassidy shook his head back and forth slowly. "Never mind, hero. Have another drink."

"I just might do that." Dalton turned the bottle up and swallowed. *Boy, if two or three drinks make me feel this good, what would a whole bottle feel like?*

The narrow streets lay in deep shadow as

the January sun cast its slanting amber light across the rooftops of the city. Drops of water from a quick shower still dotted the wooden shutters and slipped down the pastel stucco walls of the old houses. The smells of coffee and fresh-baked bread drifted through the screen doors of the neighborhood groceries. Second-story apartments with scrolled iron balconies rang with the laughter of after-game revelers celebrating LSU's victory in the Sugar Bowl's silver anniversary.

"I thought I'd just *die* out there today!" Cherry, still wearing her purple-and-gold LSU sweater, clung to Dalton's arm as they walked toward Canal Street. "When Warren broke his hand, I just about gave up."

Dalton felt like an imposter in his letter jacket. "It sure looked bad for a while, all right." Passing an alleyway, he smelled the dank, cool odor of old brick. "I knew Durel could handle the quarterbacking, but after Brodnax got his touchdown called back, it could have broken our spirit."

"But it didn't," Cherry beamed. "I'm just so proud of all our boys."

Dalton nodded, then slipped a thin, silver flask out of his inside jacket pocket. Unscrewing the thimble-like top, he took a quick sip directly from the flask, then another longer one, frowning as he swallowed.

"When did you start carrying liquor around?"

"Just something to cut the chill." He returned the flask to his pocket. "Cass gave it to me."

Cherry frowned, then pushed the brief moment of concern aside. "How does your leg feel?"

The incipient, numbing warmth that would push aside Dalton's frustration at having to sit on the bench during the game made him smile. "Gettin' better all the time," he said a little too brightly. In spite of the whiskey's help, he still had to force his lips to form the words. "It might be stronger than the other one by the time I finish this rehabilitation program."

"Oh, I'm so happy! I've been afraid to ask." In her bouncy enthusiasm, Cherry placed her hands on Dalton's shoulders, pulling her weight down and forward on him as she reached up to kiss him on the mouth.

Dalton felt a sharp stab in his left knee as it buckled outward and gave way, refusing to support him. "Uhhh . . ." He grunted with pain, slapping the flat of his hand against the side of a building to keep his balance.

Startled by Dalton's cry of pain, Cherry

recovered in time to grab his free arm, helping him to sit down on the sidewalk. "Sweetheart, I'm so sorry! I . . . I just thought your knee would be as strong —"

"It's okay . . . it's okay. Don't worry about it." Dalton tried to keep his expression and his voice calm, even though the pain caused him to break out in a cold sweat. Nausea welled up within him. "Just let me stretch it out for a minute." He straightened his left leg directly in front of him, reaching over with both hands to massage it, making sure it was in proper alignment.

As Cherry watched him, her face grew slack with concern. "Are you sure you're going to be all right, Dalton?"

"Certainly. I just lost my balance for a second and my knee got twisted the wrong way." Dalton reached up for Cherry. "Give me a hand, will you?"

"Sure, baby." She placed an arm over his shoulder and took him by the hand, helping him to stand up.

Dalton felt his face growing warm as humiliation swept over him. He looked into Cherry's eyes. A shadow of pity seemed to have crept into them — that first brief glimmering that something had changed, like the barely heard dull and distant rumble of thunder on a cloudless day.

"You want to go on back to the car?" Cherry kept her arm around Dalton, supporting him.

Dalton felt like an invalid. He eased Cherry's arm away, trying to brush aside the awkwardness of the situation with the confidence of his words. "Don't be silly. It's nothing. I'm just fine." *Settle down, Dalton, you're starting to sound like a parrot.* "We'll go eat like we planned."

Cherry nodded and slipped her hand inside his. "Good. I love the food in New Orleans."

They walked along Royal toward Canal, past the antique shops and the jewelry stores, their showcases glittering dimly in the darkened interiors. The sound of shouts, loud, harsh laughter, and Dixieland jazz carried from Bourbon Street through the intersections they passed and drifted over the tops of the old buildings. School-age boys, wearing heavy metal taps that rang like horses' hooves on the pavement, danced on street corners for nickels and dimes tossed into cigar boxes.

"Look, Dalton! Now, *that's* really New Orleans to me!" Cherry pointed at the old green-painted streetcar rocking down the neutral ground out on Canal Street.

Dalton watched the ancient iron streetcar

creak to a stop on the opposite side of Canal. Passengers spilled out onto the sidewalk, others climbed aboard, and off it went, turning right on St. Charles for the trip through the Garden District and Audubon Park. "We could take a streetcar ride after we eat, if you want to." Cherry kept her eyes on the traffic light, taking Dalton's arm as they crossed the street. "They say this is the widest street in the world."

Feeling Cherry's hand supporting him, Dalton pictured himself as an old man dottering along with his granddaughter watching over him. "Who says that?" He felt pain shoot through his knee with every step as he forced himself to walk without a limp. "Must be the people down here."

"I don't remember. Maybe I read it somewhere."

"It's pretty wide, all right," he agreed, the pain worsening. As they made their way across to the St. Charles side of the street, Dalton gazed at the palm trees lining the boulevard all the way to City Park. For reasons that escaped his logic, the sound of the palm fronds clattering in the wind off the river disturbed him.

Seems like almost everything gets on my nerves these days. Maybe it's starting the first day of 1959 down here in this strange city that bothers me. New Orleans always did remind me of something out of the old world. It looks more like it belongs somewhere in Europe than in America.

"Where did you say we're going to eat?"

Dalton pointed to the bright plate-glass front that looked out on the afternoon shadows of St. Charles Avenue. "The Pearl. It's just down the block here."

They entered the oyster bar and restaurant through doors that had been cut from heart cypress sometime during the last century. Black-and-white inlaid tile covered the floor and a long, metal-topped counter ran the length of the left wall. Twenty feet above them, ceiling fans circled slowly.

Dalton had only been there once before, but he had liked it immediately. It was airy and spacious and smelled of the sea. "What do you think?"

"I hope the food's as good as the atmosphere," Cherry replied, glancing at the tables crowded with college students, couples in their Sunday best, and bearded seamen from foreign ships wearing dungarees and pea coats.

"Looks like we'll have to sit at the bar till somebody leaves." Dalton took her arm and led her over to the row of chrome stools with red vinyl seats.

Cherry climbed up on a stool, staring at the ice bins brimming with oysters that lined the wall. Duckboards covered the concrete floor behind the bar.

A wiry, dark-skinned man wearing gray work trousers, a white apron, and a white shirt with the sleeves rolled up past his elbows walked over to greet them. "How y'all doin' today? What can I get for you?"

Dalton turned to Cherry. "Wanna try a dozen oysters as an appetizer?"

"Whatever you say, sugar."

The little man turned to the bins behind him, raking a dozen oysters out onto a plate. Using a knife with a heavy, short blade, he shucked them with surprising speed, placing them on a tray. Then he set the tray, along with fresh-cut lemon slices and Tabasco sauce, in front of Cherry. "You gonna like these, pretty girl. We got the best oysters in New Orleans."

"You like your job?" Dalton asked, making small talk with the man as he squeezed lemon onto the oysters.

"I come outta dem swamps down in Barataria," he answered in a voice thick with Cajun dialect. "My family was all trappers and fishermen," the little man explained. "Dat work burn you up in de summer and freeze you to death in de winter." He motioned around the restaurant with open palms. "Dis like dyin' and goin' to heaven."

Dalton laughed, shaking a few drops of Tabasco onto one of the fleshy, pink-and-gray oysters lying in its shell. "I see what you mean. By the way, my name's Dalton Temple, and this is Cherry Lovell. We're down here from Baton Rouge to see the Sugar Bowl."

"Curet DeJean. Pleased to meet y'all." DeJean shook hands with Dalton before wandering off to wait on another customer at the opposite end of the bar.

Dalton handed Cherry one of his doctored oysters. "First one for the lady."

Cherry made a face at the oyster, then frowned at Dalton. "I . . . I thought you had to cook them first."

"Better this way."

"I don't know what to do!"

"Let me give you a free lesson, then." Dalton lifted the oyster up to his chin, tilted the shell, and let it slide out into his mouth and down his throat in one smooth motion.

"You don't chew them?"

"Some people do," Dalton answered, handing her an oyster, "but I don't think *you'd* like to."

Cherry hesitated, a tiny furrow creasing her brow, then took the oyster and quickly followed Dalton's example. After she had swallowed, the frown on her face changed into a pleasant smile. "Hey, that's pretty good! I don't know why, but it is."

An hour later, Dalton and Cherry sat at a table in the front of the restaurant next to the rain-streaked, neon-lighted, plate-glass window.

DeJean, carrying a tray holding two cups of steaming black coffee, left his post behind the bar and crossed the tiled floor. "Anything else I could get for y'all?"

Dalton broke off a piece of French bread, mopped the last of the gumbo from the large white bowl in front of him, and popped it into his mouth. "I think we're both too full to get up, Curet."

DeJean set the cups on the table. "That's what I like to hear," the little man said and smiled. "We Cajuns all like to see people enjoy good food, expecially when we cook it ourselves."

"You cooked this?"

"No." Curet glanced back toward the kitchen and said, "But I always give our cooks good advice to make the food a little bit better for our customers."

"Everything was wonderful." Cherry smiled and patted DeJean on the arm.

Dalton slipped a ten dollar bill into his

hand, an expression of his own appreciation of the meal. "*Better* than wonderful."

DeJean unfolded the bill and inspected it. "Be right back with your change."

"Keep it."

The little man nodded, a crooked grin on his face. "I knew there was something about you I liked when you first come in dat door!" He turned to leave and called out over his shoulder, "Y'all come back now!"

"Nice little man." Cherry spooned sugar into her coffee, added cream from a small metal pitcher, and stirred thoroughly. "We will come back, won't we?"

Dalton stared out into the night. Raindrops shattered the streetlamps' reflection in the puddles on St. Charles.

"Dalton?"

"Huh. . . ? Oh, sure — we'll come back."

Cherry pushed her cup aside, reached across the table, and took Dalton's hands. "Sweetheart . . ."

Dalton felt the softness and warmth of Cherry's hands pressing on his. Her touch always made things better for him, in a way he could never explain. "Yeah . . ."

Cherry's blue eyes filled with soft light. "Everything's going to be all right."

And, gazing into those eyes, he believed that everything would.

EIGHT

The Major

★ ★ ★

"Oh, we're sorry." A plump girl with the face of a ten-year-old and her slim, dark-haired friend began removing their coats and books from Dalton's desk, which was situated between theirs. "You come to class so seldom, we thought you'd finally dropped out of school."

"Sometimes it feels that way to me too." Dalton squeezed past the plump knees, hung his letter jacket on the back of his desk, and slouched down into it.

The sound of nineteen- and twenty-year-olds settling in for an hour of lecture was subsiding as Dr. Fred C. Frey, called the Major because of his rank in World War I, bounded with an energetic gait across the platform to the lectern. In his late sixties, he had a head with more age spots than hair, a mouth like a small dinner plate, eyes that sparked with energy, and an unflagging concern for the enlightenment of his young charges. No amount of apathy on the part of any recalcitrant student seemed able to dampen it.

The Major, wearing tan slacks with a white shirt and a dark brown tie, opened his attendance book, but somehow also managed to keep his eyes on his audience. "Well, Mr. Temple, I'm stunned that you'd grace us with your anointed presence today!"

Dalton shifted uneasily in his chair, glancing about at his classmates, most of whom were trying unsuccessfully to suppress their laughter.

Up on stage, the Major began pacing, hands behind his back, with the light step of a twenty-five-year-old distance runner. "We," he paused, encompassing the room with a wave of his left arm, "all of us here — mere mortals that we are — always feel *favored* by a visit from one of the enlightened emissaries from Olympus." He then pointed toward the west. "Olympus, in this case, being the arena of battle better known as 'Tiger Stadium.' *National champions.* Just the sound of it conjures up images of golden chariots charging into battle, swords of mighty warriors flashing in the sunlight."

Soft laughter, giggles, and a few muffled guffaws that sounded like donkeys braying broke out around the room.

Dalton felt his face burn with humiliation. He almost bolted from the room, but decided he deserved whatever the Major had in mind for him, and decided to stick it out.

"Well, in conclusion, *I* want to thank you personally and on behalf of my fellow mortals" — again he encompassed the room with his wave — "for your glittering presence among us today." The Major returned to his lectern. "And now, back to the mundane world of 'Nuclear Threat and the Space Age — Crisis in the American Family.' Some of you may wish to take notes."

All of the Major's students, including Dalton, readied themselves with legal pads and pencils.

Forty-five minutes later, the Major, never having so much as glanced at a note, abruptly ended his lecture. He stole a quick look at the big clock at the rear of the room. "I see we have ten minutes of class time left, but I think I'll give you time off for good behavior. See you on Friday."

As Dalton picked up his jacket to leave, he noticed the Major motioning for him to remain. He sat back down, scribbling a few notes on his tablet to disguise from the rest of the class his true reason for remaining behind.

When the last of the students had left, the

Major stepped lightly down from the platform, walked over to Dalton, and hooked a desk around with his foot. Sitting down, facing him, he stared directly into Dalton's veiled eyes. "I think virtually no tactic's too harsh if it stops someone from throwing his life away."

Dalton found that he could not hold the little man's penetrating stare. The intent of the Major's scathing remarks directed at him today had been all too obvious. Dropping his head, he mumbled, "I don't know what you're talking about."

"You're not a fool, Mr. Temple, so I'll simply ignore that remark." War had demanded an economy of words in accomplishing his various missions, and the Major had learned this lesson well in the fire and thunder of Belleau Wood.

"Yes, sir. I'll do better."

Frey's gruff military posturing had always failed to hide the genuine concern he felt for his students. "I'd feel much better if you could be a little more specific."

"I'll come to class."

Frey rubbed the flat of his right hand across his shiny, spotted head. "Well, that's a start." Then he drove directly to the core of the matter. "How's the knee coming along?"

With an involuntarily motion, Dalton covered his knee protectively with his left hand. "Oughta be good as new for spring practice."

The Major's eyes narrowed as he caught the motion of Dalton's hand. "How about a cup of coffee?"

"Well . . ."

"I don't buy very often, son." Frey grinned. "Don't let this golden opportunity pass you by."

Dalton returned his smile and stood up. "Okay. But I can't stay long. Got to get over to the weight room and give this leg a good workout. Rehab, you know."

Frey nodded, and together they left the lecture room — the old warrior and the young athlete, both carrying the wounds of their separate battlefields. They took the marble steps leading from the lobby of Himes Hall out to the colonnade running the length of the Quadrangle and passed along the eastern wall of the new Middleton Library.

Following the sidewalk that crossed the open area between the library and Foster Hall, Dalton watched the clear, hard February sunlight shatter in the crowns of live oaks. The bright afternoon held little warmth and one couple, their books stacked beside them, sat close together on a concrete bench, hands joined, speaking in low tones. Dalton thought immediately of Cherry and how she had changed lately. She seemed almost distant.

Dalton and the Major walked down a final flight of steps with round iron railings to the coffee shop located in the basement of Foster Hall. As they stepped inside, the warm air, scented with fresh-brewed coffee, washed over them. Water and steam pipes running along the walls and ceiling gave the place the appearance of a converted boiler room.

"Grab us a booth," the Major said in a tone approaching a military command. "I'll get the coffee."

"No, I'll —"

"I told you, it's my day for buying, son," the Major cut him off, the tone of his voice dropping from command down to a firm suggestion.

"Okay. You win." Dalton walked over and slid into one of the wooden booths against the left wall. Battered, cigarette-burned, and scarred from years of students' seeking a kind of immortality by scratching their initials into the wood with their pocket knives, the booths were large and friendly and caused their occupants to want to linger over coffee and conversation.

The Major set the cups on the table and slipped in across from Dalton. The elder of the two remarked casually, "I've liked this old place since the first time I came in here. They're talking about building a new student union, but it'll never replace this."

Dalton fidgeted with his cup, spinning it slowly round and round on the table with his forefinger hooked over the handle. He stole a quick look at Frey but couldn't hold his flinty gaze. *I'm going to drink up and get out of here,* Dalton promised himself.

"There *is* life after football, Dalton," Frey said, as if he had anticipated Dalton's eagerness to leave.

"Why do you say that?"

"Easy enough." Frey took a sip of coffee, swallowed, and finished with a satisfied sigh. "Nothing like going through a war and a depression to make you enjoy the simple pleasures of life."

"Yes, sir."

"Now." He placed his cup down and folded his hands before him on the table. "I can think of only two things that would send a young man like you into the doldrums, which is where you've made your home for some time now. This is not only from my own observation — the campus grapevine is still in working order."

Dalton peered over his cup at his teacher. *Why in the world is he doing this?*

179

"First of all, and most common, are problems with the fairer sex." Frey's eyes crinkled at the corners. "And since that pretty little blond-haired cheerleader still seems perfectly enamored of you, it must be the other reason. I hope she's as constant as she is fair, my boy. She almost takes me back to those quicksilver days of my own youth."

"And what's the second?" Dalton asked, distracted by the mention of Cherry, yet still knowing in advance what the Major was about to say.

"I've already told you. There *is* life after football." The Major leaned against the high wooden back of the booth, hands folded over his flat belly. "And for someone with your background and abilities" — he paused for effect and smiled again, his eyes crinkling like an elf's — "the alternatives are bright indeed."

Dalton stared down at his cup. "I'll be back in the starting lineup next year." He looked up and held the Major's eyes. "And then, it's on to the pros."

Frey's smile still played about his face as he spoke. "Let me ask you something, Dalton."

"Fire away." Dalton kept his gaze steady, the sound of his own words building confidence in him.

"When you're inside the ten-yard line, trying to punch through for a score, there must be some of those big linemen that you just can't run over. Isn't that true?"

Dalton nodded, bringing to mind a two-hundred-and-sixty-five-pound tackle who had stood his ground like a stone tower. "Yeah. One or two I can think of."

"What do you do when that happens?"

"Just bounce off and head in another direction," Dalton replied quickly.

"That's what I thought." The Major abruptly leaned forward, hands clasped firmly around his coffee cup. "Well, now that we've got that pesky little problem under control, let's see what we can do to keep you from failing my class."

"Rack 'em up." Cassidy, wearing sun-faded Levi's and a plaid flannel shirt unbuttoned over his white T-shirt, leaned over the green-surfaced pool table after sinking the eight-ball in a corner pocket. Then he angled his face upward toward Dalton.

Dalton had on a light blue button-down oxford shirt, tan chinos, and brown loafers. He sat on a tall wooden stool, holding his cue stick lightly in one hand, its rubber-tipped end resting on the tiled floor, old and cracked and covered with chalk dust and cigarette butts. From the corner jukebox, the Everly Brothers harmonized on their hit single, "Bye, Bye Love."

"You hear me?" Cassidy straightened up, placed his cue stick on the felt surface of the table, and walked around to Dalton's stool.

Leaning his stick against his leg, Dalton rubbed his eyes with the tips of his fingers, then stared blankly at Cassidy. "What did you say?"

"You just lost another game," Cassidy repeated. "Time to pay for another rack."

Dalton turned on his stool and called across the pool room. "Hey, Red —"

A tall, stilleto-slim man with reddish-brown, wiry hair and skin that approximated the color of the Mississippi's muddy water grabbed a triangular-shaped wooden rack from a peg on the wall next to the jukebox. Wearing threadbare green work pants and a brown flannel shirt missing the second and third buttons, he slouched toward the empty table.

Dalton got off his stool, picked up a square block of blue chalk from the edge of the table, and began rubbing it onto the tip of his cue stick. Then he drawled, "My little brother here won another one, Red. I think he's found a way to cheat at pool."

Red walked around the table, collecting

the balls from the leather pockets. He dropped them with a hard thudding sound into the rack as he slid it along the green felt cloth. "Maybe you better jes' stick with football, Mr. Dalton." At the end of the table, he arranged the balls for the break, his hands flying over them in a tan blur. Lifting the rack carefully, he smiled down at the triangle filled with polished balls, bright and colorful in the yellow light cast by a hooded bulb hanging from the tall ceiling.

As he walked by, Dalton tossed him a quarter and said, "Another beautiful job, Red."

"You know, it ain't but a dime a rack, Mr. Dalton," he said, staring down at the quarter in the palm of his hand.

"It's worth a quarter just to watch a professional like you in action." Dalton placed the chalk back on the table, testing the smoothness of his cue between his joined thumb, forefinger, and middle-finger. "I love to see a man who enjoys his work."

Red nodded his thanks, slipped the quarter into his pocket, and walked away, singing along with the Everly Brothers.

Bye, bye love; bye, bye happiness. . . .

Cassidy walked to the end of the table opposite the racked balls, thumped the cue ball into position on the felt, and placed the end of his cue stick on the edge of the table. Using his forefinger and middle-finger as guides, he slid the stick smoothly back and forth twice. On the third time, he slammed it into the cue ball. The white cue ball struck the yellow one-ball at the apex of the triangle, causing a minor explosion. The brightly colored balls clacked loudly against each other and caromed off the rubber-padded rails.

"Nice break." Dalton watched the sixteen spinning balls slow down on their geometric courses across the green felt, finally coming to rest, except for the blue ten-ball. It crept slowly toward a side pocket, almost stopped, then plopped over the edge.

"I got stripes again." Cassidy chalked his cue, twisting the square around on the leather tip while his eyes scanned the table, picking out the best shot. He spread his bottom three fingers on the table, making a firm platform for the joined thumb and forefinger that cradled the slim shaft of the cue stick. Sighting down the stick, he slid it back and forth twice, then firmly stroked the cue ball near the bottom, imparting backspin as it clacked into the yellow nine, sending it into the far corner pocket. The white cue ball stopped at impact, then backed up slowly until it was in perfect position for a shot on the fifteen in the side pocket.

"Lucky shot!"

Cassidy merely grinned at his brother. "Get Minnesota Fats on the phone, will you? Tell him I'm ready."

Dalton watched his brother sink one ball after the other until only the eight and all of Dalton's balls remained. "I know where you've been spending your days, Cass."

Cassidy leaned over the table, checking the angle on the eight-ball. "In class, studying. You know me!" He squatted down and sighted across the table with both eyes open. "Then, of course, there's my devotion to training."

"Are you working out at all, Cass?"

"I ran a nine-nine hundred last year. What was your best time as a sophomore?"

"Ten flat, but I ran a nine-eight my senior year. . . ."

"And you never got any faster in college."

"That's fast enough."

Cassidy, giving Dalton his best cynical smile, stood up and leaned on his cue. "You know, you've been coming around pretty well the last month or two . . . for somebody who's led the life of a cloistered monk. Don't blow your new image by preaching to me in the pool hall." He turned around, leaned over the table, and sunk the eight in one smooth motion.

Dalton started to ask Cassidy what he meant by "coming around," but he knew the answer as well as his brother did. He walked over to the rack on the wall and slipped his cue stick into it. "I think I better get on down to the weight room and work out. This knee's not going to get well all by itself."

Cassidy placed both hands behind him on the rail of the table and leaned back. Opening his mouth to speak, he stared at the floor instead and shook his head slowly.

"What's that supposed to mean?" Dalton stepped toward his brother. "C'mon, out with it!"

Cassidy walked past him and jammed his stick into the rack. "I'm going home. You want me to pick you up at the usual time Friday in front of your dorm?"

Dalton felt anger rising in him at his brother's unspoken insinuation. He was about to confront him again, when he caught a glimpse of someone through the dingy window passing by out on the sidewalk. She had honey-blond hair, gleaming in the sunlight. His heart thudded into his ribs.

Cassidy glanced out the window, then back to Dalton. "Yep. That was her, all right."

Dalton bolted for the front door.

"Hey! Take it easy — it's probably nothing," Cassidy shouted after him.

Dalton slammed the screen door outward and burst onto the sidewalk. The door banged into the wall with the noise of a pistol firing.

Cherry jerked around, her eyes opening wide as she saw Dalton cover the ground between them in four quick strides. "Dalton, what in the world . . . ?"

Dalton saw the world through a red haze of rage. The blood seemed to roar through his head like a flame. As his right hand knotted unconsciously into a fist, his shoulder automatically turning into the punch, he took in tiny details of the tall man standing next to Cherry: the expensive gray tweed jacket and the neat four-in-hand-knotted black tie, the dark hair combed neatly above his long face with its aquiline nose and brown eyes, glassy with the shock of what was about to happen, the short chin sagging below an open mouth.

Dalton's fist exploded low on the man's jawline, below and to the right of the short chin. He heard a sharp popping noise, but felt no sense of impact as his arm carried around and through the blow. In his loss of control, he had not set himself for the punch, had not unleashed the power of his legs and the weight of his body into the blow. But it had been enough.

The man's face seemed to lose shape as though it were clay beneath the hand of a brutal potter. The glassy sheen of fear in his eyes winked out. His feet left the sidewalk as his body jerked backward, crumpling four feet behind the spot where he had last been standing. As he lay on the rough concrete, the man's left hand twitched slightly, then his body remained perfectly still except for his shallow breathing.

"Oh, Dalton!" Cherry, her right hand clutching her throat, stood gaping at her fallen companion. "Are you crazy? You've killed him!"

"Nah." Cassidy walked past Cherry to stand over the crumpled form sprawled on the sidewalk. "He ain't dead. I been hit harder than that." He noticed a couple farther down the street, arms loaded with books, who had heard the commotion and turned around to stare at the fallen man. Waving them away, Cassidy said, "Nothing to worry about, folks. He just can't hold his liquor."

They shook their heads sadly and turned away.

Cherry knelt down beside the man, lifting his bleeding head gently in her hand. "Rando! Are you all right?"

"Rando?" Cassidy glanced at Dalton, then directed the question to Cherry. "What kind of name is *Rando*?"

"I don't know. I just met him ten minutes ago." Cherry's eyes turned upward toward Cassidy, pleading for help. "His name's Rando Amara. We've got to help him."

Dalton felt he had lost the power of speech, as if his mind were somehow unrelated to his body. He stood woodenly in place on the sidewalk and found himself staring at the long, slim soles of Amara's expensive leather shoes, splayed outward to form a wide V. Three feet in front of the left heel, a stark white molar lay on the sidewalk. Fragments of soft tissue still clung to its roots, covered with a thin film of blood.

Shaking off the mild shock that held him immobilized, Dalton walked stiffly over to Cherry, kneeling beside her. "The infirmary's just down the street. We'll take him there."

Cherry winced at the sound of his words, her voice quaking as she spoke, "N-no. You wait for me here. I'll come back after I make sure he's all right." She looked up at Cassidy. "Help me with him, Cass."

Dalton felt a sense of shame and helplessness sweep over him as he saw the fear in Cherry's eyes, saw the way she recoiled from him as he knelt close to her.

"Ohhh. . . ." Amara moaned, turning his head to one side, his left hand reaching upward to his damaged jaw.

"Help me, Cass."

Cassidy stared at Dalton, then shrugged and bent over, taking Amara underneath his arms. Lifting him to his feet, Cassidy slipped one of the man's arms over his shoulder, and with Cherry holding him on the other side, he shuffled off toward the infirmary. Amara groaned louder, moving his legs in an awkward imitation of a man walking.

"Dalton, what's happened to you?" Cherry asked, her voice tinged with disapproval.

Lost in thoughts of his unraveling life, Dalton sat on the curb, oblivious to the passersby on the sidewalk. He gazed upward at Cherry standing above him. Her red sweater accented the flush of her cheeks. He wondered whether vitality or anger or embarrassment was the source of their color. "I don't know," he answered, his voice flat and dull.

Smoothing her plaid skirt over her knees, Cherry sat down next to him on the dusty sidewalk. "I don't either, Dalton. You're not the same person anymore."

Dalton stared at his feet resting in the gutter. He noticed absently that his shoes had lost their shine. *I haven't polished them in weeks. Funny, I always did that every Friday night.*

Cherry lifted her right hand, let it hang a moment in midair, then placed it lightly on Dalton's shoulder. "Maybe you should get some help, sweetheart. Talk to your pastor — somebody."

"What were you doing with that . . . that man?" A small burning began in Dalton's chest. He fought to keep it from flaring out of control.

"Aren't you even going to ask how he's doing?"

To his surprise, Dalton found that he didn't care one way or the other. "You didn't answer my question."

"I just bumped into him in the bookstore." Cherry let her breath out in a sigh. "He made some small talk and asked if he could walk with me back to the campus. I'd never have done it if I'd thought it would upset you."

Dalton felt the flame of anger dying away, his mind coming into sharp focus once more. An empty, cold ache replaced the burning in his stomach. "Is he going to be all right?"

"If you call a sore jaw and a missing tooth all right." Cherry took her hand away from Dalton's shoulder.

"Where's Cass?" Dalton asked.

191

"I told him I wanted to see you alone." She clasped her hands together in her lap. "He went on home."

"Good."

Cherry spoke in a strained voice. "When Rando came to, he threatened to take you to court, Dalton."

"And . . ."

"I told him that this wasn't New York, and that if the other football players found out that he was . . . with your girl . . ." Cherry stood up and dusted her skirt off. "Well, anyway, I convinced him that he'd be better off to just let it drop."

Dalton got to his feet, finding it hard to keep his eyes on Cherry's. "Thanks."

"I don't think the police would do a thing in the world to you, Dalton." She firmed her chin, staring up at him. "Everybody knows that the national champs don't have to obey the law like ordinary citizens. I've heard other stories about how things like this have been swept under the carpet."

Dalton knew the stories, too, but never thought he would be the main player in one.

"But that doesn't make it right," she added.

Placing his hands on Cherry's shoulders, he said in a weak voice, "No, it doesn't. I'm sorry, Cherry. Really, I am." He felt her go

192

rigid beneath his touch. "Do you believe me?"

Cherry stared into his eyes, then nodded.

"I'll even apologize to . . . what's his name, if that'll make you feel better."

"You shouldn't be doing it for me, Dalton," she said in a flat voice. "You should want to do it for yourself."

"Okay, I will." Dalton felt an easing of the pressure that had gripped like a vise against his temples. "See you tonight in front of the library?"

Cherry stared at the sidewalk, then nodded. "I suppose so." She lifted her eyes and they softened as she stepped closer, encircling his waist with her arms.

"I'm really sorr—"

"Hush," Cherry whispered, pressing closer to him. "Just hold me."

PART THREE
★ ★ ★

Dalton

NINE

Called Away

★ ★ ★

Sharon pulled over to the curb and parked the year-old '57 Chevrolet. Black, with loads of gleaming chrome and sharp-angled fins, it was not her mother's first choice for a family vehicle, but she finally relented to Cassidy's pleas for them to have a "cool" car. Sharon found, to her surprise, that she had grown to like the car almost as much as Cassidy, although she would never admit this to her brother.

"Jess is going to drop me off after our luncheon," Catherine said, opening the car door.

Sharon glanced at her mother's outfit, pearl gray dress and black heels. "You look nice today, Mama."

"Thanks, sweetheart." She shut the door and walked around to the driver's side of the car.

"I'm almost eighteen now, Mama," Sharon said before Catherine could start her discourse on driving safety. "And I'm a real good driver."

Catherine, preparing for the lecture, closed her mouth and smiled. "All right." She leaned through the open window and kissed her daughter's cheek.

As Sharon turned her head, checking the street for traffic, she heard her mother's voice, "Sharon . . . drive carefully."

Shaking her head slowly, Sharon drove away. She had only gone two blocks when she glanced to her left and pulled over to the curb again. Across the street in a vacant lot a boy of about ten wearing denim overalls and black, high-topped tennis shoes played with a small brown-and-white dog. The dog looked familiar, but strangely out of place in this neighborhood. Suddenly, it hit her. *Edgar! That's Edgar!*

Sharon wondered how the little dog had gotten so far from the yellow house on Longfellow Street. As she watched the boy scratch Edgar's ears, she thought back to the newspaper article she had written about him. She could almost remember it word for word:

Edgar's Story

Drawn to that same spot at the foot of the front steps every day, he waited for a master who would never return. For eleven years passersby would see him in the blistering afternoon sunlight, shivering in a cold winter rain, or watching autumn leaves scrape down the sidewalk in the wind — always faithful to the appointed hour, listening for that special voice calling his name.

Edgar wasn't much to look at when fifteen-year-old Linton Dulaney found him, shivering and alone, behind Bert's Records at Delmont Village. For two years Edgar would greet his master every day when he came home from school. He had no way of knowing that a German Tiger Tank had ended Linton's brief life at the Battle of the Bulge . . . he only knew that the boy who had found him never came home again. . . .

Sharon watched the boy pick up his stack of school books, bend over and give Edgar a final pat on the head, then hurry away down the sidewalk. The little dog stared after him until he turned a corner, then struggled to his feet.

Poor thing, Sharon thought, *he must have been walking all night long to have gotten all the way across town.* She pictured him lying at the foot of the steps in front of his yellow house. Each day that Linton failed to return, he would get up from his spot, worn smooth over the years, and follow the little path he had made from countless trips around the house to the back porch and his comfortable box.

I wonder what called him away from his routine of; goodness, it must be thirteen or fourteen years now! Sharon thought. She pictured him making his way across town, the sunlight splashing on strange yards and streets, the cool March breezes bringing him exotic fragrances, and most of all, the boys and girls who had petted and played with him as Linton had done so long ago.

Sharon watched the little dog walk slowly down the sidewalk in the direction of Jessie's house. She knew that his bones must be aching with weariness. *Maybe I should take him home. No! He deserves to see a little of the world after all these years.*

With a final glance at Edgar, Sharon drove away. She didn't see him stop in front of the white, hundred-year-old cottage on Napolean Street with its gray shutters that matched the color of the slate roof, flanking the tall front windows. A gallery extended across the front and partway down one side. At its south end a weathered porch swing hung in front of a white trellis that would soon be spilling over with bright purple blossoms. Between the swing and the front door, two ladder-back rockers sat side by side like old friends enjoying each other's company.

Edgar stared at the brick walkway leading up to the house. He started walking slowly toward the spot in front of the steps, stumbled twice, but made it, turned slowly around one time and lay down, facing the street. He closed his eyes as sunlight patterned the house with shadow and pale gold light. From the top of the old sycamore, a mockingbird filled the morning with song.

"I'm going to get the newspaper, Jess," Catherine called over her shoulder as she walked out onto the front porch. Suddenly, she stopped and stared at the end of the brick walkway. Then she took the steps and knelt down, stroking the dog's head and ears. "Oh, you poor little thing!"

"What are you doing, Mama?" Jessie held the baby on one hip as she pushed the door open and stepped out onto the porch. She was barefoot and wore blue pajamas topped with a light cotton robe cinched at the waist.

Catherine stood up, but her eyes gazed sadly down on the little form at her feet.

"He's still warm. Must have died not very long ago."

Jessie walked farther out onto the porch, bringing the little dog into her range of vision. She opened her mouth abruptly but cut off the gasp that almost escaped. "I wonder where in the world it came from! It's not one of the neighborhood dogs."

"He's an old dog. I expect he just finally wore out." Smoothing her dress under her, Catherine sat down on the top step, her eyes fixed on the still form at her feet. "I can't imagine, though, why he would come here to die."

"Is there a tag on his collar?"

Catherine shook her head. "The little metal ring's there, but the tag's gone." Abruptly, she stood up and walked toward Jessie. A smile pushed the look of concern from her face as she held out her arms and reached for Taylor. "How's my big boy doing this morning?"

Jessie handed the baby to Catherine. She took him in her arms and began nuzzling his neck, speaking in the nonsensical terms that most all grandmothers use with babies. The baby giggled, rubbing her face with his soft, chubby hands.

Slipping her arm beneath his bottom, Catherine held the baby's hand with her thumb and forefinger, smiling into his bright blue eyes. "No doubt about this one! He's got Cassidy's eyes." She turned her face to Jessie and added, "Cassidy's and mine." She lightly stroked the fine hair on his softly rounded head. "I think his hair's going to be dark like his father's, though." She kissed him on the cheek, then looked into his eyes. "Yes, sir, Taylor Youngblood. You're going to be a fine-looking young man someday!"

Jessie put her hands on her hips. "Well, he's got to have *something* like me, doesn't he?" She tickled the baby's bare foot. "After all, I am his mother!"

"Oh, I think there's one thing for certain." Catherine smiled, holding the child at arm's length. "He already got your discipline and self-control."

Sniffing haughtily and turning up her nose, Jessie took Taylor from his grandmother. "I don't think that's very funny, Mother."

Catherine laughed, opening the door for Jessie. "Why don't you go change him and then we'll have tea."

When Jessie had gone into the house, Catherine sat down on the steps and gazed again at the little dog. "You certainly do look familiar, old dog. I just can't quite figure out where I know you from." She shook her head slightly. "I sure hope you had a happy life." Gathering the little body up in her arms, she took it around the house toward the backyard.

Catherine walked across the dew-wet winter grass. Near the brick wall that enclosed the yard, she lay the dog down next to a willow, its limbs thin and bare and dead-looking. After the first April rains, it would form a lush green waterfall with the downward sweep of its pale bright leaves shimmering in the sunlight.

Taking a deep breath, Catherine walked over to a stone bench that rested on a brick patio beneath a mimosa tree. She sat down, enjoying the soft coolness of the morning air. A bright indigo bunting perched in one of the sweet olive trees near the back porch sang a song of warning to protect his territory. A gray cat appeared like a cloud of smoke atop the ivy-covered brick wall. Seeing that the yard was occupied, he crept along the top of the wall for a few feet, then disappeared over its edge.

"Mama, what are you doing out there?" Jessie opened the screen door of the back porch and stared out.

Glancing over at the dog's limp form, Catherine replied, "I thought we might have a funeral. Nothing elaborate, mind you —

just a simple little ceremony."

Catherine tried to make light of the situation, but somehow the little dog's death had touched her deeply. She found that an undefined and heavy sadness seemed to be seeping into her heart, as though she had lost someone or something that meant a great deal to her. *It's just a silly little dog. Why am I letting it bother me so much?*

She listened to the sound of a tugboat whistle out on the river. *I guess it's just knowing that the poor little thing died all alone. Nobody to talk to him or rub his head. He just lay down and went to sleep for the last time.*

The noise of the screen door slamming startled Catherine from her thoughts. Jessie, the baby at her hip, carried a small garden shovel in her hand. She walked down the steps and across the yard toward Catherine.

"Where's the casket?" Catherine asked, standing up and taking the shovel.

"Do we really need one?" Jessie handed Taylor to Catherine and leaned the shovel against the bench. Then she looked at the sad little form lying next to the wall. "I guess I could come up with something."

Jessie went back to the house, and Catherine turned Taylor toward her, setting him on her knees. Taking his chubby hands in hers, she began bouncing him gently up and down with her legs. "You like to play horsey, don't you, Taylor? Oh yes, that's fun, huh?" Taylor giggled his agreement as he wobbled clumsily back and forth, bouncing up and down.

"How's this?" Jessie held out an object for her mother to inspect.

Catherine glanced at Jessie walking toward her. She held a cardboard Pet Milk box, and she had put on a pair of Austin's heavy leather hunting boots. "That'll do just fine."

"I'm glad you approve." Jessie smiled. She picked up the shovel and glanced around. "You have any particular spot in mind for the interment?"

Letting her eyes wander about, Catherine pointed to a spot near the wall and beneath the outer sweep of the willow tree. "Right there, I think. It'll be so pretty when the leaves come in . . . and after the April rains."

Jessie started to dig the grave. She held the shovel's blade against the ground and stomped on it with Austin's boot. The shovel twisted at an awkward angle, pulling the handle loose from her grasp. She stared at it as though it had betrayed her. "This ground's as hard as a sidewalk! I need a jackhammer instead of a shovel."

Taylor, noticing that his horse had played out on him, began fussing for another ride.

Catherine smiled and complied with her grandson's unspoken but highly audible demand.

"Ouch!" Jessie rubbed her shin where the shovel's handle had struck it in her second attempt at grave-digging. "How do people use these things?"

Catherine shook her head, a look of impatience blended liberally with motherly understanding on her face. "Let me have a try at it, dear." She sat Taylor on the bench and waited for Jessie to trade places with her.

"I can do it, Mother! Do you think I'm still a child?" Jessie tried unsuccessfully for the third time to sink the shovel's point into the ground.

Smiling benignly, Catherine motioned for Jessie to come sit beside her. "How you ever managed to travel all over the world and make it back home by yourself is beyond me."

With a trace of a pout on her face, Jessie finally sat down and took Taylor into her arms.

"I'll need those boots," Catherine said, slipping out of her heels and placing them beneath the bench.

Jessie simply lifted her feet out of the oversized boots, shoving them over in front of her mother.

Catherine shoved her stockinged feet into

the boots, picked the shovel up, and walked over to the spot she had picked out beneath the willow. Holding the handle firmly, she placed the blade on the ground at an angle, placed her right foot on it, and transferred her weight gradually, adding extra force with her leg muscles. The blade held firm, then gradually sunk a little at a time into the ground.

"How'd you do that?" Jessie asked in genuine awe. At Taylor's insistence, Jessie had filled in as "horse" for her mother while Catherine dug the shallow hole.

"I spent a lot of my life on a farm . . . remember?" Catherine bent down, grasped the shovel closer to the blade with one hand and, keeping the other at the end of the handle, lifted the first bladeful of earth out. Placing the dirt carefully to the side, she positioned the blade next to the small hole and leaned into her work.

Jessie sat with her son on the cool concrete bench, watching with a certain wonder and admiration as her mother, a picture of femininity with her pearl gray dress, did a man's work.

Twenty minutes later, Catherine blew a wisp of blond hair back from her eyes and dropped the shovel on the ground. "I think that'll do it."

Jessie picked up the Pet Milk box, walked over, and tossed it on the ground next to the grave. "I put an old pillowcase in there to wrap him in," she said to Catherine.

Catherine nodded, her breath coming heavily now. Even in the coolness of the morning, perspiration beaded her forehead. "It'll make a good burial cloth." She took the pillowcase out of the box, stepped over near the wall, and slipped it over the still form of the little dog. Lifting him carefully, she returned to the grave, knelt down, lay him in the box, and gently placed him in the freshly dug earth.

"You want to take a rest, Mama?"

"I believe so." Catherine breathed deeply. "I'm not really in shape for this sort of thing."

"I'll fill it in later," Jessie offered. "It doesn't take any talent to do that."

"I think I'll take you up on that offer, sweetheart."

Holding a cup of tea, Catherine glanced at the white wicker furniture forming a conversation grouping on the screened back porch. She walked over and sat down in a rocker. Her eyes were drawn to the mound of earth near the brick wall.

"Well, Taylor finally gave up and went to sleep," Jessie called out through the utility

209

room door at the other side of the porch. She took a pile of diapers from the dryer, placing them on a folding table that ran the length of one wall. Glancing at the white mound of diapers, then out at her mother, she said, "I think I'll put these away later." Then she walked across the porch and sprawled on the flowered cushion of a love-seat across from Catherine.

"You look a little tired, sweetheart." Catherine sipped her tea, her eyes still staring out at the backyard.

Jessie drew her bare feet up on the cushion, pulled her hair behind her head, and slipped a rubber band over it. "I never knew that taking care of one little boy could be a full-time job. How did you ever manage to raise four of us — especially during those years when Daddy was overseas?"

Catherine smiled and turned toward her daughter, noticing the dramatic change that had taken place in her during the eleven months since Taylor's birth. The obvious difference was the lack of makeup, a slight puffiness around the eyes, and the utilitarian hairdo. But there was also a new warmth in her brown eyes and a new bearing that Catherine could only describe as a growing maturity. "Somehow, I don't remember those days as being difficult at all. Maybe it was because you were old enough to help out with the younger children, Jess."

"I don't remember helping you very much, Mama." Jessie yawned. Her smooth brow furrowed slightly. "Let's see — I was only nine or ten when Daddy left. I can't imagine that I was good for anything but playing with my dolls."

Catherine recalled those World War II days in Sweetwater, when Lane was a marine in the South Pacific. "You were an excellent baby-sitter for Dalton and Sharon."

Jessie smiled at the memories. "I seem to recall that I didn't have much luck with Cass, though."

"Well, I must admit, he was a handful for anybody," Catherine agreed with a smile.

"Sharon was always so grown-up and well-behaved, I hardly ever noticed her," Jessie added. "As young as she was, I felt sometimes that she could be looking after me." She got up and walked over to the open kitchen door, listening for a few seconds, then took her place on the loveseat.

That simple act of Jessie's somehow gave Catherine a final reassurance that her daughter had indeed become the mother Catherine always knew she could be. Jessie had been more vulnerable to emotional turbulence than Catherine's other children — more apt to make decisions based on passing fancies of the heart than on reason.

Now, Catherine could see her daughter's will directing her life rather than her emotions; could see her growing devotion to her husband and child. *She's becoming the wife and mother I had always hoped for — maybe even better.*

"Dalton never was any real problem, either," Jessie continued, sharing her recollections. She started to speak, then looked away as though she had thought better of it.

"I know," Catherine said, bringing up the subject that Jessie had feared to mention. "Dalton's not doing well at all."

Jessie jumped on board then, eager to find out about the brother who had always seemed like a haven of strength to her, much as her father had always been. "Dalton dropped by to see us last week. From the way he and Austin talked, his leg's going to be as good as new."

Catherine shook her head sadly. "I don't think he'll ever play football again, Jess." The thought had plagued her for months, but putting it into words for the first time brought a mother's pain flooding into her heart. Bright, unbidden tears welled up in her blue eyes. She brushed them away quickly.

"Mama," Jessie continued in a hesitant tone, "I hate to bring this up, but it's something we've got to face." Her voice became almost a whisper. "I think Dalton had been drinking. He was chewing mints by the handful, but that alcohol smell is something that even wintergreen can't hide."

Catherine felt the pain sharpen as she nodded in agreement with Jessie. "Daddy and I have suspected the same thing. He pretends everything is fine and changes the subject whenever we try to talk about anything personal. I don't know what else to do. He doesn't pay a bit of attention to us. It's like he doesn't *want* any help."

"Daddy's talked to him?"

"He tried to, but I don't think Dalton was even listening to him. He mumbled a few times and that was about it." Catherine took a swallow of tea, feeling its soothing warmth inside her. "I've prayed so hard for my boy, but sometimes I feel like heaven is closed against my prayers."

"Oh, Mama, you know that isn't so."

"I know, I know," Catherine agreed, her words now little more than a murmur. "It's just that Dalton's always been such a good boy — always so respectful, always worked so hard." She stared into her cup. "He's almost like a stranger now."

Jessie pulled her knees up, clasping her arms around them. "He was always such a good student. He told me his grades haven't been very good this semester. It didn't even seem to bother him very much."

"That's what worries me the most. He's just letting his whole world slip away without a fight."

Jessie stared into her mother's eyes. "It's *his* life, Mama. You just have to let go."

Catherine's eyes sparked with an intense light as she returned Jessie's gaze. "A mother never lets go — not completely, Jess. You'll learn that soon enough."

Jessie nodded, staring down at the gray-painted, heart pine floor. "I suppose so."

Over the years, there had been rare occasions when Catherine had doubted the wisdom of bringing children into the world. This brief moment of time on Jessie's screen porch, within earshot of the Mississippi River, had become one of those moments.

Then she thought of her first grandchild asleep inside the house, of the unspeakable joy she had experienced with the birth of each of her children and of the pleasure they had brought her over the years . . . and the moment vanished, as the others had, like a thin mist facing the bright and rising sun.

The light in Catherine's eyes softened. "I

214

wouldn't trade places with anyone in this world, Jess."

"Ma'am?"

Catherine laughed softly. "I guess that did seem to come right out of the blue, didn't it?"

Jessie nodded, a puzzled expression playing across her face.

"What I mean is that you and Dalton and Sharon and Cassidy have been such blessings to me all these years that I can't imagine anyone else being as happy as I've been."

"We've put you through some pretty rough times, Mama," Jessie said in a somber tone.

Catherine reached over and took Jessie's hand. "Not so rough, sweetheart. It doesn't begin to compare with all the joy you've given me."

Jessie glanced toward the kitchen door. "I'm just starting to learn what you mean. Taylor's birth was so . . . so marvelous, I just can't express it in words."

"We'll get through this trouble with Dalton, just like we have everything else," Catherine said, reassuring herself as much as Jessie. Her eyes took on a remote look. "Jesus said that we'd have tribulation in this world."

"He also said that He'd never leave us or

forsake us," Jessie noted in a voice as soft as the pale morning light spilling down through the trees into the backyard.

"Yes, He surely did." Catherine, nodding her head slowly, smiled at her daughter. "I needed to hear that, Jess." She gazed out at the early sky, bone white and empty of clouds. "We'll understand it better, by and by."

"I remember that old song," Jessie chimed in. "I sang it once or twice when I was on the road with Billy."

Dropping her gaze to the freshly turned earth out near the ivy-covered wall, Catherine acted as though she hadn't heard Jessie's words. "I wonder if there'll be animals in heaven."

"What?" Jessie swung her legs over the edge of the loveseat. "I'm having a hard time following the course of this conversation, Mama."

Catherine laughed softly. "I'm sorry. It's just that I keep thinking about that silly little dog."

Jessie rested her chin on her clasped hands. "Well, there're horses. The Bible tells us that. And there's a river, so there just might be some fish."

"It's strange, the things we think of when . . . or at least *I* think of, when I'm in one

216

of these dark times. Sometimes I can't seem to keep my mind focused on a single train of thought."

"You're doing fine, Mama," Jessie reassured her. She sniffed the air, sniffed again, then jumped up from the loveseat. "Oh no! The cake's burning!" As she ran for the kitchen, she called back over her shoulder, "I was going to bake one for practice before Taylor's birthday next month!"

"Good thing you did!"

"Isn't it, though?" Jessie called from inside the kitchen.

Catherine heard the oven door open, and at the same moment, Taylor's cries rang down the hallway. She stood up and walked into the house. "Life goes on!"

TEN

Promises

★ ★ ★

"I don't know, Mrs. Temple."

Cherry wore a red jumper, black leotards, and a pained expression. She glanced at her left thumbnail, then lifted it close to her face, inspecting it as though her choice of words depended on its polished perfection. "I don't think I can take this much longer."

Catherine, sitting with Cherry in one of the high-backed booths, had kept her tan all-weather coat on to ward off the chill in the drafty coffee shop beneath Foster Hall. "I understand how you feel, Cherry."

"He . . . he just doesn't seem to . . ." She let her voice trail off as she waved at a tall, broad-shouldered man standing in the serving line. "To care about . . . much of anything anymore."

Glancing around the noisy, crowded room with its exposed conduits and pipes running along the walls and ceilings, Catherine wondered what attraction this cavern of a coffee shop could possibly hold for people. The tables and booths were packed with students and faculty, and cluttered with stacks of books, coffee cups, and plates of half-eaten doughnuts. Sugary pastry smells mixed with that of freshly brewed coffee.

"Mrs. Temple . . ." Cherry leaned forward, her elbows on the table. "Did you hear me?"

Catherine flinched slightly, turning her attention to Cherry. "Oh, I'm sorry, dear. I've been kind of . . . distracted lately." She sipped her milk-whitened coffee from a thick mug, then placed it on the table, warming her hands on it. "Cherry, I thought you might have a suggestion about how we could get through to Dalton."

Cherry merely shrugged and turned her head to speak to a couple walking by on their way out.

Catherine persisted in trying to recapture Cherry's full attention. "I *do* know that young men are more likely to listen to their girlfriends than anyone else, Cherry. Can't you talk some sense into him?" Catherine felt a sense of hopelessness as she gazed at Cherry's face; pretty and cheerful and as devoid of care and concern as a house cat's.

Cherry shook her head, her bouffant twist holding firm. "He won't listen to me."

Keeping silent, Catherine allowed Cherry to find her own way in their conversation.

"Since he hurt his knee . . ." Cherry winced slightly as she mentioned the event that had brought such discomfort and uncertainty into her life.

Catherine's spirit lifted as she saw Cherry's reaction at the mention of her son's injury. *I guess she does have some true feelings for Dalton, after all.*

". . . since then, all he can think of is getting it strong enough to play again." Cherry let her breath out in one long sigh. "He wouldn't even pose with the team when the people came down from New York to do a story on the best football team in the country."

"He didn't mention that to us."

"Oh yes, ma'am." Cherry brightened. "They're gonna be in one of the big national magazines" — her face dropped abruptly — "and Dalton's been left out."

"Well, I guess having your picture in a magazine is not that important."

"It is to me!" Cherry's eyes grew intense as she spoke. "Dalton and I had all these plans for our future. He was going to win the Heisman Trophy — at least, I thought he would — and then go on to play professional football." She gazed into a remote and unattainable future.

"Football's not the whole world, Cherry." Catherine had begun to believe that Cherry could perhaps be relegated as part of the problem rather than a part of the solution.

Cherry stared at something only she could see in the smoky air above the tables.

Catherine continued her role as Dalton's sole advocate. "As much as Dalton loves football, and with all his experience, he could finish his education and go to work as a coach — in high school and maybe later at the college level."

"I have a confession to make to you, Mrs. Temple." Cherry dropped her eyes to the table, then glanced at Catherine before staring out at the coffee shop's controlled bedlam. "I picked Dalton out when I first came to school here."

"You *picked him out?*" Catherine felt that she already knew the main plot of Cherry's story and waited only for her to fill in the details.

"Yes, ma'am." She seemed unable to meet Catherine's eyes. "I did a lot of — research, I guess you'd call it."

"I see."

Cherry held Catherine's gaze. "No, I don't think you do, Mrs. Temple." She turned her cup in a slow circle. "You see, I came here to LSU to find a good husband. Education had very little to do with it."

Nine-o'clock classes had let out, and the din rose in volume as even more students crowded into the already overflowing coffee shop. Catherine noticed several of the varsity football players and was saddened that she could no longer number her son among them. She felt as though she had been injured as badly as Dalton had that November night in Tiger Stadium.

"Well, anyway," Cherry continued her selective biography, "I decided a long time ago that I wasn't going to live the rest of my life dirt poor, the way I was brought up. I never would have been able to go to college if it hadn't been for my uncle. He always liked me, for some reason, and told Mama he'd pay for my education."

"He must be a nice man."

Cherry shrugged. "I guess so." She glanced at the big clock on the wall beyond the serving line. "You've got a wonderful son, Mrs. Temple."

"I think so." Catherine found herself surprised at the cool and distant sound of her words.

"Look, I admit that I deliberately picked Dalton out of all the boys on this campus," Cherry said, a slight flush coming to her cheeks. "I talked to a lot of people, and everybody said he was the nicest, most dependable person they'd ever met . . . or things that meant the same thing."

"Why are you telling me all this, Cherry?"

Cherry stared down into her cup, then lifted her head. "I don't really know." Her eyes held Catherine's without wavering. "I promise you this, though — I fell in love with Dalton after our first date." A smile started in her eyes, then spread to the rest of her face. "He was just the best thing that ever happened to me — a knight on a white charger, everything that I had dreamed about while growing up in that crummy little town where I was born."

"But —"

"But, I'm not going to throw my life away on a dr—" Cherry couldn't quite say the word out loud. "A man who drinks. A man who's a quitter. And I'm afraid that's what Dalton is turning into. . . . I really am."

At the bluntness of Cherry's words, Catherine felt hot tears well up in her eyes. She quickly brushed them away but could do nothing about the pain that gnawed at her insides.

"I'm sorry to tell you all this, Mrs. Temple, but it's just the way I see things." Cherry gazed back into a past filled with painful memories. "My daddy was a drunk. I never saw much of him, but I saw what he did to my mama . . . and I'm never going to let that happen to me."

"I wouldn't want you to, Cherry." Catherine's eyes held an intense light as she spoke for her son. "But Dalton's made of better stuff than you give him credit for, and he'll make it through this hard time — with or without you."

Cherry dropped her eyes. "I hope he does, Mrs. Temple. I really do."

Dalton drove along Dalrymple, past the Sigma Chi House, its antebellum facade a white glare of columns in the night. Turning left on Lakeshore Drive, he spun along out of the glow of streetlamps and windows into an area that provided a touch of wilderness in the sprawl of the LSU campus. This stretch of lakeshore between Dalrymple and Stadium Drive was heavily utilized by students for one of the most popular of their extracurricular activities known as "parking."

Pulling onto a hard-packed area of shoreline beneath a spreading willow tree, Dalton switched off the engine, jammed the gearshift of Lane's '39 Ford coupe into reverse, and turned off the lights. He stared out across the lake toward Stanford Avenue running along the opposite shore. A single car, no more than a speck of light, moved at a snail's pace through the darkness.

Dalton gazed at Cherry, her pink sweater pulled around her shoulders against the night chill. Her profile was clean and smooth, the nose slightly uptilted, her face shadowed by the mass of honey-blond hair that she had worn down instead of in her usual bouffant twist. *I wonder why she's changed her hairstyle? Oh, well, she looks great anyway she wears her hair.*

"Are you cold?" he asked.

Cherry stared straight ahead. "No."

"I could let you have my jacket if you are." Dalton slipped out of his purple-and-gold letter jacket. "You sure?"

"Yes."

Dalton tossed the jacket into the backseat. Turning back to Cherry, he noticed that she had begun to chew on her thumbnail, held it close to her face for inspection, and then put it between her teeth once again. He suddenly felt a coldness like a sliver of ice inside the pit of his stomach. Searching for words that refused to come, he flicked on the radio. Its faint glow searched the contours of Cherry's face, then the music gradually came alive as the vacuum tubes warmed up.

. . . the day we tore the goalpost down . . .

"Hey," Dalton commented, rejoicing that he had found an opening in the growing barrier of silence, "that's 'Moments to Remember'! It was playing the first night we went out."

Cherry took her thumb away from her mouth and clasped her hands together in her lap.

"Did you hear me?"

"I heard."

"Well, do you remember or not?"

A deep sigh escaped Cherry's lips. "I remember."

Dalton felt the sliver of ice in his stomach grow to the size of a knife blade. "What's the matter with you, Cherry?"

"Nothing."

"Didn't you like the movie?" Not waiting for Cherry to give him another non-answer, Dalton pushed ahead, "I guess westerns aren't your favorite, but everybody likes John Wayne — don't they?"

"I guess."

"I know you like Ricky Nelson. He played the young gunfighter part real well, I thought." Dalton slid over on the seat, placing his arm along the backrest. *What's the matter with me? Why am I talking so much?* He found himself rattling on, the words spill-

226

ing out seemingly beyond his control. "And he and Dean Martin sang pretty well together. It wasn't even all that corny . . . at least, I thought they sounded pretty good together. And Walter Brennan's always good for a laugh."

"And Dean Martin played a drunk." Cherry turned toward Dalton, her face bland and expressionless except for the hard glint in her eyes. "I don't like drunks."

Dalton felt the words hit him like a slap in the face. He moved his arm away. "What's *that* supposed to mean?"

Cherry stared through the windshield at the lake. The full moon cast a glossy pathway across its star-filled surface. At its marshy edge among the willows, a chorus of frogs sang their favorite rain song.

"You didn't answer me."

Keeping her eyes on the scene ahead of her, Cherry spoke in a flat, controlled voice. "It means that I'm not going to get hooked up with a drunk like my mother did."

"You think I'm a drunk? Is that it?"

"Not yet."

"What do mean, *not yet?*"

Cherry kept her voice at a quiet pitch, as though her words themselves needed no help from volume. "You haven't been drinking long enough yet."

"I assume there's more to come in your little symposium on the evils of demon rum."

"Yes, there is. In less than two months, you've already reached the point where you're drinking every day."

The truth of Cherry's words stung Dalton like a lash. He opened his mouth to defend himself, but a hopeless, sinking sensation silenced him. All the things that meant the most to him in life seemed to be slipping from his grasp, one by one, in spite of all the years of hard work and discipline. He could almost see the future he and Cherry had planned shatter before his eyes, like thin porcelain beneath a hammer blow.

Cherry folded her arms across her chest as if to protect herself from what was sure to come.

Dalton refused to believe what was happening. He felt himself sliding into a dreamlike state. Desperate now, he burst in, in a voice that he forced himself to control. "Cherry . . . we've been together for over two years now."

"I know that." She seemed to respond more favorably now to Dalton's quiet tone.

Encouraged, he continued, "I know I haven't been easy to get along with for the last few months, but I'm going to do better. As soon as my knee —"

"No!" Cherry turned to face him, her hands grasping for his. "It's not going to get any better, Dalton! You've got to stop kidding yourself. You'll never play football again!"

Dalton had thought the very same thing many times, but the sound of the actual words spoken by Cherry was more terrible than he could have imagined. "Don't you ever say that again!" His voice rose into a shout.

Cherry instantly pulled away from him.

"I've worked too long for this!" Dalton felt hot tears spill out of his eyes. Ashamed, he turned away, wiping his eyes on the sleeve of his shirt. He spoke finally, his breath clouding the car window, his voice quaking as he fought for control. "All those years . . . all that hard work. It can't be for nothing. . . . It can't!"

Confronted by Dalton's relentless sorrow, Cherry seemed now to regret her words. She slid over on the seat, placing her hand on his shoulder. "I know what you've been going through, sugar. It's the worst thing that could have happened."

Dalton turned around abruptly, encircling her with his arms, pulling her close. Feeling Cherry's warmth and softness, losing himself in her fragrance like a dream of summer,

Dalton thought for one heart-stopping moment that all was well with them — that her angry words and her coolness toward him had only been a waking nightmare.

Then he felt her hands against his chest, pushing him away. On the edge of his hearing, he listened to the soulful voice of Johnny Mathis singing "Chances Are." He remembered that it had been *their* song during the first few months they had gone together. Fastening his eyes on hers, he saw a remote look in their blue depths that told him more than words could say.

"I can't face this anymore, Dalton." Cherry's voice was almost a sob. "I just can't!"

Dalton knew with certainty then that she had stepped beyond his reach. He turned the key in the ignition, firing the engine to life. *I could just step on the gas and run this thing right out into the lake. All of this pain and trouble would just vanish . . . like my life has.*

"I'm so sorry, sugar."

Cherry's words sounded almost ludicrous. Dalton fought down the rage that was building like a storm inside him. He eased the gearshift up into reverse and backed out into the road. Driving slowly back toward campus, he gazed out the window at the lake, still shimmering under the full moon as the night breeze ruffled its dark surface. Off in the distance, he heard the wail of a siren.

"Dalton, I really do love you." Cherry leaned against the door as she spoke. "It's . . . it's just that all the things we planned together . . . well, now they . . ."

Cherry's voice had become little more than a dull, droning noise, just another source of grief to be contended with in Dalton's blighted world. Turning right on Stadium, he glanced at Campus Lake, remembering against his will the picnics they had shared on its grassy banks. He turned right on Highland, continuing on to Evangeline Circle, where he turned again and pulled up in front of Evangeline Hall. Couples walked arm in arm along the sidewalks, sat together on the old weathered stone benches, or stood holding hands in the shadows.

Dalton forced himself to look at Cherry. The Ford's idling motor made a familiar, reassuring sound that reminded him of the many times he had sat next to his father on the way home from football games or innumerable practice sessions. *Maybe it's not as bad as I'm making it out to be. We've had arguments before.* "It's still early." His words seemed to catch in his throat like fish hooks. He swallowed and continued, "We could go somewhere and grab a bite to eat."

Cherry shook her head, her hair catching the light from a streetlamp. "I don't think so, Dalton." She gave him a weak smile. "I'm kind of tired."

"Okay. I'll walk you over to the dorm."

"No thanks." The words leaped from her mouth. She leaned over and gave Dalton a quick kiss on the cheek. "Thanks for a wonderful evening," she called back over her shoulder as she shoved the car door open and got out.

The slamming of the door felt like yet another slap in the face to Dalton. *"Thanks for a wonderful evening." That's what she used to say when we first started dating. A person doesn't say that after more than two years together.*

Dalton watched Cherry head toward the lighted archway that formed the entrance to the lounge area of Evangeline Hall. Her skirt swayed with the rhythm of her steps as she walked. Beyond her, through the glass doors, he could see a girl in a white blouse stooped over her studies at the reception desk. He switched off the headlights and waited.

He saw Cherry enter the dorm, walk over, and say something to the girl at the desk. The girl reached behind her and placed a black telephone on the counter. After signing in, Cherry lifted the receiver, dialed, and held it to her ear. Speaking a few words, she returned the telephone, walked over to a wing-backed chair against the wall, and sat down. Taking a compact from her purse, she applied fresh lipstick, then ran a brush through her hair.

Dalton watched Cherry as she sat primly on the edge of her chair, her head turning toward the door every time it opened . . . as if she was waiting for someone. He forced himself to put the car into first gear and slowly drive away.

Seconds after Dalton had willed himself to leave Cherry to her obvious plans, he changed his mind. Letting the Ford idle around the curve of Evangeline Circle, he parked on the opposite side, backing beneath an ancient magnolia tree. Then he sat, slumped behind the steering wheel, staring at her, a distant and indistinct figure behind glass.

Fifteen minutes passed before a gleaming Cadillac, its huge fins reminding him of pale yellow sharks, pulled into the spot where he had parked the Ford. A tall man with a sparse frame opened the Cadillac's door. In the glare of the interior light, Dalton recognized the long face with its aquiline nose and short chin, the neatly combed dark hair, and the tweed jacket. The last time he had seen him, the man had been lying unconscious on the Chimes Street sidewalk.

Anger flamed in Dalton's chest, rising to his face, pounding inside his head. He reached for the door handle, gripped it tightly, then let his arm go limp at his side. *What's the use? What difference does anything make now?*

As soon as Amara reached the entrance of Evangeline Hall, Cherry rose from her chair and hurried across the foyer to greet him. Taking both of his hands, she rose on tiptoe to give him a quick kiss on the lips. After signing out, she slipped both hands around his arm and, leaning on his shoulder, walked out toward the Cadillac, her face smiling and animated as she spoke with him.

A cold, smothering darkness seemed to press down on Dalton as he stared at Cherry, lavishing all that affection on Amara. He fought against the burning rage in his chest. In his mind, he clutched Amara by the throat and sent his fist crashing into his arrogant, grinning face.

Stop this! For a moment, Dalton thought he had actually spoken the words aloud, then he forced the thoughts from his mind. *If it wasn't him . . . it'd just be somebody else. What difference does it make?*

Reaching beneath the seat, Dalton pulled out a square bottle with a black-and-white label. Pulling the cork, he stared out the windshield at Cherry as she slid into the front seat of the yellow Cadillac. Amara closed her door, then took a few gangly strides around the car and climbed in behind the wheel. He started the engine, lay his hand along the back of the seat, and pulled away from the curb.

Dalton watched Cherry slide across the seat toward Amara, his hand caressing her hair; saw, as though in a blurry dream, her head tilt slightly upward as Amara kissed her lingeringly on the mouth.

As Dalton watched the Cadillac disappear into the night, he thought it strange that his chest could hold so much pain and still not burst.

Raising the bottle to his lips, Dalton felt the whiskey spilling into his mouth, burning its way down his throat and into his stomach. Swallowing as much as he could stand, he pulled the bottle away and lapsed into a coughing spasm. The whiskey did its work quickly, sending an insidious warmth outward from his stomach to his chest and neck, and finally coursing with a numbing heat through the dark recesses of his brain.

Dalton sat and watched the couples coming in for the night, kissing at the doorway of Evangeline Hall beneath the arch, standing with their arms around each other until the minute-hand reached its apex on the big clock behind the reception desk. *Making promises they never intend to keep,* Dalton thought bitterly, hardly noticing the March chill had seeped into the car.

Reaching into the inside pocket of his jacket, he pulled out a small box covered in black velvet. He opened it, staring at the clear white diamond glinting in the amber light from the streetlamp. "Promises they never keep," he said, although he was barely aware that he had spoken the words aloud.

ELEVEN

A Father's Love

★ ★ ★

Wearing a khaki shirt with sleeves rolled up above his elbows and jeans soft from washings and faded by sunlight, Lane sat in his study, located at the rear corner of the house just off the kitchen. A bookshelf built into the wall held the heavy volumes of the Louisiana Criminal and Civil Statutes, along with biographies, novels, and a few books of poetry.

Black-and-white prints of Lane in the company of other youthful and uniformed athletes on high-school and college playing fields hung on the pecan-paneled walls. In some shots, they were caught unaware by a photographer's flashbulb; in others, the young athletes stood in relaxed poses, squinting toward the camera lens in the slanting Southern sunlight.

Hearing the familiar sound of the Ford's engine as the car crept past his window at a snail's pace and pulled into the garage, Lane got up and went out into the kitchen. In the glow of the stove light, he poured a cup of freshly brewed coffee, strong and black and steaming.

Returning to his study, Lane placed the cup of coffee on his desk and sat down in the leather chair that Catherine had bought for him in an antique shop on Royal Street in the French Quarter. A creaking sound reminded him that he had forgotten to oil its swivel mechanism.

He glanced at the envelope lying on his desk. It held Dalton's grade sheet from the LSU Registrar's office. *I never thought I'd see the day when Dalton would fail everything — well, almost. He did pass Dr. Frey's class.*

Bowing his head, Lane prayed out loud, "Lord, give me wisdom for what I have to do. Give me the right words — and give me silence when You would have me remain quiet. I thank You for this . . . and for Your grace and mercy that sustains us. Father, bless my son. I ask for him what Jesus did for all of us — that You keep him from the evil of this world. In Jesus' name."

Lane heard someone fumbling with the lock at the back door, the sound of the door opening and closing, then the floor creaking under slow footsteps. He pulled his gold-rimmed reading glasses off, laying them on his desk. "Dalton?" he called.

Four seconds of silence were followed by, "Yes, sir."

"Would you come in here, please?"

"Yes, sir."

Lane gazed up at Dalton as he appeared at the door, leaning against the frame for balance. He noticed his son's eyes, red and swollen and rheumy. *From alcohol,* he thought, *or grief — or maybe both.*

Shifting uneasily, Dalton asked in a husky voice, "What is it, Daddy?"

"Sit down, son."

Dalton slumped down in a chair at the side of the desk, his eyes staring at the floor. He ran his hand through his hair, placed his elbow on the chair arm, and leaned the side of his face on the palm of his hand.

"You want some coffee?" Lane asked.

Dalton shook his head.

Suddenly, pictures from the past filled Lane's mind like a slide projector flashing behind his eyes; he held Dalton in his arms for the first time with Catherine, pale and drained and glowing with joy, lying next to him on frosty white sheets; heard his son's laughter spilling in through the kitchen window as he played with his childhood friends; saw him running the football again with that natural balance of speed and controlled power beneath the towering arc lights of countless playing fields; watched Dalton walk across the stage in cap and gown. . . .

Lane had agonized for days about how to approach Dalton. What could he say? What could he do to change his son's life? How could he help to make right all the things that had gone wrong? All the words he had labored so carefully over escaped his mind. He had only his heart to speak from. "I love you very much, son."

Dalton raised his head slowly. His eyes, holding a sorrow too deep for words, fastened on Lane's. He seemed unable to move; his mouth opened to speak, but no sound came out.

Lane stood up, reached down, and taking Dalton by the shoulders, he lifted him from the chair. Placing his arms around his son, Lane hugged him as he had done when Dalton was a boy and the world had come too hard against him.

Dalton began to shake as the grief poured out of him. Sobs racked his body as he stood in his father's arms. He became a child again in the shelter of his father's love.

Father and son stood like that for a long time. The house creaked, making sounds never heard during the day, settling down for the night. A car sped by out on the street, its tires making a dull, humming noise on the blacktop.

Finally, Lane put an arm around Dalton's shoulder and walked with him out of the study. "You'll feel better after a good night's sleep."

Dalton merely nodded as he let himself be led through the kitchen and up the stairs to his room. He sat on the side of the mattress as Lane slipped his shoes off, then lifted his legs onto the bed. Lying back on his pillow, he closed his eyes, his breath escaping slowly between his lips.

Lane walked to the closet, took a blanket from the top shelf, and spread it over Dalton. The moon shone through the partially opened blinds, laying slats of pale light across the bed and the hardwood floor. Lane gazed down at his son for a few moments, then turned and headed out of the room.

"Daddy . . ."

At the sound of Dalton's voice, Lane stopped in the doorway.

"Thanks."

Dalton awakened with a start. His head felt as though someone had driven several sixteen-penny nails into it. The second thing he felt was an almost overwhelming sense of shame — shame that made the final decision for him. He glanced at the alarm clock on his nightstand — 3:00 A.M. In the shadows, he swung his legs over the edge of the bed and walked to his closet. Ten minutes later, he was ready.

Slowly opening his bedroom door, Dalton glanced both ways out into the upstairs hall. He wore brown loafers, jeans, a white button-down shirt, and his letter jacket. Slinging Lane's marine duffel bag over his shoulder, he stepped carefully onto the wood floor, trying to keep it from creaking. When he reached the head of the stairs, he glanced once more at the door of his parents' bedroom, then placed his foot on the first stair.

"Where you goin', hero?"

At the sound of his brother's voice, Dalton froze, one foot on the first step, the other on the landing. He made out Cassidy's form in the shadowed doorway of his bedroom, his hair white, almost glowing in the dim light filtering through the window.

"You runnin' away from home?"

Dalton turned to face Cassidy. "If you wanna talk, come on downstairs," he whispered in a barely audible voice, then adjusted the duffel bag over his shoulder, grasped the railing with his other hand, and walked close to the bannister on the way down.

As he reached the downstairs hallway,

Dalton looked over his shoulder for Cass but saw only the empty stairwell and moonlight streaming in through the window behind it. Easing his duffel bag down onto the kitchen tile, he walked over to the cabinet and took out a glass and a package of Alka Seltzer. He filled the glass half-full at the faucet, dropped in two of the big white tablets, and stared at the fizzing, bubbling water.

Taking the glass with him, Dalton walked over to the kitchen table, pulled a chair out, and sat down. As Dalton was finishing the last of the Alka Seltzer, Cass sauntered into the kitchen, wearing jeans and a white T-shirt. He had washed most of the sleep from his face and had taken an extra minute to rake a comb through his hair.

"Bad head, huh?"

Dalton simply stared at the fizzing contents of the glass, knowing that his brother didn't really expect an answer.

Cassidy jammed his hands into the front pockets of his jeans. "You've thought this over?"

"Yep."

"Where you goin'?"

Dalton shrugged, then picked the glass up, inspecting the white residue on the side. "I haven't decided for sure. You got any suggestions?"

"How 'bout back upstairs to bed?"

Dalton glanced up at his brother, a hint of a smile on his face. "Too late for that."

Cassidy's voice rose in anger as he took his hands out of his pockets, gesturing wildly. "Whadda you mean, it's too late? Too late for what? You're —"

"Shhh," Dalton hissed, waving his hand downward, then pointing up to the ceiling.

"Okay, okay," Cassidy said softly, holding his hands in front of his chest.

Dalton glanced at the clock above the stove. "Look, it's almost three-thirty. I gotta get goin'." He took his glass to the sink and rinsed it out.

"You're something else, you know that, big brother?" Cassidy said and grinned.

Drying the glass, Dalton turned toward Cassidy. "What are you talking about?"

"Your life's going down the drain, and you're worried about keeping Mama's kitchen clean." Cassidy shook his head slowly back and forth. "I bet I haven't washed a glass in a month."

"Habit," Dalton muttered as he walked over to the table and picked up the duffel bag.

Cassidy pulled a chair out from the table and sat down. "You got any money?"

"A little. I saved a lot of what I made

working construction last summer."

"How much?"

"A hundred and seventy-three dollars."
Dalton dropped the duffel bag and sat down.

"That's all?" Cassidy reached into his back
pocket for his wallet. "You made good
money on that job. What happened to the
rest of it?"

Dalton glanced at the duffel bag resting at
his feet, his mind picturing the engagement
ring he had left behind while he was packing.
"I spent it."

Cassidy took a twenty and two fives from
his wallet, handing them to Dalton. "Here.
You need this more than I do. It's all I've
got, except for a little change."

Dalton shook his head. "I'll be all right.
After I get a place to stay, I'll go to work."

"Call me nutty, big brother, but I can't
figure out what this is all about." Cassidy
slipped the wallet into his back pocket, then
gazed directly into Dalton's eyes. "What's
the point in leaving home? If you want to
work, you got all kind of contacts right here
in Baton Rouge."

"I guess I don't really know all the reasons
myself." Glancing at the clock, Dalton ran
his hand through his hair and added, "It's
. . . it's just that everything's . . . I don't
know . . . coming apart here. Everything that

I've worked for and . . ."

"And Cherry," Cassidy finished the sentence for him. "I could have told you that."

Dalton's eyes flashed with anger. "Told me what?"

"That she wouldn't stick with you," Cassidy explained, as though it should have been perfectly obvious. "You know, if things got tough."

The anger slowly drained from Dalton's face. "Yeah." He stared at the floor. "You tried to tell me that all along, didn't you? How could I be so stupid?"

"Guess it just comes easy for some people."

Dalton, a rumor of a smile flickering in his eyes, glanced at Cassidy. "Well, this sure isn't getting me anywhere. I better hit the road."

"You gotta decide where you're goin'."

"All right," Dalton agreed, standing up and pushing his chair back under the table. "New Orleans."

"What are you gonna do down there?" Cassidy shook his head disdainfully. "I thought you might at least try Sweetwater. You know a lot of people there who could help you out."

"That's the point. I want to go someplace where I *don't* know anybody."

"Well, we'd better get goin'."

"What do you mean, *we?*"

"I'm gonna take you to the bus station."

"How?"

Cassidy reached into his front pocket and fished out a set of keys, dangling them in front of Dalton's face with a tinkling sound. "With these. That's how."

"I didn't know Daddy gave you a key to the Ford! I sure don't have *my* own key."

"He didn't." Cassidy grinned. "But they do a good job making them over at Morgan and Lindsey." He pointed to another of the keys. "Got one made for Mama's Chevy too."

"You're gonna do great in Angola, Cass." Dalton slung the duffel bag over his shoulder. "Yes, sir, you'll be running the whole prison in two months time."

Cassidy let the remark pass without a counterattack. "It's a good thing you've got me looking out for you, big brother. You'd be walking to the bus station if I wasn't."

Dalton set the duffel bag down. "Cass, would you do me another favor?"

"Don't push your luck."

"Trade jackets with me."

Cassidy glanced at his leather jacket hanging on the back of a chair near the stove, then back at Dalton. "You mean for your letter jacket?"

"Yep."

"Man, that'd be great!" Cassidy walked over to the chair, grabbed his high-school jacket, and tossed it to Dalton.

Dalton slipped out of his LSU jacket, handing it to Cassidy. "You don't mind?"

"Mind? Are you kidding?" Cassidy put the heavy leather-and-wool jacket on, admiring his reflection in the kitchen window. "Man, the women will go crazy over this! They think football players are the next best thing to James Dean. Especially since y'all won the national championship last year."

"Everybody at Istrouma knows you're not on the LSU football team."

"Istrouma?" Cassidy seemed appalled at his brother's lack of imagination. "I'm not talking about some silly high-school chicks. I'm talking about college women!"

Dalton gave Cassidy a puzzled look.

"Don't you have a creative bone in your body, boy?" Cassidy adjusted the jacket on his lean frame. "I'll just hang around the campus in the right spots. You know, the Quadrangle, the coffee shop, the Field House. Most of 'em can't know *everybody* on the whole football team." He stuffed his hands into the side pockets of his new jacket. "With my good looks and charm, those coeds will just eat me up."

"Won't work."

"Whadda you mean?"

"You'll never pass for a college football player," Dalton explained. "You look like a little boy."

Cassidy grinned at his brother. "That just makes me all the more lovable."

"Okay, lover boy, but don't say I didn't warn you when you end up looking like a dunce." Dalton realized that for the past few minutes, his mind had been free of torment and worry. *You're a pleasant distraction — I'll give you that, little brother.* He put the black leather jacket on.

"You ready to go?"

Again Dalton glanced at the clock. "I'm ready for just about anything but what I've been doing the past few months." He shouldered the duffel bag.

"All right," Cassidy said, walking over to the kitchen door and listening briefly for any sound that might be coming from the upstairs bedrooms. "I guess the coast is clear. We gotta be quiet, though."

"You don't think they'll hear the motor?"

"Nah. The garage muffles the noise when you start it, and I'll just let it idle down the driveway." He walked across the tiled floor toward the back door. "Besides, their bedroom is on the opposite side of the house."

Dalton followed Cassidy out onto the back

porch, pulling the door too quietly. "You act like you've done this before."

Cassidy merely grinned and skipped down the steps into the backyard.

"You have, haven't you?" Dalton followed after Cassidy, keeping close so he wouldn't have to raise his voice. "You've taken the car out at night before. Admit it."

Cassidy stopped in his tracks, gazing upward, both arms extended toward the starry night. "There are more things in heaven and earth, Horatio, than dreamed of in . . ." Dropping his arms, he walked into the garage. "Well, I think the lines went something like that. I never paid much attention in class when we studied Shakespeare."

The bus door whooshed shut. The big diesel engine roared, spewing fumes into the night air as the driver backed carefully out of the lined parking space. Friends and relatives and well-wishers stood on the oil-stained pavement, waving to the passengers smiling behind thick glass windows.

Dalton stared at Cassidy leaning casually against a metal pole, hands jammed into the pockets of the oversized letter jacket. As the bus pulled forward down the side drive toward the street, he waved at Dalton, turned, and walked across the lot toward the Ford.

I'm gonna miss you, little brother, Dalton thought sadly as he lost sight of Cassidy when the bus made a left-hand turn onto the highway.

Settling back in his seat, Dalton felt a sense of isolation totally different from anything he had ever experienced before. He realized that for the first time in his life, he was truly on his own. This wasn't like the isolation of the basin during the times he had gone to Coley's camp alone. Then, he had known that in a few days, he would again be in the company of his family and friends.

Now he had cut free of those ties, and even the fact that it had been his choice, that he could return whenever he wished, didn't prevent that sudden and unexpected feeling of loneliness that had overtaken him; that he was somehow drifting alone in a vast, endless night.

As the bus headed down Highland Road toward the Airline Highway that ended in New Orleans, Dalton took a final look at the campus that had been his home for almost three years: live oaks stood like massive sentinels along the roadside, reaching out with their great limbs to form a green canopy over the bus; the Memorial Tower, dedicated to students who died in World War II, with its lighted facade overlooking the expanse of the parade ground; the buildings of the Quadrangle behind it; the French House, a girl's dormitory constructed in 1935 in the style of a French chateau.

As the bus rumbled past Evangeline Hall, Dalton looked away, fighting against the memories of what had happened there only hours before. He willed such thoughts from his mind, lay his head back against the seat, listened to the big tires drumming against the blacktop, and drifted into an uneasy half-sleep.

"New Or-leeens!"

Rubbing his eyes with his fingertips, Dalton sat up in his seat and glanced at the red-faced driver who had just announced their arrival. *You certainly aren't from around these parts, not pronouncing New Orleans like that, you're not.*

Dalton roused himself from his seat, grabbed his duffel bag from the overhead rack, and walked down the bus steps into the noisy crowd milling around the parking area. Walking through the glare of the bus station, he found himself standing on a sidewalk in the strange New Orleans night.

Taxicabs whizzed past, and people walking by carried on conversations in voices loud and nasal as though they were talking to someone on the opposite side of the street.

A woman wearing net stockings, spiked heels, and a heavy coat of rouge and mascara that could not conceal the hopelessness in her eyes stopped a few feet away and gave Dalton a hard stare. "How you doing, darling?"

Dalton cleared his throat, glanced away, and pretended interest in an ancient black man in a tattered suitcoat trying desperately to light a sodden cigar.

"What's the matter, sugar, your girlfriend don't understand you?" The voice was as harsh and raspy as whiskey and cigarettes could make it.

Dalton turned around, unable to hold the hard stare. "Maybe she understands *too* much." As soon as the words died away in the chill night air, he wondered why he had said such a thing to a complete stranger.

"What you need is a little time with Monique. Make you feel like a new man."

Dalton tried to speak but found that his words stuck inside his throat. He shook his head, grinned sheepishly, and stared down at a crumpled paper cup on the sidewalk.

Deciding he was not worth any more of her effort, Monique turned away and hailed a cab.

Dalton watched her climb inside, blowing

him a kiss as she sped off down the street. *What a town! That would never happen in Baton Rouge in a hundred years!*

Although Dalton had never been in this part of town before, he knew the general direction of Canal Street, the river, and the Quarter. He readjusted his duffel bag to make it more comfortable on his shoulder, flinched as a horn blared from a passing car, and trudged off down the sidewalk.

"Coffee and beignets, please."

"Yes, sir. Be right back with your order." The dark-skinned young man, balancing a tray of empty cups on his fingertips, wrote Dalton's order down on a pad he had placed on the table. He glanced up as he wrote. "You from out of town, ain't you?"

Dalton nodded. "How'd you know?"

"Easy," he answered cryptically, then straightened up with his pad and tray. "You gonna love these beignets and coffee. Best in the world."

As he watched the waiter hurry away toward the kitchen, Dalton thought it strange that the waiters would wear black waistcoats during this early breakfast hour. Then it occurred to him that New Orleans was like no other city in the country, in far more interesting and mysterious ways than formal dress at seven A.M.

He sat beneath a blue awning in the Café du Monde located on Decatur Street across from Jackson Square. All the tables in the large patio area were occupied. The people were dressed in every imaginable type of attire: formal wear, khaki work clothes and heavy boots, business suits, and the theatrical and fringe crowds whose dress was so uniquely bizarre and outlandish that it defied description or imitation.

Dalton found that he enjoyed the animated conversations of the diners as well as the rich smell of brewing coffee and the pastries covered with powdered sugar. He listened to birds singing in the live oaks along the street and in the square. Palm fronds clattered in the wind off the river.

Then the memory of the past night pierced his mind like a dagger. He saw again in the streetlight's amber glow Cherry leaning toward Amara, kissing him on the mouth. "No!" The word escaped his lips before he could stop it.

Around him, a few of the diners paused, cups in the air and beignets half-chewed, giving him oblique glances. Then they resumed their breakfast hour, the mild disturbance forgotten in food and drink and the promise of another day.

Dalton forced a smile as the young waiter returned with steaming, milk-whitened coffee in a thick mug and crusty brown beignets on a matching plate.

"Anything else, sir?" The waiter stood at attention, a white dishcloth draped over his crooked arm.

Dalton fished a dollar out of his pocket and handed it to him. "Is this enough?"

"That'll be just fine, sir." The waiter spun around, heading for a couple just sitting down two tables away.

Stirring sugar into his coffee, Dalton bit into one of the hot pastries. Crisp and warm and flaky soft inside, with the powdered sugar melting in his mouth, it helped restore his spirits at once. He washed it down with hot coffee, then took another big bite, chewing slowly, savoring the sweet, delicate taste.

Then his mind turned to thoughts of home. *Mama'll be getting up to make a big batch of pancakes like she does every Sunday morning. I hope Cassidy tells them that I'll be all right; that I just needed a little time by myself to sort things out. They'll worry some, but I'll get in touch pretty soon; as soon as I have something good to tell them.*

Dalton finished his breakfast, ordered a second cup of coffee, and drank it slowly, watching the Quarter come to life. Trucks loaded with bananas, grapes, apples, tomatoes, squash — every kind of vegetable and fruit imaginable — drove past on the way to the French Market located just down the street.

Across the square, early churchgoers filed through the massive doors beneath the towering Gothic spires of St. Louis Cathedral. The artists strolled down the sidewalks, carrying their canvases, setting easels up at strategic points, preparing for the onslaught of tourists.

Realizing that he had no job and no place to stay suddenly ended Dalton's pleasant idleness. *I've spent enough time just doing nothing . . . except trying to work this pitiful knee back into shape. It's time I got to work at something . . . anything.* He could think of only one person who might be able to help him, and he could not even remember the man's name.

TWELVE

The Pearl

★ ★ ★

"We can always use a little extra help around here," the wiry, dark-skinned man admitted. He wore gray work trousers, a white shirt with the sleeves rolled up above his elbows, and a long white apron. *Curet DeJean — that's his name!* Dalton remembered suddenly. Dalton watched as DeJean drove the short-bladed knife into an oyster, splitting the shell apart. He placed the oyster on a metal Dixie Beer tray and wiped his hands on the apron. "I can gar-roantee you ain't gon' get rich at dis place, no."

"Mr. DeJean, I . . . I just need a job. . . ."

"DeJean," he interrupted, "jes' plain ol' DeJean. That 'mister' stuff make me feel old as my daddy." DeJean stared at Dalton's downcast expression, remembering him as a confident-looking young man with his pretty blond girlfriend the last time he had seen him. He looked completely different now.

"You don't mind hard work?"

"No, sir."

"Jes' plain *no* will do."

Dalton glanced about the restaurant at the black-and-white tiled floor, the long metal-topped counter, and the ceiling fans turning slowly, twenty feet up. "Do you own the place?"

"No, but I might as well, as far as the work goes. Now the money — that's a different t'ing."

Noticing an oily haired man in a pea coat drinking coffee at a table near the window, Dalton asked, "Do y'all serve breakfast here too?"

"You writin' a article for the *Times Pica-yune*?" DeJean shucked another oyster, dumping it on the tray. "I thought you said you needed a job."

"I do."

"Well, get to work cleanin' dat back alley," DeJean muttered. "And do a good job too. If de Health Department close dis place down, we both out of work."

Dalton glanced about uneasily.

"There's a bucket and push-broom in that little room outside the back door." DeJean pointed to the service entrance of the restaurant. "You can change in there too. I hope you got something besides dem fancy clothes in dat sack."

"Yes si — I mean, I do."

DeJean set the tray on the counter, adding lemon slices and a bottle of Tabasco. Taking a bottle of Jax Beer from the cooler beneath the counter, DeJean pried the top off with his teeth and took a long swallow. Then he turned his attention to the oysters, pink and fleshy in their shells.

Dalton wondered how the man could drink beer and eat raw oysters so early in the morning.

Seeing Dalton staring at him, DeJean added Tabasco and lemon to an oyster and dumped it down his throat. "Eat 'em every day for my breakfast. Sometimes I fry 'em," he said, answering Dalton's unasked question. "You better get to work. Last boy dat stood around wid a blank look like dat on his face lasted about two minutes in dis job."

Nodding quickly, Dalton turned, grabbed his duffel bag, and hurried out the service entrance. The door to the small utility room had rotted at the bottom, the dark, damp wood swollen and warped. The sound wood that was left bore scars and markings of various passersby and disgruntled ex-employees. Someone had carved *Mama Didn't Love Me* above the doorknob.

Dalton stepped inside the musty-smelling

cramped room, pulled the string that turned on the sixty-watt bulb in the ceiling, and looked around. Empty paint cans, an assortment of boxes and crates, odds and ends of tools, and a few cleaning supplies cluttered the small room. At one end, stacks of old newspapers, magazines, and other papers and posters lay in dusty disarray. Spider webs spanned the corners of the ceiling.

Quickly changing into an old pair of black, high-topped Converse tennis shoes, threadbare khakis, and a flannel shirt, Dalton stepped into the alley, picked up the bucket, dumped some powdered soap into it, and filled it with water. As he left the small concrete area at the back door and walked into the main part of the alley, he froze in his tracks, his face going white with disgust.

Walking back inside and over to the counter, Dalton found himself gagging. "Did you see what's in that alley?" He stared wide-eyed at DeJean.

"Mais yeah." DeJean finished his last oyster, wiping his mouth with the bottom of his apron. "You done got it all cleaned up already?"

"There's a dead cat out there . . ." Dalton's voice carried a sharp edge of disbelief, honed by anger. "And about a hundred dead, stinkin' fish."

"Everyt'ing stink when it's dead." DeJean walked down the duckboards behind the bar, carrying a case of Dixie Beer, bent down, and began stocking the cooler. He grinned up at Dalton. "I'm surprised a college boy like you didn't know dat."

"How'd you know I went to college?"

"Yo' clothes. De way you act." DeJean gave him a sober look. "You ain't smart alecky, like a lot of 'em, though."

"Thanks," Dalton said, wondering if it was really a sensible reply. Then his mind returned to the alley. "You expect me to clean *that* up? The cat's already started to rot."

"The last boy that worked wouldn't clean up all dat mess. Das why he quit. I guess he musta had a weak stomach or somet'ing. You don't want de job?" DeJean returned to his stocking. "Somebody else come along and take it."

Dalton thought it over for a few seconds, scowled at DeJean, and walked out the back door.

Dalton came inside from the alley, his khakis and tennis shoes soaked and stained, his hair hanging down in his face, and fire in his eyes. He kept his anger to himself, though, mumbling under his breath, "A stinking rotten cat and rotten catfish!"

"You want some lunch?" DeJean asked, his arms up to the elbows in a sinkful of soapy water.

At the sound of the word *lunch*, Dalton suddenly realized he was famished. *How could I be hungry after that mess I just finished cleaning up?*

"Well?"

"Yeah. I could eat something."

"Go back to the kitchen, then, and tell them I said to give you something to eat," DeJean ordered. He glanced at Dalton's wet and dirty clothes, then added, "But clean up a little first."

Dalton went out back to the little utility room, took off his soggy clothes, cleaned up as best he could, and put on the clothes he had worn down to New Orleans only a few hours before. *Has it only been a few hours?* he thought. *Seems like I left home such a long time ago.*

Walking across the back part of the restaurant, Dalton entered the swinging double doors that led into the kitchen. A large black man in a white apron and tall chef's hat stood before an array of pots and pans heating on the burners of a huge stove. A rich, spicy smell permeated the air. The big man stirred and added ingredients and stirred some more, moving in his work like an overweight matador before a bulky black bull.

On the other side of the stove, a chunky woman in her midtwenties wearing a black hair net over her head was busy chopping celery and onions and peppers with a gleaming knife that looked like a small sword.

Dalton hated to disturb either of the two people, hard at their jobs, by asking for something to eat. Then he saw a slim woman in a white uniform wringing out a mop at the back of the kitchen. As he walked up to her, she turned around and gave a slight gasp, placing her left hand against her throat.

"Oh! You startled me. I didn't think anyone else was back here."

The young woman's eyes caught his attention first — green as the midday sea and full of light. In them, Dalton saw something that somehow lightened his burden of loss that had become increasingly heavy over the past few months. He realized this only later, however, as he was fully occupied with the remainder of this unexpected encounter.

A slim nose and full lips that curved in an understated Cupid's bow had been set by an artist's hand in her oval face. Her skin was pale but gave off an underlying apricot glow that spoke of vitality. A wisp of reddish-brown hair, touched by gold highlights, peeked from beneath the blue scarf she wore over her head. She looked like a cross between a fashion model and a Russian peasant heading out for a day in the fields.

"Can I help you with something?" The girl held her mop with both hands, poised to clean the floor.

"Uh . . ." Dalton thought that words were becoming increasingly difficult for him in the past few days. *Maybe that Ole Miss halfback damaged more than just my knee.* "I . . . well, DeJean told me that I could come back here and" — he then found himself staring at the hint of a dimple in her softly rounded chin — "you know, get something to eat."

The girl leaned her mop against the wall. "Sure, I'll be glad to fix you something. What would you like?"

"I don't know." Dalton wondered what she would look like in something other than the shapeless uniform dress. "I guess I'd like to know your name."

Her lips parted in a smile that found its way instantly to her eyes. "Justine," she answered in a soft, slightly husky voice. "Justine Coday. What's yours?"

"Dalton Temple."

"Nice to meet you." She offered her hand.

Dalton took it, feeling a warmth that seemed to flow into him. "You too." *I'm in worse shape than I thought. First time I meet this girl and I'm getting mushy inside. Just grabbing at anything to make me feel better, I guess.* Reluctantly, he let her hand go.

"You want some shrimp gumbo? They haven't started frying anything yet, but the gumbo's already cooked."

"Sure. That'd be fine."

Justine leaned her mop against the wall. "C'mon. You'll have to eat back here, though."

"That's all right with me." Dalton nodded and followed her over to the far end of the big stove.

Justine took a large, white bowl from a shelf and stepped over to the stove. She added fluffy white rice from a stainless-steel cooker, then ladled the rich, thick, deep-red gumbo over the rice. Slicing off three pieces of crusty French bread, she smeared them with garlic butter and put the food down on a small table, covered with a red plastic cloth, that sat in the rear corner of the kitchen next to a window.

Dalton pulled out a wooden chair and sat down. "This looks great!"

Justine took a bottle of Barq's Root Beer out of a glass-front cooler against the back wall, popped the cap off with an opener, and set the tall, cold bottle on the table. "I hope you enjoy the gumbo," Justine said and smiled. "I made it."

"You did?" Dalton asked with surprise, thinking she looked nothing like a cook.

"Yes. After six months, Hubert — he's the cook — said I'd finally made something good enough to serve to the customers. That's a real compliment, coming from him."

"You gonna be cooking full time now?" Dalton had temporarily forgotten the steaming, succulent meal before him, his hunger for food replaced by a greater hunger — to learn more about Justine Coday.

"No. Actually, this is my last day."

Dalton felt disappointment, touched by a heavy sadness, well up inside him. His face reflected it.

"Oh, it's for something better," Justine assured him. "At least, I believe it is. I don't think I'm really cut out for the restaurant business, anyway." She turned to leave, then smiled back at him. "Enjoy your meal!"

Dalton spooned some of the rich gumbo into his mouth, the shrimp tender and spicy in their thick sauce. The French bread was fresh-baked, crusty and flaky on the outside, soft and white and chewy on the inside.

As Dalton ate, he watched Justine mop the kitchen, dragging the heavy bucket along with her. Never had he seen someone so out-of-place as Justine looked at her work.

It brought to mind a scene from Walt Disney's *Cinderella*. He had seen the movie years before, and he now hoped Justine's story would turn out as well as Cinderella's had.

Customers started coming in by twos and threes from the St. Charles Street entrance. Two waitresses hurried in the back way and went to work, taking orders and carrying trays to the tables from the kitchen's serve-through counter and from the bar, where DeJean continued to serve up oysters and an assortment of drinks.

Finishing the last bite of gumbo and the final crust of bread, Dalton chewed slowly, swallowed, and let out a sigh of approval. "Ummm, that sure was good!"

Justine, having put her mop and bucket away, set a cup of strong black coffee on the table next to Dalton's plate. "I'm glad you enjoyed it."

"Better than my mama makes," Dalton said, his gaze fixed on Justine's eyes. "And I thought she was the best."

Offering her hand once more, Justine said, "Well, it's been nice knowing you — for this little while, anyway."

"You leaving so soon?" Dalton stood up and took her hand, holding it longer than was polite.

Justine nodded. "I'm just working a half-day." She slowly pulled her hand free of Dalton's. "Maybe I'll see you again sometime."

Dalton wanted to say a dozen things at once to Justine; to tell her how she made him feel somehow better, just being near him; how things suddenly didn't look quite so hopeless; and much more — but he didn't. What he said was, "Yeah, maybe," and sat back down at the table.

"Well, good-bye, then." Justine turned and walked away, her hair catching the light through the window in a shimmering flash of red and gold. Dalton wanted to get up and run after her, to ask her to wait for him . . . somewhere. But he didn't.

"Good-bye." He watched her disappear through the swinging doors, then sat staring into his coffee cup.

"Hey! If you finished, college boy, you got a truck to unload."

Dalton gazed at DeJean's head poking through the partially opened door. "You mean I got the job?"

"Yeah, it's yours. That alley looks real good now." DeJean kept his head between the two swinging doors, as though it was stuck there. "You got a place to live?"

Dalton shook his head.

"I didn't think so." DeJean disappeared,

then cracked the door one more time. "I might have a place for you to stay by the time you finish with that truck."

Dalton stopped in front of the narrow, tan-painted house on Chartes Street, located on the fringe of the Quarter. Fishing out the crumpled piece of paper from his back pocket, he squinted at the address DeJean had scrawled on it, then stepped up onto the stoop and knocked on the door.

A sturdy woman with iron gray hair as straight as if it had been starched and pressed poked her head around the doorjamb. "Your name Dalton?"

"Yes, ma'am." Dalton glanced at the piece of paper again. "Are you Mrs. Costello?"

The woman gave her head a quick downward jerk. "DeJean called. Said you was okay." She held out a key in her hand dotted with age spots.

Dalton took the key. "Thanks."

"That'll be ten dollars for the first week — in advance. This ain't no charity ward."

"Yes, ma'am." Dalton fished a ten-dollar bill out of his wallet and placed it in her hand.

The woman crooked her finger toward the side of the house. "At the end of the alley. You can't miss it."

"Thank you," Dalton said to the slamming door. He hefted his duffel bag onto his shoulder and pushed open the scrolled iron gate that led into a narrow, dark alley. As he walked alongside the house, he could smell the dank, cool odor of the old brick that floored the passageway. From two blocks away, the din of Bourbon Street already drifted on the evening air.

At the end of the alley, Dalton saw a tiny stucco apartment enclosed by banana trees that had just started to put forth the first green shoots of spring. The last of the sunlight glinted on its red-tiled roof. Outside the front door, a cast-iron bench and matching chair stood on the brick patio near an ancient fig tree. Weeds had long since taken over the flower beds.

Using the heavy brass key, Dalton opened the door and stepped inside the cottage. Then he dropped his duffel bag on the varnished pine floor, scuffed and dusty, and flipped the wall switch. A single forty-watt bulb cast a smoky light over the apartment's drab and musty-smelling interior.

A sink, two-burner stove, and small refrigerator built into the cabinet along with a scarred wooden table and two chairs served as the kitchen and dining area. On the other end of the single room sat a sofa, rocking chair, and an end table holding a lamp and a blue plastic radio. An iron bed with a blue chenille bedspread sagged against the back wall across from the sofa. Double windows with Venetian blinds flanked both sides of the front door.

Dalton crossed the room, entering a short hall with a bathroom to the right and a closet on the opposite side. He pulled the blinds apart and looked out onto a brick wall overgrown with ivy and frost-burned weeds from winters past.

Returning to the front room, Dalton flicked the overhead light off and collapsed on the bed. He stared at the ceiling, dimly lit by the fading light at the burnt-out end of a long day. The activity of mind and body had served well to insulate him from the sorrow that stalked the edge of his thoughts like a predator at the fringe of firelight. Now the activity had died away like the last flickering flames, and the predator was once more on the prowl.

Reaching behind him, Dalton flicked the knob of the radio. As it warmed up, the tubes glowed faintly in the gloom of the apartment, then the volume increased, the speaker blaring a harsh stream of Dixieland jazz. He quickly turned the knob, tuning in another station. The sound of Elvis' unmistakable version of "A Fool Such as I" filled the room. Dalton lay on his narrow bed and listened to the song as the last rose-colored afterglow filled the room, then faded away to darkness. *Ol' Elvis has really got it made. Money, fame, and any girl he wants in the whole country. What I wouldn't give to trade places with him!*

"I can't stay in this oversized coffin anymore," he finally said aloud. "Not tonight, I can't."

He got up, flicked the light on, and dumped his belongings out of the duffel bag onto the couch. After sorting out a few clothes, he took a shower, shaved, and dressed in tan slacks, a pale yellow button-down shirt, and his brown loafers.

Walking to the bathroom, he stared at his reflection in the water-spotted mirror. As he combed his towel-dried hair, Dalton found his mind traveling back to that final night in Tiger Stadium. He felt the thudding of shoulder pads against his churning legs as he broke tackles, felt the cold autumn air burning deep inside his lungs as he sprinted down the sidelines, saw the end zone stripe blazing white beneath the dazzling arc lights . . . then —

"No!" He shouted the word. It sounded almost like a gunshot as it ricocheted off the bathroom tile. Suddenly, the terrible weight of grief and loss bore down on him as it had so many times during the past months. He fought against the images that filled his mind: the sound of the band thundering through the stadium after a touchdown, the bedlam in the locker room after a victory, that unbearable sight of Amara's hand caressing Cherry's soft hair as she leaned toward —

"No!" Dalton stared at his face in the mirror, at the glistening tears that spilled from his eyes. "I'm going out of my mind! How did this happen to me? How did I lose everything?" The comb dropped from his hand onto the cracked linoleum as he spun around, banging into the door. He grabbed Cassidy's jacket from the sofa on his way out of the apartment.

After his hot shower, the cool night air hit Dalton's face like a bucket of water. The shock seemed to settle him down. He took a deep breath, staring upward. In the absence of neon, the sky glittered with a shower of stars.

Dalton was already falling into the habit of speaking his thoughts aloud. "There really *is* something up there! A real sky, just like Baton Rouge or Sweetwater or anyplace else, right up above New Orleans."

He sat down on the bench next to the fig tree in the dim light cast by the streetlamp at the end of his little alley. Propping one knee up, he leaned back on his elbows, wondering why the sight of the night sky, the stars, and the waning moon fascinated him on this ordinary night.

Letting his thoughts carry him back to the morning and The Pearl, Dalton saw again the face of Justine Coday, heard her soft voice speaking, not in words of love or passion or hate, but of the ordinary things that connect one day to the other — the small things that carry people from one hour to the next.

Dalton suddenly realized that he had grown weary of the extremes of life — the heart-stopping excitement of seventy-thousand people coming to their feet to cheer him on as he ripped through the line, rocking the linemen back on their heels for a ten-yard gain; the crowd roaring their approval as he returned a punt for a seventy-five-yard touchdown. He was tired of extremes: like Cherry's embrace, and the touch of her soft, warm lips on his that sent his heart soaring; the sight of her with another man that sent it plummeting on a downward spiral to grief and misery.

The window next to the patio creaked upward. Mrs. Costello's square face appeared beneath the lifted blind. "You crazy or something?"

"Ma'am?" Dalton sat up straight on the bench, squinting into the gloom.

"You gonna get a chill out there," she went on. "I ain't got time to play nurse if you come down with pneumonia."

"Yes, ma'am." Dalton stood up. "I was just going back inside. Gotta be to work in the morning."

The window creaked back down, thudding against the sill.

PART FOUR
★ ★ ★

Justine

THIRTEEN

Bernice and Elwood

★ ★ ★

Dalton watched the truck he had just finished unloading rumble off toward the street. He sat down on the concrete steps that led down to the alley from the low concrete platform that served as The Pearl's loading dock. Taking the red handkerchief DeJean had given him out of his back pocket, he wiped the sweat from his eyes. His khakis were wet and dirty and his high-topped black tennis shoes squished when he walked.

"You a worker — I'll give you that." DeJean walked out the back entrance, letting the screen door bang shut, and sat down next to his newest employee. "I seen a lot of boys come and go, but none of 'em worked as hard as you do."

Dalton grinned his thanks.

DeJean handed Dalton a frosty cold bottle of Barq's Root Beer. "Here. You look like you could use one of these."

Dalton noticed the tiny flakes of ice floating in the brown liquid. "Boy, you got that right!" He turned the bottle up, draining half of it in one long gulp. Setting it down on the flat concrete next to him, he leaned back on his elbows, letting his body relax. He had learned during those bone-grinding years of football practice as well as during games how to conserve his energy.

"You played football for LSU, didn't you?" DeJean sipped strong black coffee from a thick white demitasse cup.

The question hit Dalton right out of the blue. "Uh — yeah. I didn't think you knew. You never said anything." During his three days so far in New Orleans, no one had mentioned football to him at all, unlike home, where football was a usual topic of conversation. It had been sort of pleasant.

"I ain't all that interested in sports, except for huntin' and fishin'."

"How'd you know?"

"Just this morning, I remembered your picture from the newspaper."

Dalton took two more swallows of his root beer. "I hurt my knee. That ended it for me."

"I remember that too — now."

"I tried real hard to get it strong enough to play again," Dalton said with little emotion.

"I bet you did."

Dalton finished his root beer, holding the cool bottle against his forehead and the back of his neck. One of the old iron streetcars rumbled by out on St. Charles Avenue. A policeman's whistle shrieked above the traffic noise. The smell of frying fish and bubbling gumbo drifted through the back screen door of The Pearl like a preview of the supper menu.

"I kinda like this job," Dalton said, as though no one else was with him. "I didn't think I would, but it's not so bad."

"Glad you do."

Surprised at the sincerity of DeJean's reply, Dalton smiled. *Three days on my own, and already I'm talking to myself even when someone else is around.*

"What happened to your girlfriend?"

Dalton could carely conceal his surprise at DeJean's question. "What do you mean?" He had the feeling, however, that DeJean somehow knew much of what had happened.

"What happened to her?"

"How do you know anything *did* happen?"

" 'Cause you a different person than the one I served that day with your girlfriend." DeJean sipped coffee from his tiny cup. "That's how I know."

"We're . . . not together anymore. That's all."

DeJean nodded his head. "I seen that kind of woman a lot down here in New Orleans. I guess they ain't particular where they do business."

"You make her sound like a —"

"It ain't my business to judge anybody. I ain't even saying she's a bad woman." De-Jean stared at the slate roof of the building next door glinting in the morning sunshine. "But she's gonna take care of number one, no matter who gets hurt . . . don't matter what kind of promises she's made either."

"She had a rough time growing up."

"Don't we all," DeJean remarked and grinned. "Looks like you ain't exactly found yo' laughing place yet either."

For some reason, Dalton found the reference to Brer Rabbit's briar patch funny and laughed, even though he knew he really hadn't found his "laughing place."

DeJean resumed his brief treatise on a certain kind of woman. "That little blonde of yours has a special kind of life inside her; one that she's built up over the years." De-Jean gazed directly at Dalton. "She's gonna get it for herself too. She can't live no other way, and that's all there is to it."

"And you think that makes her a bad person?"

"I told you," DeJean answered, his voice

flat, "it ain't my business to judge nobody. I got enough to do keeping my own self straight."

Dalton felt that sick feeling returning to the pit of his stomach at the mention of Cherry. He also felt that DeJean had probably told him more truth about her than he had learned on his own in the years they had been together. Had it not been for his injury, he told himself, Cherry would probably have left him somewhere down the line if something else had gone wrong. And it would have been much worse after marriage and children. But knowing the truth didn't make losing her any less painful.

"How you like Justine?"

DeJean had a way of cutting through the amenities of polite conversation that was unsettling to Dalton. "Like her? She only talked to me a few minutes. I don't even know her."

"Minutes, days, years even ain't always what matters. You was around 'Blondie' for a long time, wasn't you?"

"Well . . . yeah."

"Did you know her?"

Dalton stared at a pigeon waddling across the peak of a steep roof. "Probably not."

"You see?" DeJean rested his case. "Now, Justine is the kind of woman that's the same when she's with you or when you ain't around."

"How do you know that?"

"I jes' know," DeJean insisted, as though some things should be accepted as irrefutable even in the absence of a factual basis. "She was a little different when she first come here, but something changed her over the months."

"What changed her?"

DeJean shrugged. "Don't know. She was always nice, you know, but before she left, she was even better." He downed the last of his coffee. "Don't know how else to say it."

Dalton found thoughts of Justine crowding in on those of Cherry. "Where did she go to work?"

DeJean's smile was private and full of portent. "You want to see her bad enough . . . you'll find out."

"What kind of answer is that?"

"The only one you gonna get," DeJean answered, laughing.

Dalton shook his head and stretched out on the bare, cool concrete, folding his hands behind his head.

"I wouldn't get too comfortable if I was you. Here comes another truck."

Sitting up slowly, Dalton listened to the rumble of the truck backing in from St.

Charles. He stretched his muscles, loosening up for the work ahead. "They bring enough seafood in here for three restaurants. I feel like that walk-in cooler's getting to be my second home."

"Dis place *is* kinda like three restaurants," DeJean said, standing up and brushing off the back of his trousers. "The downtown business people during the day; the long-shoremen, warehouse workers, bus drivers, cops, and all dem other night people, and den you got weekends, when anybody could show up. They always a crazy bunch dem."

Dalton grinned at DeJean's unique and usually accurate way of expressing himself. "Well, looks like I get to pack vegetables this time," he said, glancing at the lettering on the door of the big blue truck.

"This work ain't so bad now."

"Not for you," Dalton said good-naturedly. "You get to go back inside."

DeJean fixed his dark eyes on Dalton's. "I worked back here two years. Take it from me, it ain't so bad now." Then he grinned. "When July and August roll around — den you got all de right in de world to complain, you."

Dalton watched DeJean disappear behind the screen door. The grief and pain returned in a rush of heaviness. *Why can't I get rid of these thoughts? That part of my life is over.*

As the truck backed into sight, Dalton leaped down from the platform to direct the driver into position. Pain shot through his knee as it buckled under him. He forced himself to walk over and get the driver to park close against the ramp, knowing that every trip he made into the cooler carrying a crate or box on his shoulder would be an exercise in torture.

Bone-tired and dirty, Dalton waved goodnight to DeJean and walked down the alley toward St. Charles. "I need to buy some new work clothes," he said out loud, glancing down at his stained khakis that now had holes in both knees. His red flannel shirt had a tear in the right elbow, and ragged holes gaped open where two of the buttons had been. "Mama would die if she could see me in these clothes."

He recalled the brief conversation with Catherine, two nights before, when he had summoned up the courage to call home and let his family know that he was all right. In spite of his reassurances, he could tell that his mother was on the verge of tears. He had promised her that he would call more often and that he would be home for a visit in a few weeks.

Dalton turned left on St. Charles, and then right when he reached Canal Street. Walking along the broad, palm-lined thoroughfare, he listened to the traffic noises, the harsh grating voices of a middle-aged couple arguing next to an open car door, and the ferry's urgent whistle as it summoned its passengers across the wide gangplank.

Stopping at the corner of Tchoupitoulas, he gazed at the big white ferry pulling away from its landing on the way across the muddy, mile-wide river. Beyond it the sun, a huge blazing red coal, slipped out of sight behind Algiers Point. He felt the breeze off the river, smelled hot dogs and chili cooking at a sidewalk vending stand, and watched the lavender sky begin to darken.

"I just can't stand to go back to that little apartment alone." Even as he spoke the words, Dalton thought something had gone terribly wrong inside his head for him to talk out loud so much when no one else was around. But he continued, "I'll just take a walk, maybe get something to eat."

He walked along Tchoupitoulas, turning right on Poydras, then left on Magazine. After two or three blocks, he recognized where his wanderings had taken him.

"The Irish Channel. I've heard this is a tough neighborhood." He passed a dingy bar with a Jax Beer sign in the window and loud rhythm-and-blues music spilling out the door.

"So what," he continued his one-sided conversation. "It's not as bad as going back to that apartment with nothing but that crummy little radio for company." Glancing down at his clothes, he thought this time, *I'm not exactly dressed for Commander's Palace, anyway.*

Looking into the windows of hardware and furniture stores and the assortment of shops, Dalton strolled along the cracked and tilted sidewalks of Magazine. He smelled the hot, fresh bread from the bakeries and noticed the plums and peaches and apples in their bins in front of neighborhood groceries. Then he saw a purple neon sign that spelled "Mary's Bar" in a flowing script.

"Mary's Bar," he said, pondering out loud. "How tough can a place with a name like 'Mary's' be?"

As Dalton stood on the sidewalk in front of the bar, a skinny man with white shaggy hair and a bulbous red nose rode slowly past him on a bicycle with white-wall tires. "How ya' doin'?" the man called, his speech adenoidal like that spoken in most New Orleans neighborhoods.

"Good," Dalton replied. "How 'bout

you?" But the man's attention was diverted by a willowy blonde in a red dress sashaying down the other side of the street.

DeJean had told Dalton that the unique New Orleans accent had originated with the Irish and Italian immigrants of the late nineteenth century. It reminded him of the "Bowery Boys" movies he had seen at the Regina and Rex and Dalton theaters when he was growing up in Baton Rouge.

Dalton opened the heavy oak door, weathered and scarred over the years, and stepped inside. The interior held a smoke-filled gloom that almost turned him around. But he walked across the scuffed linoleum to the bar and sat down on a high wooden stool.

Men and women seated in the booths and at square tables covered with red plastic tablecloths stared at Dalton briefly, then returned to their cigarettes, drinks, and conversations. A beefy-faced man, roughly the same shape as the jukebox he leaned on, gave Dalton a toothy grin, then turned to the short, swarthy man standing next to him and made a remark that brought uproarious laughter to both of them.

Dalton coughed as he breathed in the thick cloud of smoke that seemed as much a part of Mary's Bar as the dilapidated pool table and the Christmas lights still strung behind the bar. *Maybe I oughta leave this place before I suffocate.*

"What'll it be, sport?" The bartender wore a bright green nylon shirt with yellow buttons stretched tight over his round belly. His graying brown hair was parted low over his left ear in a style that swooped and swirled around the hairless top of his scalp.

Dalton stared at the elaborate hairdo, wondering how long the man spent combing it each morning so that the bald spot was equally covered.

"You got a problem, sport?"

Glancing at the man's heavy-knuckled and gnarled hand gripping an empty Dixie Beer bottle, Dalton said, "No, I don't think so."

"Well . . ."

"Oh . . . ah, I'll take a shot of whiskey."

The man leaned over and dropped the empty beer bottle into a wooden case on the floor. "You don't look like the type to drink straight whiskey," the bartender observed.

"Better make it two shots," Dalton ordered. He grinned, feeling that hard drinking was probably near the top of "Mary's" most-admired-qualities list.

"You got it, sport." The bartender set two heavy shot glasses on the counter, its bare wood covered with dark rings from countless other wet shot glasses. He poured from a bottle with a green label and a chrome-colored measuring device screwed onto the neck, then scooted the glasses in front of Dalton. "That'll be seventy cents."

Pulling a dollar bill from his wallet, Dalton laid it on the counter. The man stuffed it into his front pocket, walked to the other end of the bar, and started talking to a sailor in a uniform that Dalton didn't recognize. *Guess I don't get any change. No sense in causing trouble in this place, though. Not for thirty cents.*

Dalton stared at the whiskey, gleaming with blue and green and amber light from a half-dozen neon signs hanging behind the bar. He picked the first shot up and glanced at the bartender, who in return was staring at Dalton. Lifting the shot toward the bartender in a toast, Dalton downed the whiskey. It burned his throat like a hot saw blade, then sent glowing coals rolling around in his stomach. He wanted desperately to cough but managed to give the bartender a weak smile instead.

The whiskey fire, as it always did, gradually turned into a seductive warmth that cradled Dalton's mind, rocking him on a sea of forgetfulness and fantasy. The harsh voices in the bar seemed to take on a mellower tone; the glaring lights dimmed and softened.

"Oh, the shark has pretty teeth, dear . . ."

Dalton recognized the song as "Mack the Knife" by Bobby Darin. He had never liked it before. But then, he had never heard it when he was drinking. He turned up the second shot glass, draining it in one gulp also. The second shot of whiskey had lost some of its bite. "This is really some smooth stuff," Dalton remarked to the bartender, who was filling a schooner with draft beer.

"Yeah," the bartender scoffed, "it starts tasting like twelve-year-old Scotch after three or four."

"Give me two more, then." Dalton felt a silly grin spreading across his face. He didn't even try to stop it, feeling that it would be right at home in "Mary's."

"Here you go, college boy." The bartender tilted his bottle, filling both of Dalton's glasses.

Dalton held the first drink just below his mouth. "Why'd you call me that?"

"It's what you are, ain't it?"

"Was," Dalton corrected him. "But how'd you know?"

"We don't get many in this place — that's how. You wasn't all that hard to spot." He glanced at Dalton's clothes. "Besides, you don't look at home in that outfit."

The bartender put the bottle down and

turned and carried his sloshing schooner to the other end of the bar. Dalton turned up his glass, letting the amber liquid flow into his mouth and down his throat.

A chunky woman with thin shanks encased in net stockings and hair of that peculiar inky shade of black that only comes in a bottle tottered over to the jukebox. Patting her lacquered hair in place, she leaned against the glowing plastic front, scanning the titles, a nickel poised in one puffy hand.

Gazing through blue-white clouds of smoke, Dalton watched the woman plunk her nickel into the slot, then slowly reach out and push a button. She produced another nickel and held it at the ready, tapping the pointy toe of one shoe as she decided on another selection.

"In 1814 we took a little trip. . . ."

Dalton sang along with Johnny Horton's best-selling record, "The Battle of New Orleans," as he stared at the woman standing at the jukebox. Her face carried an expression of intense concentration, as though her selection of a song would carry cosmic and profound consequences.

"You enjoy lookin' at my wife, pretty boy?"

Dalton turned his head slowly to the left and looked up at the jukebox-shaped man he had noticed when he first came in. "Not particularly."

The man wore bibbed overalls, a striped T-shirt, and a three-day growth of dark stubble on his heavy jowls. "Why you doin' it, then?"

Giggling, Dalton felt a numbness in his lips and cheeks. "I'm having a hard time following this conser . . . this converstation. No, that's wrong. This con-ver-sa . . . tion." He felt proud of himself for finally getting the word out.

"You gettin' smart with me, boy?"

"Who, me?" Dalton glanced around at the bar behind him, picking up his last shot of whiskey. "No. Not me. I ain't smart at all." He lifted his glass in front of his face. "Wait a minute! I think I found the problem!"

"You some kind of nut or something, boy?" The man glanced over at the bartender, who shrugged.

"No, no. Look." Dalton held his glass in front of the man's eyes. "See it?"

"I don't see nothin'."

"In the glass — it's my brain. No wonder I got so stupid all of a sudden." He downed the whiskey, then tried to force the silly grin off his face. "Now we can talk."

The man's tiny dark eyes narrowed as he spoke. "I don't know what ya problem is, boy, but if you think you can come in here and try to make us look stupid," he said and pointed toward his short, swarthy friend who now sat at their table, cluttered with Regal Beer bottles, "then you got another think comin'."

"I'd never try to make you look stupid."

"Oh, yeah?"

"Yeah," Dalton said, his voice rising. "You're doing too good a job of it yourself."

The man motioned with his head toward his friend, who pushed his chair back noisily and walked over to stand in front of Dalton.

"This punk says we're stupid," Jukebox growled, moving his weight from one heavy brogan to the other.

"Oh, yeah," the swarthy friend said, as though no one else had ever thought of using those two words in conjunction. "Maybe we oughta learn him better, then."

Jukebox doubled up his fist, drawing it back level with his right shoulder.

"Elwood, you leave that little boy alone!" The raspy, cigarette voice of the lady with the bottle-black hair stopped Elwood's fist in midair.

"You stay out of this, Bernice! Me and smart-mouth here," he said, scowling at Dalton, "got some business to finish. Jes' git on back to the table."

Bernice clomped over to the bar on her high-heels, stopping six inches from Elwood's belly. "You big dumb ox, I said leave this little boy alone! He ain't hurtin' nobody."

What happened next was only a blurred and disjointed scene of rapid motion, physical violence, and pain, as though Dalton had been abruptly thrust into a surrealistic black-and-white movie.

"You don't never know when to keep yore mouth shut, Bernice!" Elwood moved with surprising speed as he pushed his wife with his hamlike hand and sent her reeling backward.

With no conscious thought, Dalton found himself crouched in front of Elwood just as the big man turned away from his wife. Dalton's legs, hips, and shoulder were already turning into the blow, all the force of bone and muscle and tendon concentrated at the apex of his knuckles.

Elwood's eyes bulged with hopeless fear. Then his mouth flew open as though it were spring-operated when he saw Dalton's fist a split second before it slammed into his nose. His eyes blinked once, then rolled back in his head. Arms slowly flailing the air, he slumped to the floor.

Still moving forward into the blow, Dalton

fought for balance, grabbing the edge of the bar. He desperately sought Elwood's swarthy friend, knowing where the next strike would come from. Something heavy thudded into the back of his skull, exploding with bursts of white and orange light — the colors of the blinding pain. Then suddenly he felt himself sucked downward into a howling darkness.

FOURTEEN

Come Home

★ ★ ★

Something soft and wet slipped across his cheek. Dalton moaned, struggling to open his eyes as the pain in his head tried to siphon away all his strength, all his life. He cracked one eye. Ten inches away, a black-and-tan puppy, his tongue lolling out, stared at him. Then he leaned forward and licked Dalton's cheek, his tail wagging in pure joy that he had found someone to play with.

Dalton propped himself up on one elbow, then sat upright in the gravel and leaned back against the side of a building constructed of rough concrete blocks. Yellow sunlight spilled down the side of a corrugated iron wall streaked with patches of orange rust that formed the other side of the alley.

To his right, he could see a clutter of garbage cans and heaps of trash. At the other end of the alley, an open wagon with wood sides clattered along the street behind a bay horse. A nondescript man in a long black coat sat on the spring-mounted seat, holding the reins loosely in one hand.

The puppy got down on his belly, sliding himself forward until he was between Dalton's spread legs. Then he pawed slowly at one hand, his face turned upward, peering through the shaggy hair that almost hid his shiny dark eyes.

Dalton scratched the puppy behind the ears, watching his tail sway slowly back and forth. "Hello, pup. I hope you're not feeling as bad as I am." He gingerly touched the back of his head with his fingertips. "Somebody must have hit me with a baseball bat — or a sledgehammer."

The puppy whined for more attention, pawing now at Dalton's other hand. He rolled over on his back, his head at an awkward angle, staring up at Dalton.

Dalton scratched the puppy's belly, rubbed his ears a few seconds, and then got carefully and painfully to his feet. Walking slowly to the end of the alley, Dalton found that he was on Camp Street. He followed it to Canal and crossed against the red light in the absence of traffic, knowing that Camp became Chartes Street on the other side.

As he entered the Quarter on Chartes, the bell in St. Louis Cathedral began chiming, calling the parish flock to Sunday morning mass. Dalton strolled aimlessly through the quiet streets full of Saturday-night litter — cans and bottles and paper wrappers of all sizes and shapes and colors.

When he reached the corner of St. Peter Street, the pain in his head had changed to a throb, sending a wave of nausea through his stomach. He sat down on the sidewalk and leaned carefully against a building. Latecomers, a middle-aged couple and a girl in her early teens, hurried into the cathedral. Diagonally across from him, the artists had begun to set up for the Sunday afternoon sightseers. A rainbow suddenly formed in the glistening shower sent up by a network of sprinklers behind the massive piked-iron fence surrounding Jackson Square.

A whining noise caught Dalton's attention. He saw the puppy lying ten feet away in the shadow of a cast-iron lamppost. Distracted and disoriented by the pain in his head, he had forgotten about the dog. "Well . . . look who's here."

The puppy cocked his head to one side, stared at Dalton for two seconds, then whined once more.

Dalton snapped his fingers and beckoned, "You might as well come on over here. I didn't even know you were following me."

Instantly, the puppy leaped up and loped over to Dalton, lying down between his legs. Dalton sat for a long time in the yellow sunlight, petting the dog and watching the people stroll around the square. Mass ended, and the parishioners spilled out of the cathedral.

Ever so often, a fringed carriage pulled by a tired-looking old mule would clatter along St. Peter Street to its starting point on Decatur. Each time, new occupants would be aboard, exclaiming the wonders of the Quarter or simply sitting quietly, admiring the ancient buildings, or perhaps dreaming of an earlier, simpler time when carriages such as the one they rode in were the last word in transportation.

Finally, Dalton's head eased up a bit. He stood up, tested his balance, and walked off down St. Peter with his new companion at his heels. They crossed Royal, then turned right on Bourbon, heading toward Esplanade.

As Dalton continued his unplanned morning wanderings, he heard the sound of a clear tenor voice coming through the door of the Sho Bar, an infamous Bourbon Street strip joint.

Softly and tenderly, Jesus is calling,
Calling for you and for me . . .

Dalton shook his head and rubbed his eyes, thinking that he must be hallucinating. He walked over to a banged-up metal garbage can standing just inside the edge of an alley and sat down on its off-center lid.

Come home, come home,
Ye who are weary . . .

"It's real," Dalton said aloud.

The puppy cocked his head to one side and whined, then reared up on the side of the can.

Dalton reached down and scratched him behind the ears. "I think we'll just sit here awhile and rest, pup." He managed a weak grin at his new companion. "You don't have any pressing appointments, do you?"

The puppy wagged his tail in pleasure, holding the rest of his body still.

"I thought not." Dalton stepped across to the shady side of the alley and sat down. Listening to the soft, sweet sound of the singing that floated across the street, he drew his knees up and rested his head on his crossed arms.

An angel . . . music and an angel. In Dalton's half-conscious mind, this thought merged with the reality of the relentless noonday glare on the sidewalks and white stucco walls of the building across the street.

The music was a memory made just before he drifted off to sleep, sliding over to lie on his side in the alley. Across the street, the woman, looking like an angel in a cream-colored dress trimmed with lace at the bodice, was a dreamlike reality seen through his sleep-dimmed eyes.

Resting his head on his arm, Dalton stared up at the woman, her hair full of red and gold light. She stood next to a thin-shouldered man wearing a gray suit and red tie, who was only two or three inches taller than she.

Several other people stood near them on the sidewalk in front of the Sho Bar, talking, taking obvious pleasure in each other's company. Dalton noticed that all of them carried Bibles. He felt, without understanding why, that the Bibles were somehow as much a part of their outfits as their shoes.

Then Dalton turned his eyes on the woman. He watched the graceful movement of her slim hands as she spoke, waved good-bye to a friend, or brushed her wind-tossed hair back from her face. Soon, he lost sight of her as a great weariness overtook him, pushing his eyes closed.

"I don't think he's hurt." Justine Coday knelt next to Dalton, laying her hand on his forehead.

Dalton slowly brought his hand up, touching Justine's, then raised up on his elbow. He opened his dazed eyes, trying to focus on her face. "I . . . I must have fallen asleep."

Justine took his hand, helping Dalton to sit up. Only then did she recognize him. "You're . . . you're Dalton, isn't it? Dalton Temple, I believe."

Dalton nodded, rubbed his eyes with both hands and stared at her. Then he glanced at his disheveled and grimy clothes, imagining what his entire appearance must look like to her. *How does she even know who I am?* Understanding slowly began to filter through his foggy state of mind and he replied, "And you're the girl who fixed my lunch." His thoughts seemed wrapped in cotton, fuzzy and hard to identify. "Your name's . . . wait a minute — Justine!"

Justine nodded, then stood up next to the man she had been talking with across the street. "Dalton and I worked together . . . for one day," she explained to him. "And this is J. E. Cutshaw. He's my pastor."

Dalton looked at up at Cutshaw. Lean, almost to the point of being gaunt, his face looked chiseled and sharp, the nose slightly hawklike. Dalton had seen men before with this unmistakable, hollow look of having grown up in abject poverty. The lack of nourishment as children marked them for life.

Then he noticed Cutshaw's eyes — warm brown, with a deep, abiding glow of goodwill in them that somehow made Dalton feel better almost instantly. "I didn't know there was church in the Quarter, except for the St. Louis Cathedral. It's kind of hard to miss that."

"Stranger things have happened in the Kingdom, son," Cutshaw remarked and laughed. "Here, let me give you a hand." He took Dalton's arm, helping him to his feet.

"Thanks," Dalton said weakly, his eyes returning to Justine. "He's really your pastor?"

Justine glanced at Cutshaw. "He certainly is . . . and I wouldn't trade him for *anybody*."

Cutshaw smiled at Dalton, his eyes crinkling with unadorned merriment. "Not many wise men after the flesh, not many mighty, not many noble, are called . . ." His voice still carried that undertone of joy as he spoke. "Well, I'm certainly not wise, or mighty, or noble," he said, turning his humor on himself, "but then, you may have noticed that already."

"Oh, I didn't mean . . ." Dalton let his words trail off, not knowing exactly what he *did* mean.

"It's all right, son," Cutshaw went on. "No, sir, Jesus didn't get much of a bargain when He called me to preach His gospel . . . but He called me, anyway."

Dalton remembered the sweet singing he had heard as he drifted off to sleep in the alley. Something of it came through in the conversational tone of Cutshaw's voice. "Was that you I heard singing 'Softly and Tenderly'?"

Cutshaw raised his eyebrows in mock alarm. "You're not going to report me to the Music Lover's Society, are you? They'll ride me out of town on a rail!"

"Not hardly," Dalton laughed, the pain in his head cutting it short. "I thought it was real pretty."

Cutshaw turned to Justine. "A fan," he proclaimed, spreading his hands wide.

Justine glanced at Dalton, a look of concern on her face. Then her eyes found Cutshaw's. "Everybody in the Quarter's heard how good the French Quarter Chaplain sings, whether they like the message or not."

"French Quarter Chaplin?" Dalton found that he could not keep his eyes off Justine.

"That's what everybody calls him," Justine explained.

Cutshaw held his Bible across his chest with both hands, as though protecting himself from attack. "I got saved on a street-corner in Memphis, Tennessee, Dalton, while listening to a preacher not much older than me." At the memory, his eyes focused on another time. "That was *some* day! Right in front of a little place called Taylor's Café." He shook his head slightly, coming back to the present. "Then God called me to preach to other people like myself — the ones who just didn't fit in with the regular Sunday morning church crowd."

"How'd you get to New Orleans?"

"Preaching on street corners." Cutshaw's brown eyes held a private light, like a single candle burning in a darkened room. "You might find this hard to believe," he continued, "but everybody didn't exactly welcome me to their town with open arms. I learned a little bit of what Paul went through, I guess."

Dalton was starting to understand that the word *Christian* meant remarkably different things, depending on who you were talking to. "It got pretty rough?"

"Once in a while," Cutshaw nodded his head slowly. "Oh, I never got flogged, and nobody threatened to have me stoned or cut my head off."

"What then?"

"Let me just put it this way," he said and

grinned. "I can tell you a whole lot more about the jailhouses in some towns than I can about the motels."

"I don't find that hard to believe at all," Dalton said, the pain in his head beginning to subside. "I'm finding out that everybody doesn't love *me* either."

"Well, you must be doing *something* right, then," Cutshaw added without explanation. "Anyhow, to answer your question about how I happened to be down here — when the local citizenry got too hostile, I just up and moved on to the next town . . . one after the other." He made a sweeping gesture with his right arm. "And I ended up here, in New Orleans."

"On Bourbon Street?"

"Yep," Cutshaw said enigmatically, his left hand still holding the Bible to his chest.

Dalton, a puzzled look on his face, glanced up at Justine.

"I made such a nuisance of myself preaching out in front of the nightclubs on Bourbon," Cutshaw explained, "that the owner of the Sho Bar finally told me he'd let me use it on Sunday mornings for church if I'd stay off his block the rest of the week."

"Sounds like you made a pretty good deal."

"I think so," Cutshaw agreed quickly.

"I'm thinking about trying a service for a couple of hours on Wednesday morning next . . . for the people who can't make it on Sunday."

Hearing a whining sound, Dalton turned toward the puppy just behind him.

"Oh, my goodness!" Justine stepped close to Dalton, staring at the blood clotted at the back of his head. "You're hurt! What happened to you?"

Dalton found her eyes with his. He felt good, having Justine concerned about him. "A memento from one of those people who doesn't love me." He noticed that Cutshaw didn't appear to take his injury seriously. *Guess he's had a lot worse happen to him*, Dalton thought.

Justine lay her hand on Dalton's head and said, "Lean over so I can take a look at it." She pulled the hair apart carefully, gently inspecting the wound just behind his right ear.

"Think I'll live?"

"It needs to be cleaned and bandaged," she proclaimed. "Let's get you home, and I'll take care of it."

Dalton thought of Justine walking into his dingy little apartment. "Aw, it's all right. I'll just wash it off with a little soap and water when I get home."

Justine gave Dalton a once-over. "*You*

need the soap and water. The cut needs some peroxide so it won't get infected." She inspected the area closer. "I can't tell for sure, but after I get it cleaned out, it may need stitches."

"Might as well do what she says, Dalton," Cutshaw broke in. "I've only known this little girl for about a year, but I've found out that when she sets her mind to something, she can be pretty stubborn."

Dalton found that he was perfectly willing to place himself in Justine's care. "Guess I don't have much choice in the matter, then . . . do I?"

"Want me to go along, Justine?" Cutshaw asked.

"No. We'll be just fine," she assured him. "Besides, you need some rest."

"That, I do," Cutshaw said. "Seems like people never need preachers at decent hours here in the Quarter."

As they turned to leave, the puppy barked once, then trotted off down the alley. He sat down, scratched behind his right ear, then disappeared behind the building.

"Is that your puppy?" Justine asked.

"I don't know who he belongs to." Dalton shrugged. "We only met this morning. I think he may have adopted me for a couple of hours."

★ ★ ★

"I'm really sorry about the way this place looks." Dalton sat at the table in the kitchen area of his apartment. He had showered and put on Levi's, a blue-striped pullover shirt, and a pair of sweat socks. The sunlight streaming in through the blinds behind him formed bands of shadow and pale gold light across Justine's dress as she stood at the little stove, pouring boiling water into a cup.

Justine turned around, carrying two cups, both chipped, one with most of the price tag still stuck to its side. "I wish you'd quit apologizing. I've seen worse places than this — believe me." She placed the cups on the table and sat down in the wobbly chair across from Dalton.

"Thanks for taking care of my head." He touched the lump behind his ear.

"Are you feeling better? It's not still throbbing, is it?" Justine scraped coffee from the two-ounce jar with a bent teaspoon, dumping it into the cups.

"I'm fine."

She added sugar from a torn Colonial bag, stirred it into the coffee, and handed it to Dalton. "I'm glad the cut isn't bad, but that bump still has me worried. Maybe you should let me take you to the emergency room."

"No, I'm okay, really."

Justine added a spoon of sugar to her coffee and stirred it in, then gazed at Dalton. She lifted the cup with both hands, holding it just below her lips. *There's such sadness in his eyes. I wonder what happened to him. He certainly doesn't fit in down here.* As though her thoughts had suddenly become vocal of their own accord, Justine said, "What are you doing down here?"

Dalton's brow furrowed slightly. "I don't think I know what you mean."

"Well, let's just say you're not the French Quarter type," Justine asserted, then smiled. "And certainly not the type to be doing all the dirty work over at The Pearl."

"I just needed to get away for a while." Dalton drank a swallow of coffee and set the cup on the table. The March wind moaned outside the open window. Leftover winter leaves scraped across the brick patio.

"Get away from what?" Justine felt a growing need inside her to ease the grief she saw in Dalton's eyes, heard in the empty, remote tone of his voice. And there was something else about him that intrigued her — something beneath the loss, a sense of strength and discipline and loyalty . . . somehow gone wrong.

She had hoped he would ask to see her

again that first day at The Pearl when she told him she was leaving. But he hadn't. Though it had only been a few days, it seemed like such a long time ago. She didn't understand how this man she had been with for such a short time — who seemed so lost and alone — could affect her the way he did. But she felt those not-quite-familiar stirrings deep inside — those faint, nearly forgotten whispers of the heart that could not be denied.

"Maybe I ask too many questions."

"No, it's all right." Dalton glanced at a wisp of Justine's hair flowing like a shiny thread along the delicate curve of her ear. "I got hurt playing football and — well, after that . . ." He stared at his coffee cup. "It just seemed like everything started going wrong and I . . . needed to get away."

"Where'd you play football?"

Dalton smiled, thinking how fleeting and fragile his moments of fame had been. In a way, it was almost comforting not to have to perform for the fans, to be relieved of the constant pressure of making the big play, scoring the crucial points that would put the team over the top. But what could replace something that he had lived for most of his life? "LSU," he answered.

"Were you any good?"

Dalton laughed out loud. "You're not much of a football fan, are you?"

Justine shook her head slowly. "I guess I'm supposed to know you. I'm sorry."

Dalton felt much better, although he didn't quite know why. But that laugh was the first real burst of joy he could remember in a long while. "It's not important."

"Where're you from?" Justine asked, continuing to move the conversation forward.

"Mississippi, but we moved to Baton Rouge when I was eight, so that's my home." He noticed Justine's long, curving lashes, a little darker than her hair. "How about you?"

She sipped her coffee slowly, then held the cup with her fingertips. "All over, I guess, no place in particular."

"I never knew anybody from there before."

Justine laughed softly. "My dad was a career-army man. We traveled all over the world."

"I bet that was an interesting life."

"The main thing I remember is the loneliness." Justine felt as though someone else had spoken the words. Never did she remember revealing her feelings to anyone she had known for such a short time. And there had been very few people in her life that she had confided in at all.

"You mean with just you and your mother?"

"No." Justine saw herself waiting at the living-room window peering through the drapes of one of a long succession of homes she had shared with her father, waiting for him to come home. And she remembered the sameness of the bases, no matter where in the world they were located, and the drabness, like a world wreathed in a dun-colored mist. "Just me."

"What happened to your mother?" Seeing the reaction on Justine's face, Dalton winced at his own question. "I'm sorry. It's none of my business."

"No, I don't mind." She gave him a hint of a smile that made its way only as far as her eyes. "She died when I was born. I only knew her from pictures . . . and what Daddy told me about her, which wasn't very much."

Dalton thought it strange that he didn't feel uneasy with the intimacy of their conversation. "Didn't he love her?"

"I think he did — very much." Justine nodded slowly. "Maybe that's why he didn't talk about her very much. I think he never got over losing her."

Dalton felt drawn to Justine like a growing plant reaching out for the light. She did, in fact, seem like light to him in a world that had grown very dark over the past few months. He was not very good at pretense

315

and deception, having had no practice at it, so he told her, "Justine, I hope you don't think I'm making a pass at you or anything, but this is the best I've felt in a long time. I don't know how else to say it."

Justine started to speak, then thought better of it. She reached across the table and took Dalton's hand. She looked at a cut that ran from the knuckle of his forefinger along the veins at the top of his hand to the wrist. Turning his hand over, she traced the callus on his palm with the tips of her fingers. Then she slipped her hand inside his and gazed into his eyes.

The breeze picked up outside, rustling the dry leaves of a banana tree next to the house. From somebody's open window, the sound of Johnny Mathis singing "A Certain Smile" drifted as softly as thistledown on the afternoon air.

FIFTEEN

Sudden Storms

★ ★ ★

In the backyard a folding table, sagging under the weight of a huge birthday cake, soft drinks, a cut-glass punch bowl, and paper cups and plates, stood on the lawn among the tender shoots of pale green grass. Darker clumps of clover blossomed with white flowers. Balloons and streamers of colored crepe paper hung from the myrtle and sweet olive trees and formed a bright canopy stretched along the top of the brick wall at the back of the yard.

Out front on Napoleon Street, Dalton stood on the cracked sidewalk in the shade of a towering sycamore tree. Taking a deep breath, he headed down the brick walkway leading to the gallery of the white cottage. Hesitating, as though the cypress steps might not hold his weight, he walked up onto the porch, paused at the front door, then sat down in the weathered swing hanging from the ceiling on chains. He listened to the singing that drifted around the house from the backyard.

Happy birthday to you; happy birthday to you;

Happy birthday, dear Taylor; happy birthday to you.

Pushing on the gray painted floor of the porch with his foot, Dalton let the swing rock him gently to and fro. He stared at the pansies, white and yellow and deep purple, in the flower beds lining the front walk. A blue jay, out of sight in the crown of the sycamore, celebrated in song the coming of spring.

Reaching inside the breast pocket of his navy sport coat, Dalton slipped a silver flask out, unscrewed the top, and took a long pull. He blew his breath out softly as the whiskey burned its way down, then he took another swallow. Taking a roll of wintergreen mints out of the pocket of his blue button-down shirt, he sliced the foil with his thumbnail, popped a mint into his mouth, and put the roll away.

Dalton listened to the backyard party sounds for a while, then got out of the swing, and walked over to the front door. He opened it quietly, letting himself into the living room. Then he walked back to the kitchen, the heart pine floor creaking beneath his feet in the silence of the empty, darkened house.

Pausing at the back door of the kitchen that led out onto the porch, Dalton gazed at the backyard party. Taylor Youngblood, the first and only Temple grandchild, sat at the head of the table in his varnished wood high chair with a decal of a big teddy bear on the backrest. Jessie and Austin stood on each side of him, proudly holding his cake, the single candle already blown out.

Taylor let out a sudden grunt and dug his chubby hand into the side of the cake, tearing out a chunk and stuffing it in the general direction of his mouth.

"Strange how family traits show up so early," Jessie said, her voice faint in Dalton's ears. "He's already got your table manners, Cass!"

From the shadowed porch, Dalton stared out through the screen door at his family, knowing that they couldn't see him. They still wore their Sunday suits and dresses from church. *That's Mama's idea, I'll bet, everybody dressing up for Taylor's first birthday party.*

Dalton watched Austin cutting the cake, serving everyone on paper plates. Catherine walked with Connie Youngblood to the brick patio beneath a mimosa tree, where they sat down together on a stone bench. Balancing their plates on their laps, they chatted and ate together like the best of friends, although Dalton knew his mother and Jessie's mother-in-law had very little in common and saw each other only at family get-togethers like these. He couldn't hear their conversation but knew what it concerned by their constant glances in Taylor's direction.

Lane, Austin, and Marvin Youngblood stood near the brick wall, talking and holding their paper cups of punch like stage props. Lane occasionally glanced down at his watch. *He's afraid he's gonna miss his Sunday afternoon nap,* Dalton thought.

Jessie and Sharon sat in the grass with Taylor among the boxes and torn wrapping paper that had held his presents. He pounded on a bright rubber ball with his chubby fists, squealing with glee and glancing at his mother for approval.

Suddenly, Dalton had the feeling that he stood in a darkened theater watching a movie of his family. He gazed out at these people, his flesh-and-blood kin, in their ordinary and enduring celebration of a birth. The porch screen gave the whole sunlit scene a gauzy, unreal quality, as though he dreamed that he watched them in a movie as real as life.

Where's Cassidy? He was there just a minute ago.

"How's it going, hero?"

Dalton turned carefully around and stared at Cassidy. He had taken his tie off and wore a white shirt and a pale blue suit.

"You going to the party?"

Dalton shook his head.

Cassidy looked beyond Dalton. "Well, come on in here, then, before somebody sees you."

Glancing first out through the screen, Dalton walked across the kitchen tile, stepped into the living room, and shook hands with his brother. "How'd you know I was here?"

"I didn't know till a minute ago. Somebody's supposed to pick me up in a little while, so I went around to the front yard." He slipped a silver flask out of his back pocket. "Then I saw this on the porch swing."

Dalton took the flask and put it back inside his jacket. "Thanks."

Cassidy sat down in an overstuffed chair, leaned his elbows on the arm rest, and crossed his legs casually. "You know, big brother, if you're going to be a professional drunk, you gotta remember the basics . . . like keeping your bottle out of sight."

"Always right on top of things, aren't you, Cass?" Dalton's eyes narrowed in the dim light. "Always got your guard up — one step ahead of everybody else."

"I try," Cassidy said with a smirk. "It saves a whole lot of trouble in the long run."

Dalton stared at the back screen door, seeing the people in the yard as shadowy images. "Maybe I ought to take a lesson from you, little brother."

"Aw, don't take things so serious, hero," Cassidy countered and grinned. "You gotta be able to take a joke to get along in this world." He glanced through the glass of the front door at the street. "How you getting along down in the Big Easy?"

"Not too bad. I got a little apartment in the Quarter and a job at The Pearl right across Canal." Dalton walked over and sat on the couch at a right angle from his brother. In his guileless way, he blurted out, "I met a girl, Cass. I know it sounds stupid after what's happened, but she's really something. . . . I don't know how to describe her — special, I guess."

"Special, huh?" Cassidy stood up and paced the floor slowly. "I don't know about you sometimes, hero. You get dumped by this blond barracuda up here, and then you head straight to New Orleans where you immediately get tangled up with somebody from the Quarter. Where'd you meet her, in some strip joint on Bourbon?"

Dalton laughed, seeing the image of the Sho Bar and the strange and grateful congregation gathered on the sidewalk after Sunday morning services. "Not exactly."

"Special," Cassidy spat the word out as he paced. "Man, you're something else. You just *beg* women to break your heart." He stopped and stared at Dalton. "You're like somebody who just stepped out of one of those stupid Victorian sonnets."

"You reading Victorian sonnets these days?" Dalton knew he had caught Cassidy with his guard down.

"For school. We had to, or fail."

"Sure you did." It was Dalton's turn to smirk. He felt like he did when he and Cassidy were growing up together, sharing the same room and always trying to get the best of each other. "I bet you've been sneaking into Sharon's room and taking her poetry books when she's not looking."

As always when he wasn't winning, Cassidy changed the game. "You better get going if you don't want them to know you're here. They probably won't be out there much longer."

Dalton stood up, the humor gone from his face. "How's Mama doing?"

Cassidy shrugged. "Okay, I guess. She worries about you, but she still says you're too strong to let anything get you down for very long."

"She does?"

"Yeah. You know Mama. She always was a poor judge of character." Cassidy glanced again out the front door.

Dalton followed with his eyes. "Must be pretty important. Who you expecting, anyway?"

"Nobody special." Cassidy dismissed the question with a shake of his head. "She probably got hung up, trying to check out of the dorm."

"You got college girls picking you up these days?"

"Now and again, I run across one who's not too smart." Cassidy walked over to the front door, then turned around. "I hate to rush you, big brother, but if you want to keep being the 'mystery guest,' you better hit the road. That little shindig in the backyard is about to break up."

Dalton glanced toward the kitchen door. Through the porch screen, he could see shadowy figures moving about outside, cleaning up around the tables. "I guess you're right."

"Yeah, it's almost nap time for the guest of honor. How did you get up here, anyway?"

"Bus."

"I'd give you a ride down to the station, but she'll probably be too late."

"I don't mind walking a few blocks." Dalton crossed the living room, pulling a small box wrapped in white paper from his front coat pocket. "Here, give this to Jessie. It's a little something I picked up for Taylor."

Cassidy took the box, shaking it near his ear. "Kinda small. What is it?"

"A little silver spoon. I had his name put on it."

"Cute. Jess will like that."

"How's Daddy?" The words had been in the back of Dalton's mind since Cassidy had come into the house. He had decided not to ask, but the question seemed to roll out of him of its own volition.

"You know him better than I do," Cassidy replied, not really answering the question.

Dalton nodded. "I gotta go." He opened the front door, stepped out onto the porch, then looked back at Cassidy. His mind filled with things to say, but he decided against all of them.

Cassidy followed his brother out onto the porch. "Hey —"

Dalton turned around, one foot on the first step and the other still on the porch.

"Take care of yourself, hero."

★ ★ ★

Even with all the bulbs in the ceiling fixtures burning, the light in the room had a murky quality, as though it had been filtered through all the misery and hopelessness of the patrons who frequented the place every other day of the week. The tiny round tables had been pushed against the walls, and the straight-backed chairs arranged into rows of seven. In front of them, a chrome-plated microphone rested on its heavy metal base.

Dalton turned to Justine, sitting next to him. She wore a smile that seemed to brighten the air around her and the same cream-colored dress she had on the day she found him in the alley across the street. "I don't feel much like I'm in church." Dalton shifted uneasily in his chair.

Justine laughed softly, placing her hand on his forearm. "I think that'll change as soon as the preaching starts."

"Do you know many of these people?"

Shaking her head, Justine glanced around her. "Just one or two. Most of the people in the Quarter are pretty transient."

"From the way everybody was hanging around visiting out front that Sunday, I thought they must have known each other for a long time."

"No, it's not that," Justine explained.

"There's just a . . . I guess you'd call it a kind of friendly spirit about the services that makes everybody feel at home."

Dalton noticed that most of the people were in their twenties and thirties and wore suits and dresses that were out of style, but clean and neatly pressed. Several, with their beards and wrinkled clothes, looked as though they had just wandered in off the street. Some of them glanced furtively around the room; others stared vacantly into space.

Suddenly a blaze of yellow sunlight split the gloom as the door leading out to the street opened. Cutshaw, wearing his cheap gray suit and red tie and clutching his Bible, hurried down the aisle to the microphone, speaking as he went. "Sorry I'm late folks, but the local constabulary insisted that I answer a few of their questions before they'd let me leave."

Dalton turned to Justine. "What's he talking about?"

She leaned over and whispered, "Sounds like the police are harassing him again."

Cutshaw placed his Bible on a shaky wooden podium and opened a hymnal that looked as though it had been in use since Billy Sunday was a boy. "If you'll turn with me to page one hundred and twenty, we'll lift our voices in praise to the Lord. Best way I can think of to start the day. You should find some songbooks scattered around on the chairs."

Dalton leaned closer to Justine, looking onto the page with her. When he saw the title of the song, he knew he didn't need the hymnal to sing it. It was a song he had grown up with — one of his mother's favorites.

"I'll start us off with the first verse so those of you who haven't heard the song before can hear how it goes, and then y'all join in on the chorus." Cutshaw's smile transferred itself to most of the faces in his audience. "Then we'll all sing the last verse and chorus together — hopefully, on key."

Blessed assurance, Jesus is mine!
Oh, what a foretaste of glory divine!

Dalton had almost forgotten the hauntingly sweet quality of Cutshaw's voice that he had heard that first time from the alley across the street. He sensed a new meaning in the song — something that his mind couldn't quite fit around.

Heir of salvation, purchase of God,
Born of His spirit, washed in His blood.

Dalton joined in with the rest of the congregation, noticing the perfect pitch of Justine's clear alto voice. The song took him back to a white-frame church in Sweetwater,

Mississippi, where he had first learned the words.

This is my story, this is my song,
Praising my Savior, all the day long. . . .

During the remainder of the singing, images flashed through Dalton's mind: the little Sunday school room where he had colored pictures of David hurling his one smooth stone at Goliath and of Jesus gathering the little children around Him to bless them; the hard, wooden pews and his legs dangling over the edge during a long sermon; dinner on the grounds, and long tables laden with home-cooked garden vegetables, fried chicken, tender, juicy roasts, and pies and cakes — chocolate and pecan and coconut.

Cutshaw led them in several more songs, then asked Justine to come forward. After apologizing for her lack of training, she sang "The Old Rugged Cross." Her voice broke once on the chorus, but it didn't seem to bother her.

When Dalton heard Justine sing the line, *Till my trophies at last I lay down,* he thought of the gleaming wood-and-glass cabinet in his bedroom at home, filled with football and baseball trophies from elementary school through college. The excitement had faded quickly after he received each one.

It occurred to Dalton that as the years had

passed, he seldom looked at his shining collection that spoke of his various victories on the playing fields. Now, in this nightclub-turned-church, his mind turned to trophies that would not tarnish nor fade away, and to that final victory.

As Justine settled into her chair beside him, Dalton watched Cutshaw step to the podium and open his Bible. He gazed out at his transient, but attentive congregation, his eyes seemingly fixing on each of them. "I'd like to speak today on the subject of 'Unexpected Storms.' "

Cutshaw scanned his audience again. "How many of you have been hit by 'unexpected storms'?"

Most of the hands in the audience went up. Dalton's did too.

"I'm in good company, then," Cutshaw remarked and nodded. "Things seemed to be going well for you. Your life was clear and full of sunshine. You thought all the clouds must surely be on the other side of the world." He looked toward the ceiling, holding his right palm out, as though testing for rain. "The sky was as blue as you'd ever seen it."

A noise like thunder exploded through the room as Cutshaw pressed his mouth to the microphone. A few people jerked in their seats, startled by the sudden noise; others laughed nervously. "Then out of nowhere, a storm hits and blows your dreams over the edge of the earth — rips your life to shreds."

With all eyes now riveted on him, Cutshaw said in a level voice that commanded obedience, "Turn with me, if you will, to the fourth chapter of Mark's book, and let's read verses thirty-seven to thirty-nine.

" 'And there arose a great storm of wind, and the waves beat into the ship, so that it was now full.' " Cutshaw lifted his eyes from his reading. "I know some of you are going down — or you *think* you are. The winds of alcohol, drugs, hate, lust, sorrow — they're pounding against you like storm waves, trying to tear you apart and send you under."

Turning back to his Bible, Cutshaw continued to read, " 'And he,' that's Jesus, you know, 'was in the hinder part of the ship, asleep on a pillow: and they awake him, and say unto him, Master, carest thou not that we perish? And he arose, and rebuked the wind, and said unto the sea, *Peace, be still.* And the wind ceased, and there was a great calm.' "

Cutshaw left the podium, walking down one of the aisles. He touched his chin with joined thumb and forefinger. "Now, what was the first thing the disciples did when they got into trouble?" Glancing around the room, he continued his walk along the narrow aisle. "Anybody?"

A man of indeterminate age, wearing an ancient tweed sportcoat and a toothless smile, raised his hand, waving it before he spoke. "They went to Jesus."

Nodding his agreement, Cutshaw continued, "Now, that doesn't take a whole lot of explanation, does it? They went to Jesus."

Dalton listened to every word of the sermon, keeping his eyes riveted on the speaker. Cutshaw told of storms in his own life, and of how this same Jesus had always delivered him. He encouraged others to tell their stories of storms and deliverance, and several of them did — some with downcast looks, some with faces radiant and shining with joy.

As he was closing, Cutshaw walked back to the podium. "Sometimes it's not necessary to state the obvious, but I'll do it anyway this time. You must come in faith, believing that Jesus will deliver you. I could quote Scripture all morning on that subject, but I'll just use one example. Jesus said that if you have faith as big as a mountain, you could move a mustard seed with it . . . didn't He?"

The listeners, knowing something wasn't quite right about that statement, glanced around at each other. Some knew right away and laughed at this reversal of the faith message, joking among themselves about it. Dalton could see that Cutshaw had made his point.

"Now, I can tell you from personal experience, and from the lives of some of the greatest saints in this Book" — Cutshaw lifted his Bible in his left hand — "and as an example, Job comes to mind. You might not get delivered from your storm as soon as you ask."

He held his Bible in his left hand, thumbing through it with his right. "But let's just say a word about that. First Peter, chapter one, verse seven, says, 'That the trial of your faith, being much more precious than gold . . . might be found unto praise and honour and glory at the appearing of Jesus Christ.' " He gazed at his audience. "Remember, a trial is a test that has an end. And God lets us go through trials to produce patience, endurance, and a character perfect and lacking nothing. But that's another sermon."

Again, Cutshaw placed his Bible on the pulpit. "As I do at the end of every service, I want to extend an invitation to those of you who have never accepted Jesus Christ as your Savior. Romans ten and nine says, 'That if thou shalt confess with thy mouth the Lord Jesus, and shalt believe in thine heart that God raised him from the dead, thou shalt be saved.' "

Cutshaw looked out over his audience again. "It doesn't say you *might* be saved, or that there's a *chance* you'll be saved. God's Word says that you *shall* be saved."

"Now," Cutshaw stepped from behind the podium, "the message today was mainly for those who have drifted away from the Lord. Life's storms and trials have wounded you so deeply that you think you'll never be healed." A radiant smile lit his face. "But what did Jesus say? He said He was sent to 'preach the gospel to the poor, to heal the brokenhearted . . . to set at liberty them that are bruised.' "

Cutshaw extended his arms to the people. "All of you who are bruised and broken-hearted — come to Jesus. He said that all those who come to Him, He will in no wise cast out."

Dalton noticed Cutshaw's eyes fall on him. He felt as though this man could see inside his heart. Dalton remembered walking down the aisle of the little church in Sweetwater when he was only eight years old and how that day had changed his life. Even before the preacher could give the invitation, Dalton found himself on his feet, walking down this aisle to the altar.

Dalton fell to his knees in front of the makeshift podium, hardly aware of his surroundings. His voice was choked and barely audible as the words poured out of him. "Jesus, only You can heal me! I'm hurt too bad. There's no other way." He didn't feel the tears on his cheeks, only the lifting of a great weight from his heart and a lightness in his soul, as though he would float toward heaven, and a great peace flowing through him like a river.

SIXTEEN

The Past

★ ★ ★

Spring had invaded New Orleans in full force. Flower beds blazed with color. The trees seemed to transform from stark, barren sculpture to lush green canopies almost overnight. And a yellow sun bathed the city in a soft warm shower of light.

The streetcar swayed and rocked along the grassy esplanade that divided St. Charles Avenue, heading away from the downtown business section toward Audubon Park. At the intersections, it would whine to a stop, loading and unloading passengers, then continue on through the tunnel of oaks.

The Garden District's antebellum and late-Victorian houses stood like aging royalty among their clipped lawns, black with shadow beneath the ancient live oaks. Stone walks led up to broad galleries painted marine-gray and decorated with intricate lattice work. Their roofs, sharply pitched and slate gray, rose high above the mundane happenings of the city below.

Dalton, in faded jeans and a white cotton shirt, sat on the hard wooden bench next to Justine. "I'm glad we could both get the day off," he told her.

Justine wore sandals and white cotton slacks with a pale green blouse a shade lighter than her eyes. "I used to dream of living in a house like one of these." Her voice had a faraway quality as she kept her eyes on the elegant old homes.

Dalton gazed at Justine's profile, her lips slightly parted, as the breeze through the open window of the streetcar tousled her hair, fanning it out from her face. "Let's get the conductor to stop this thing, and I'll buy you one."

Justine turned from the window, a smile lighting her eyes. "That was a long time ago, when I was a little girl," she said absently. "It doesn't seem so important now."

"But it did then?"

Gazing back out the window, Justine let the past flow back in. "We traveled around so much, living in apartments or those shoddy little houses on the army bases. Every one just like the one next door." She nodded her head slowly. "You know, I think that's what I disliked the most. They were all alike. Sometimes I think it made

337

all the people act alike."

"And the soldiers' uniforms," Dalton joined in, "they're all just alike."

"Yes, that's it." Justine's face stayed toward the window as she spoke. "I used to think sometimes that we were all robots, or puppets, with the colonels and generals sitting in their big offices, pulling our strings."

"You may be getting pretty close to the truth."

Justine laced her slim fingers inside Dalton's. "Don't get me wrong; it wasn't a bad life. It's just that everything seemed so . . . so shallow, I guess you'd call it . . . and temporary."

Listening to Justine's tale of moving from place to place, of not having a mother, Dalton realized how fortunate he had been to have his own family.

Justine let the words trail out in bits and pieces, wandering around in the years past. "We never got to make any friends. Not any *real* friends; people that you could get close to and count on to help you.

"I remember when I was in the third grade, there was a girl named Rosemary who sat in the desk behind me. She had pigtails and more freckles than anybody I ever saw."

"And she was your best friend."

Justine nodded. "I had the best time of my life. We told each other secrets, and spent the night with each other, and talked about boys." Her smile reflected the memory that still flickered in her mind; then the smile slipped from her face. "Six months later, Daddy got transferred to another post." She looked into Dalton's eyes. "I never saw her again."

Dalton saw the fleeting sadness in Justine's eyes, smelled the fragrance of her next to him, like summer honeysuckle. He touched her cheek with his fingertips, leaned close, and pressed his lips against hers. Justine responded to Dalton's kiss, closing her eyes and curling her fingers into the hair at the back of his neck.

Then she pulled away. "Goodness! What's wrong with me?" She glanced around her, then kept her eyes on Dalton's, her cheeks flushed. "We're in a public place!"

"That's all right, darling," a plump, gray-haired woman sitting across the aisle said. She wore fuzzy pink house-slippers, a green-and-yellow print blouse, and carried a D. H. Holmes shopping bag. "You and your young man go right ahead! I remember how springtime used to affect me and my boyfriend."

Dalton grinned at her. "I bet you still got

a boyfriend or two hangin' around your door."

The woman pushed the remark aside with a wave of her hand. "You go on with yo' bad self! I'm way too old for that foolishness now!"

Laughing along with the woman, Dalton turned back to Justine, speaking under his breath. "I bet she was really something thirty years ago!"

"I'll bet she's still something right now!"

"You just may be right about that." He led the way back to their conversation, glad that Justine had begun to tell him something about her past. "Do you see your father often?"

Justine stared at Dalton's hand, still clasped around her own. "He was killed in combat in the Korean War." She glanced up. "Funny, they called it a 'police action' instead of a war." Her eyes held a remote gaze. "The men who got killed, though, are just as dead whether it's called a 'police action' or a real war. Somehow, it demeans their sacrifice to call Korea a 'police action.' Maybe it's just me."

Seeing the expression on Justine's face, Dalton asked no more questions.

"My mother's sister took me to live with her family, but they never were really *my* family. I left the day I turned eighteen." She gave Dalton a half-smile. "I'm sorry to ramble on like this. You must be bored to death."

"Nothing about you is boring." Dalton gave her a blank stare, shaking his head slowly. "I can't believe I said something so corny. It just popped out." He smiled again at the lady with the D. H. Holmes bag, then rubbed the corners of his mouth with thumb and forefinger. "That sounds like something out of an old Andy Hardy movie."

"Corny's okay," Justine told him, a soft light filling her eyes. Then she squeezed his hand tightly. "You're so fortunate to have a family like yours! From what you've told me, they sound perfect — like the family I would have picked out of a mail-order catalogue if I could have done that when I was a little girl."

"Maybe it's not too late," Dalton said quickly before he realized what he had said and where the words were leading.

"You mean, to find a catalogue that sells families — like garden hoses or women's nightgowns?"

"No . . . I don't mean that at all."

Justine's eyebrows raised slightly. Her lips parted, then three seconds later she spoke the words. "Just exactly what do you mean, Dalton?"

"I . . . I guess," he hesitated, "I mean, it's not too late for you to become part of a family like that . . . like mine."

"Is this a proposal?"

The conversation had somehow jumped from the subject of catalogues to the subject of matrimony so quickly that Dalton felt light-headed. "I suppose it is," he responded slowly.

"You *suppose?*"

"I do."

"That's what you're supposed to say when you get married!"

Dalton took both Justine's hands, gazing directly into her eyes, bright with the wonder of what was happening. "Will you, Justine Coday, be my wife? There! Is that plain enough for you?"

"Dalton," Justine said, a tiny furrow creasing her smooth brow just above the bridge of her nose. "We only met a few weeks ago. You don't even know me!"

"I know all I need to know about you," Dalton insisted, realizing that this decision had been working in him for several days now. "I know that when I'm not with you, there's a pain inside me," he said, touching his chest, "that won't go away till I'm with you again."

Justine listened with a rapt, almost

shocked, expression on her face, as though Dalton was releasing some profound revelation to her bit by bit.

And, in fact, Dalton came to know as he spoke the words how precisely they defined the feelings that had become a part of him in such a short time. "I know that there's an emptiness inside me that's only filled when I'm with you."

Justine's eyes brightened with an unspoken joy. A single tear slipped down her cheek. "I . . . I don't know what to say. This is all happening so suddenly!" Her voice broke with emotion as she spoke.

"Maybe you should get to know more about me, Dalton," Justine continued.

"I love you, Justine. That's all I need to know."

"But if we had more time —"

Dalton gazed at Justine as he spoke, taking in every curve and feature of her face. "Time doesn't always tell the story, Justine." He glanced out the streetcar window at the parade of passing houses, the perfectly manicured lawns, at a man in khakis and a plaid short-sleeved shirt walking behind a reel-type push mower, the blades churning up a green cloud of grass clippings.

"I went with the same girl for more than two years," Dalton said, his voice freighted with the sad remnants of the past. "Then I found out I didn't know her at all. Didn't know a thing in the world about her — nothing that mattered, anyway." His face brightened as he turned back to Justine. "So you see, that ol' argument about taking a lot of time to get to know each other doesn't mean much to me now."

"This is absolutely insane!" Justine let her breath out in a rush of words.

"Ain't it, though?" Dalton grinned.

Justine's eyes filled with tears as she spoke. "I love you so much, Dalton. I think I have since I saw you that first day in The Pearl with your messy ol' clothes and . . . and your eyes so full of sorrow, like a little lost boy."

"I feel like a boy again right now." Dalton threw his arms around Justine, holding her close, lost in her fragrance and the softness of her pressing against him.

The lady in the fuzzy slippers stared at the couple, her eyes moist as she whispered, "Lord, bless these young people! Keep them in the shadow of Your love."

DeJean twisted a white dish towel inside a shot glass, held it up to the light, then placed it up on the shelf behind the bar in the company of its sparkling kin. "I sure hate to lose a good worker like you."

"I'm glad I got to meet you, DeJean." Dalton wore a new pair of Levi's and a white T-shirt with the folds in the cloth still showing. He turned up a bottle of Barq's Root Beer, downing the last drop. "It's time for me to go home, though."

"Yeah, you right about dat," DeJean agreed, polishing another glass. "You finish dat college degree, you won't have to work at no place like de Pearl no more."

"This ain't such a bad place." Dalton surveyed the restaurant, noticing a late diner lingering over his bowl of gumbo at a table next to the window that looked out onto St. Charles. He remembered the day he had sat at the same table with Cherry. *It doesn't bother me anymore. Thank the Lord for that!* "And you're sure a good man to work for."

DeJean nodded, rubbing his next glass with renewed vigor. "Sometimes you don't know if people like you or not. It's good to hear t'ings like that." He turned his head from his work toward Dalton. "You gonna coach football when you get out of college — you know, like we talked about?"

"I think so."

"Good. I think maybe you gonna like coaching better than playing."

Dalton nodded, then stared reflectively at

DeJean, intent on his work. "I think you're right."

"But since you ain't got no degree now, and it's three hours till quitting time, how 'bout you go out there and clean out that utility room?"

"Sure thing," Dalton replied, then turned toward the back door and walked out onto the loading ramp. He stepped inside the utility room and grabbed a broom and dustpan leaning against the wall. After sweeping the cleared area, he began to pick up trash: broken boards and pieces of brick, old brooms and mops that had been worn down to nubbs and handles, a 1953 Ringling Brothers Circus poster complete with an elephant rearing ponderously on its back legs, and an "Earl Long for Governor" sign.

After taking the first stack of trash out to the garbage cans, Dalton returned for another load. A nightclub flyer, advertising their latest exotic dancer, caught his eye. Beginning to feel a cold, prickling sensation at the back of his neck, he picked the half-crumpled poster up from beneath a stack of old *Times Picayune* newspapers, brushed the dust off, and took a closer look.

The dancer, her back to the camera and her face turned in a coy glance over her shoulder, was doing her best Betty Grable imitation. The photographer had done his job well, but he had not been able to hide the hollow, lifeless expression that the eyes held behind the painted-on smile. The pose reminded Dalton of an old black-and-white photograph of the famous movie star that he had run across in a *Life* magazine, but the girl in this advertisement had on less clothes than World War II's top pin-up girl who wore a modest one-piece bathing suit.

Dalton's face took on an expression of shock, his eyes growing wide. Then the life seemed to drain out of him as he backed against the wall, his knees buckling like an invalid's as he slid gradually down into a sitting position on the cold concrete floor.

Dalton sat there for a long time, staring blankly at the picture. The smiling face on the dirty, wrinkled poster seemed to mock him. A spark flickered deep inside his glazed eyes, then flamed suddenly into an anger bordering on rage. Crumpling the poster in his hand, he sprang up and stormed out of the utility room.

A red haze seemed to hang between Dalton and the world he saw around him. He walked down the alley, turned left on St. Charles, and headed toward Canal. A streetcar clanged and clattered by, but Dalton heard only the roaring inside his head.

Crossing Canal against the light, he heard the screeching of tires on pavement and barely dodged a shiny red Edsel, its driver cursing him behind the window glass.

Barging along the sidewalk, Dalton bumped and pushed his way through the crowd until he saw the big clock in front of D. H. Holmes. He shoved the heavy glass door open, finding himself in the relative hush of gleaming counters and racks of clothing attended by well-dressed and professionally polite salespeople.

Dalton followed his nose straight to the cosmetic counter. The fragrances of perfumes and powders and bath oils guided him as surely as a compass.

Justine, wearing a simple black sheath, reached beneath the counter, taking a gift box of perfume from one of the glass shelves. As she stood up to hand it to her customer, an angular woman with black hair piled up on her narrow head, she saw Dalton heading for her. A rumor of a smile quickly vanished from her face when she saw his dark expression.

Placing the box on the counter in front of the woman, Justine said, "Excuse me. I'll be right back," and walked away to intercept Dalton.

Dalton stopped at the counter, his eyes

blazing at Justine. "How could you?" He threw the crumpled-up poster at her. It bounced off the counter and onto the floor.

Astonished at Dalton's behavior, Justine stooped over and picked up the paper.

"Go ahead — look at it!"

At the sound of Dalton's voice, the lady a few steps down the counter gave him a glance of alarm.

Justine, flushed and speechless now, unfolded the grimy poster, holding it at waist level. She stared at it for three seconds. Then her eyes, bright with unshed tears, turned upward toward Dalton, pleading with him for understanding.

Dalton's chest rose and fell rapidly with his breathing. He stared at Justine, a fury of love and hate and confusion raging inside him. Storm winds howled inside his mind; his thoughts blown about like so much confetti.

"How could you! You . . . you . . ." Dalton suddenly realized that something in his innermost being gently tugged him away. He fought for control, his anger gradually fading to be replaced by an almost unbearable sense of betrayal. He gazed into Justine's face, streaked now with tears. A desperate longing filled his chest. He could almost see himself taking her in his arms, comforting her, telling her it was going to be all right.

But Dalton found that he could not. He merely shook his head sadly, his heart as empty and hollow as the face in the poster, and turned and walked away.

Dalton sat beneath a live oak whose huge, low-hanging limbs, touching the hard-packed ground in places, spread outward fifty to seventy feet from its massive trunk. Dusk drifted down through the leaves like a purple mist. He stared at the New Orleans Museum of Art across the lake, its white-columned facade gleaming in the afterglow like a Greek Temple.

He remembered bursting through the heavy doors of D. H. Holmes onto Canal, walking along in a daze for what seemed like hours, then turning right on Carrolton. His pace had slowed and he drifted aimlessly along until he had ended up in City Park, walking along the lake.

Dalton sat against the tree for a long time, took a last look at the museum, then stood up and walked away into the night. Crossing Bayou St. John at the Esplanade bridge, he continued on toward the Quarter, where he saw the neon glare of the liquor store beckoning him inside.

"That'll be two and a quarter, buddy."

The skinny man with eyes so pale they were almost without color slipped the bottle into a brown paper bag and banged it down on the counter. He held his thin palm toward Dalton like a beggar.

Dalton dropped the bills and change on the bare plywood counter, grabbed the bottle, and left the stale, smoky air of the tiny liquor store.

Continuing down Esplanade, Dalton reluctantly made his way to his apartment. Entering into its gloom, he fumbled for the bulb dangling from the ceiling on its cord, found it, and switched it on. He slumped down at the kitchen table, took the bottle out of the bag, and placed it in front of him.

Glancing around the tiny apartment, Dalton saw Justine everywhere: at the stove preparing gumbo or red beans and rice; sitting with him on a Sunday afternoon in the living area, reading or talking or just lying on the couch, her head pillowed on his lap as the lavender light outside the window darkened. He could almost feel her softness and warmth against him, siphoning away all the day's troubles, taking away all the sharp-edged remnants of the past.

Dalton got up, taking a water glass from the drain next to the sink. He placed it next to the bottle on the table. Sitting down, he pulled the cork on the bottle, picked the glass up, and lay the neck of the bottle against its rim. Whiskey gurgled from the bottle as he filled the glass almost to the brim.

Suddenly he stood up. *I can't do this!* Dalton realized. He emptied the glass and the bottle into the sink and walked out the door into the night. Dalton hardly noticed the tourists and the heavy traffic that jammed the streets and sidewalks as he ambled aimlessly through the Quarter. Loud music and raucous laughter spilled out of the nightclub doors.

Past Jackson Square, Dalton climbed the levee and walked south past Algiers Point on the opposite bank of the river. On his way back upriver, he noticed the first pink tinge of light in the east as he neared Café du Monde. He found an outdoor table, ordered a café au lait, and watched the sunrise and the city come to life.

"God bless you, brother." Cutshaw, wearing khakis and a white dress shirt, got up from his bench next to the walk inside the piked-iron fence of Jackson Square. The man standing with him rubbed the brown-and-gray stubble on his pointed chin and gave Cutshaw a smile that was minus three teeth but not short on warmth. "I shore 'preciate everthang you done for me, Rev'rand," the man said with sincerity. He pulled his ragged brown topcoat about his chest and walked through the gate toward Pirate's Alley.

"You must have done something great for him," Dalton said, still sitting down on the bench. "He looked like he just found the end of the rainbow."

"I didn't do much," Cutshaw replied, taking a seat next to Dalton. "But I hope I was able to point him to the One who can." He crossed his legs, rested his elbows on the back of the bench, and took a deep breath. "Now, what can I do for you this fine May morning, Dalton?"

Dalton gave Cutshaw a short version of what had happened during the past sixteen hours, including the bottle of whiskey that he sent gurgling down the drain.

"You don't need whiskey anymore, son. God took care of that the morning you came down to the altar." Cutshaw spoke with the confidence of a man who had been given all the authority and knowledge he needed to do his job. " '. . . A broken and a contrite heart, O God, thou wilt not despise.' God knows your heart, Dalton. He took you in His arms, forgave you, and healed your wounds that morning. Am I right?"

Realizing that Cutshaw had put into words exactly what had happened to him that Sunday at the Sho Bar, Dalton merely nodded his agreement.

"Now, is there anything else on your mind?"

Shocked, Dalton thought that Cutshaw must have misunderstood what he had just told him. "I . . . I don't know what to do about Justine."

"Why, marry her, son. She'll make you a fine wife."

Dalton felt that Cutshaw surely didn't grasp how terribly wronged he had been. "What about . . . the things she did?"

" 'Ye do err, not knowing the scriptures, nor the power of God.' " Cutshaw's eyes grew intense. "That's what Jesus told the Pharisees when they asked Him a stupid question."

"But how can I marry her when —"

"You don't deserve her!" Cutshaw's words again carried that unmistakable authority. "Are you going to worry about something that God doesn't even know happened?"

Dalton's face reflected the bewildered state of his mind.

" 'Though your sins be as scarlet, they shall be white as snow.' You think God put that in the Bible just for the fun of it? The blood of Jesus washed Justine's sins away. When God looks at her, He sees her just as pure and innocent as a little child."

Cutshaw's voice softened as he gazed at Dalton. "It's all right to be a little ignorant, though. You'll learn."

Dalton forced a smile, feeling like a truant boy standing in the principal's office.

"Justine came to New Orleans to go to Tulane . . . to get a degree in English literature." Cutshaw snapped his fingers. "Now, listen good. I'm only gonna tell you this once.

"She got hooked up with the wrong man at a party, and he hooked her up with drugs. Once he got her addicted, he could control her.

"Now, about that poster that bothers you so much. That man made a lot of money off her dancing. Not at the joints on Bourbon; he knew he had something better than that. He booked her in dinner clubs, expensive private parties — places like that. And" — Cutshaw fastened his eyes on Dalton's — "not that it makes any difference in her life now, but she never wore anything more revealing than a two-piece bathing suit — the kind you can see on Ponchatrain Beach all summer long."

Cutshaw lay his hand on Dalton's shoulder. "I know it hurts, son. Maybe I was too hard on you, but I wanted to put this thing in the light God sees it. I was with Justine when she was getting off drugs. It wasn't pretty — but she stuck it out. Now, God's given her a new life," he said. A smile lit his face as he added, "Just like He has you.

"I don't think it was an accident that you met Justine at The Pearl, or that you just happened to end up in that alley across from our church service that Sunday morning." Cutshaw's brown eyes shone with the never-ending wonder of the work he had been called to do. "I believe God put the two of you together because you've each got what the other needs.

"Justine loves you very deeply, Dalton. I don't know how it happened so quickly — it just did. But if you condemn her for her past — if you can't love her as she is right now — then I'll say it again, 'You don't deserve her.' "

"But why didn't she just tell me?"

Cutshaw lifted his hands toward the sky. "Another dumb question!"

A smile worked around at the corners of Dalton's mouth as he watched Cutshaw's antics.

"Because she's ashamed, that's why. All this happened before she met you, anyway, so quit making such a big deal out of it, will you?"

Without understanding why, Dalton found that the terrible darkness that seemed to have fallen upon his soul was being bathed in light. Somehow everything that Cutshaw said made perfect sense to him. Justine's past now seemed as remote as . . . as his desire for whiskey, as remote as the pain that Cherry's betrayal had brought into his life, and as unimportant as winning the Heisman.

"What a beautiful day!" Cutshaw stood up, looking back at the towering facade of the cathedral gleaming in the morning sunlight. "Let's go get some beignets."

"I'm not —" Dalton started to say that he wasn't hungry, then realized that he was famished. "That's a great idea! What a beautiful day!"

SEVENTEEN

Mobile

★ ★ ★

"I don't usually drink malts at nine o'clock in the morning." Wearing a mint-colored dress, Justine sat on a round cushioned stool at the fountain in Woolworth's. She watched the young man in his white paper cap pour her thick chocolate malt from a tall chrome container into a heavy glass. Frothy and cold, it quickly beaded the glass with drops of moisture.

"Me either," Dalton agreed, watching his own glass fill up. He took a big swallow that left a light brown mustache on his upper lip. "Umm . . . I think they're better in the morning."

Dalton thought back over the past two hours. He had gone to Justine's apartment as soon as he and Cutshaw had finished their breakfast, deciding that he could bear to wait no longer to ask her forgiveness. Afterward, in her embrace, he could almost feel her love flowing through him, becoming a part of him.

"I'm sorry I didn't tell you, Dalton." Justine poked in her malt with a paper straw.

Dalton placed his hand on top of hers. "We've already been through all of that. From now on, it's just something that never happened. Like my drinking."

Justine turned her face toward him, then a smile curved her lips, quickly turning to laughter.

"What's the matter?"

"You look like a little boy!"

"What are you —" Dalton glanced at himself in the long mirror on the other side of the counter, smiled back, then wiped his chocolate mustache off with the back of his hand. "That just means it tastes good. It's an old Mississippi custom."

"I'll bet."

"Sure, it is," Dalton insisted. "In some Arab countries, the polite thing to do is burp if you enjoy your meal." He kept his tone somber as he explained, "In Mississippi, we make sure we get some of the meal on our face to show our approval."

Justine gave him a skeptical look that didn't quite replace her smile. "I think you're losing your mind."

"You ain't heard nothin' yet," Dalton said.

"I'm not sure I want to." Justine sipped her malt, savoring the rich, sweet taste.

Dalton took a big swallow, taking time to point out to Justine the now thicker brown coating on his top lip. "Oh, yes you do. You're gonna love this!"

Glancing at her watch, Justine sipped more malt, then said, "Whatever it is, you'll have to do it in a hurry. I've got to be at work in less than an hour."

"That's one of the things we need to talk about," Dalton said, attempting to sound casual.

Justine turned toward him again, trying to decide whether the expression on his face as he gazed back at her belonged to a ten-year-old boy waking on Christmas morning or one plotting a way to play hookey from school.

"You finished?" Dalton drained the last of his malt.

Nodding, Justine slid off the stool and turned toward the door that led out onto Canal.

Dalton took her hand. "Let's look around for a while. You've got plenty of time."

"Might as well." Justine shrugged. "I'd just have to wait around for someone to let me in the store. What do you want to see — the toy department?"

Dalton smiled and said, "You didn't miss it far."

They left the soda fountain and walked through the toy department past the helium-filled balloons, fanning upward in a bright cloud at the end of their strings, past cones of fluffy pink cotton candy, rubber balls and cap pistols, past Betsy-Wetsy dolls peeking through the cellophane windows of their boxes.

At the jewelry counter, Dalton stopped and inspected the rings gleaming on shelves behind the glass counter.

A saleslady wearing a red smock and a placid look greeted him. "Good morning. May I show you something?"

"Yes, ma'am," Dalton answered. She reminded him of his second-grade teacher. "I'd like to see those." He pointed to a flat, velvet-covered tray holding gold bands inserted into slots.

The lady gave Justine a look of disapproval, shaking her head slightly so as not to alert Dalton.

Standing behind Dalton, Justine merely shrugged, holding her hands out palms upward.

Placing the tray on the counter, the lady spoke in a tone of mild disapproval. "I don't think you'd be interested in these. They're our one-dollar rings."

Dalton winked at Justine, then surveyed

the array of rings studiously, rubbing his chin with thumb and forefinger. "Maybe you're right. Do you have something a bit cheaper?"

Slightly flustered, the woman quickly regained her composure. "No, I'm afraid not."

"What size do you wear, Justine?"

"Five, I think."

The lady plucked a ring from the tray, holding it as she would a dead insect.

Dalton slipped the ring onto Justine's left finger. "That's a perfect fit." He admired it, holding her hand in front of his face to inspect it. "Now, give me a size ten." Slipping the ring on his finger, Dalton held it side by side with Justine's. "I think these are exactly what we've been looking for. How about you?"

Justine decided to play along with the game. "Oh, darling, they're even better than I had hoped!"

Dalton placed two one-dollar bills and two nickels on the counter. "I believe that's right, isn't it?"

A bewildered expression climbed onto the lady's face as she stared at Justine. "You really like them?"

"Of course! What woman wouldn't?"

"Shall I put them in a box for you?"

Justine held her hand up to the light, admiring the cheap gold band. "No, thanks. I'll wear it."

Dalton slipped his hand around Justine's waist. They walked through the store and out onto the sidewalk. The morning traffic roared and honked and screeched along Canal Street. Out on the neutral ground, the old streetcar whined to a stop, discharging salesclerks and attorneys and government workers out into the bustle of rush hour.

"Now, for the rest of the plan."

Justine raised her eyebrows a quarter-inch. "You mean, there's more?"

"Most definitely." Dalton plucked a set of car keys from his left front pocket.

"You don't have a car."

"These belong to J. E."

"What are you doing with them?"

Dalton shoved the keys back into his pocket. He took both of Justine's hands, lifted the left one, and kissed it just above the shiny one-dollar ring. "We're going to Mobile to get married."

"We are?" Justine thought better of her response. "I mean . . . we're not. We can't."

"Why not? There's no waiting period there."

"I . . . I don't know. We just can't, that's all."

"Do you love me?"

Justine gazed into Dalton's eyes, then pressed close to him, slipping her arms around his waist. "Oh yes! Yes!"

"Then that's your answer."

She spoke the words softly, her head resting against his chest, asking, "Are you sure?"

Dalton stroked her hair with his left hand, then kissed her on the forehead. "I've never been more sure of anything in my whole life."

Justine stepped back and glanced at Dalton's clothes. "I think maybe you need to clean up a little first."

Dalton had forgotten that he had left straight from work the afternoon before and had been up all night long in the same clothes. "I'll go clean up and then tell De-Jean what's happening. You tell them at the store that you're resigning, and I'll pick you up in forty-five minutes in front of the clock."

Feeling light-headed at the whirlwind rush their lives had been swept into, Justine hesitated. "Do we have time?"

"Sure. It only takes three hours to get there."

Justine pressed close to him again. "Hold me for just a minute. This doesn't seem real."

Dalton held her in his arms on the

crowded sidewalk, then kissed her gently on the lips. When his hair had turned white and he would need a walking cane to get to his mailbox, that moment would come back to him as sharp and clear as the day it happened. The traffic noises, the whine of the streetcar, being bumped and jostled by passersby, the feel of Justine in his arms, and the honeysuckle fragrance of her.

"That's him." The clerk in white shirt and tie pointed down the hall, then hurried off in the opposite direction, carrying a stack of manila folders. "His name's Boone, I think," the clerk called back over his shoulder.

Dalton spotted the justice of the peace, a tall man with iron gray hair in a charcoal gray suit. His athletic build appeared to be settling nicely into a middle-age spread.

"C'mon." Dalton, who now wore his tan slacks and navy blazer, grabbed Justine's hand and pulled her along after the man, their footsteps on the marbled floor echoing with a hollow sound off the vaulted ceiling.

Justine felt swept away in this headlong rush to marriage: the drive along the Gulf Coast from New Orleans; filling out the forms for the license; a quick trip to the hospital for the blood tests and a hurried meal while they waited for the results; then, back to the courthouse.

As they hurried after Boone, who had just turned a corner, Dalton gave her an opening. "Last chance to change your mind. Are you sure you want to marry me?"

A little breathlessly, Justine replied, echoing Dalton's answer earlier that morning on Canal Street, "I've never been more certain of anything in my life."

"Mr. Boone," Dalton called out.

Boone turned around, folding his arms across his chest. "Let me guess. You want to get married. Am I right?"

Dalton and Justine smiled their answer.

Boone glanced both ways, then pointed to a door down the hall. "Let's go in here. I think it's empty now."

Dalton and Justine followed him into an eight-by-ten room with a green wooden table and three straight-backed chairs. They stood stiffly next to the table, Justine grasping Dalton's hand as though something might snatch her away.

Boone took a slim black book from his inside jacket pocket, opened it, and found his place with a ribbon marker. "Now, repeat after me."

Justine would remember little of their vows with any clarity. Boone's voice sounded muffled, as though he were speaking through a blanket. She and Dalton repeated his words, binding them together through sickness and through health, through riches and through poverty.

Dalton's expression was that of a man standing before a judge's bench, waiting for the gavel to fall, as he followed Boone's lead.

Two minutes later, they placed their one-dollar rings on each other's fingers, ending the ceremony.

Boone offered his opened book on the table in place of congratulations. Dalton fumbled in his back pocket for his wallet, took out a ten, and placed it inside the book. Boone shut the book, shoved it back into his pocket, then quickly filled in the marriage license, adding in names for witnesses, and disappeared through the door without word.

Justine stared at Dalton, thinking that her expression must be just as stunned and blank as his. "This *can't* be legal!"

Dalton sat next to Justine on a wooden bench on Church Street in Mobile's downtown historic district. The buildings, used for professional offices as well as private residences, were of federal, raised cottage, and Victorian styles from the mid-nineteenth century. Traffic moved past them at a leisurely pace.

"This is a picture of my dad and me when I was five." Justine handed the black-and-white print to Dalton.

He gazed at the slim man in uniform holding hands with his fair-haired daughter. Squinting into the bright sunshine, they stood in front of a black thirties-vintage Ford. "You don't look much like him."

"No." Justine spoke in a hushed tone. "People say I looked just like my mother. I don't have a picture of her with me, though."

"Well, let's see what I've got in here." Dalton took his wallet out, opening it to the cellophane sleeves that held his snapshots. "Here's one of Mama and Daddy right after the war."

Justine placed her hand over Dalton's and gazed at the blond woman and her husband in his marine uniform. "She's so pretty. I hope she likes me."

"Don't worry about that," Dalton reassured her. "Mama will love you to death."

"Your daddy was an officer?"

"Yep. Fought in World War II and Korea." Dalton flipped to the next picture. "Here's my sister Jessie. She's married to Austin Youngblood, and they have a boy named Taylor. He's a year old now, but I don't have any pictures of them yet." He smiled at a private thought. "Their wedding was a little different from ours."

"I think most people's weddings were a little different from ours."

Justine pressed closer to Dalton while he showed her his family, seeing the love he felt for them reflected on his face. His was the kind of family she had thought about so many times growing up from one army post to another, from one strange classroom to another. Would they accept her? In the midst of her happiness, the thought haunted her.

"And here's Sharon. She makes all A's." A shadow crossed Dalton's face. "She's got leukemia, but it's been in remission for about two years. I hope she's well." He flipped to one more picture. "This is Cass."

"He looks like a little angel."

"Boy, he's got you fooled already, and you haven't even met him yet!" Dalton put his wallet away. "Well, it is an old picture and his white hair and that big grin always did make him look like an innocent lamb."

"What's wrong with him?"

"You'll find out soon enough," Dalton predicted. "I'm just kidding. He's not so bad. Besides, he's the only brother I've got."

"I just can't wait to meet your whole family."

Dalton put his arm around Justine's shoulder. "We've got a garage apartment out behind the house. It'll be perfect for us until I get out of college."

"You don't think your mother will mind having me around?" Justine still felt uneasy about fitting into the family. "I don't know what I'd think if my son just showed up one day, married to someone I'd never seen before."

"You just wait. She'll be the first one to suggest that we live there." He kissed her on the cheek. "Now, where do you want to spend your wedding night?"

Justine gazed thoughtfully at a woman in a flowered dress pushing a baby carriage down the sidewalk across the street. "I don't know. What about you?"

"Biloxi. We'll stay right on the Gulf." Dalton took both her hands, staring into her eyes. "We'll walk on the beach, leave the window open and feel the breeze and listen to the sound of the waves all night."

"That sounds lovely." Justine suddenly felt a deep sense of belonging that she hadn't thought possible. She knew then that whatever happened, she would be happy as long as she and Dalton were together. A silent prayer of thanksgiving rose from her heart as she leaned forward, taking Dalton's face in her hands. "You know something?"

"I know I like you touching me."

"You haven't kissed the bride yet." Justine felt Dalton's lips pressing against hers, felt herself becoming a part of him in a way far deeper than their kiss.

Dalton stood up, taking her hands and pulling her to her feet. "What do you want to do now?"

Justine slipped her arm around his waist as they walked away in the sun-dappled shade of the old trees. "I don't know, but there's no hurry. We've got the rest of our lives."